REIGN

THE ITALIAN CARTEL #3

SHANDI BOYES

Edited by
NICKI @ SWISH DESIGN & EDITING

Illustrated by
SSB COVERS & DESIGN

COPYRIGHT

Copyright © 2020 by Shandi Boyes

All rights reserved.

No part of this book may be reproduced in any form or by any electronic or mechanical means, including information storage and retrieval systems, without written permission from the author, except for the use of brief quotations in a book review.

Written by: Shandi Boyes

Editing - Nicki @ Swish Design & Editing

Proofreading - Kaylene @ Swish Design & Editing

Cover: SSB Covers & Design

Model: Jonny James

Photography: Kruse Images & Photography

❈ Created with Vellum

DEDICATION

To the voices in my head,

Thank you for convincing people I am not crazy.

Shandi xx

ALSO BY SHANDI BOYES

Perception Series

Saving Noah (Noah & Emily)

Fighting Jacob (Jacob & Lola)

Taming Nick (Nick & Jenni)

Redeeming Slater (Slater and Kylie)

Saving Emily (Noah & Emily - Novella)

Wrapped Up with Rise Up (Perception Novella - should be read after the Bound Series)

Enigma

Enigma (Isaac & Isabelle #1)

Unraveling an Enigma (Isaac & Isabelle #2)

Enigma The Mystery Unmasked (Isaac & Isabelle #3)

Enigma: The Final Chapter (Isaac & Isabelle #4)

Beneath The Secrets (Hugo & Ava #1)

Beneath The Sheets (Hugo & Ava #2)

Spy Thy Neighbor (Hunter & Paige)

The Opposite Effect (Brax & Clara)

I Married a Mob Boss (Rico & Blaire)

Second Shot (Hawke & Gemma)

The Way We Are (Ryan & Savannah #1)

The Way We Were (Ryan & Savannah #2)

Sugar and Spice (Cormack & Harlow)

Lady In Waiting (Regan & Alex #1)

Man in Queue (Regan & Alex #2)

Couple on Hold (Regan & Alex #3)

Enigma: The Wedding (Isaac and Isabelle)

Silent Vigilante (Brandon and Melody #1)

Hushed Guardian (Brandon & Melody #2)

Quiet Protector (Brandon & Melody #3)

Bound Series

Chains (Marcus & Cleo #1)

Links (Marcus & Cleo #2)

Bound (Marcus & Cleo #3)

Restrain (Marcus & Cleo #4)

Psycho (Dexter & ??)

Russian Mob Chronicles

Nikolai: A Mafia Prince Romance (Nikolai & Justine #1)

Nikolai: Taking Back What's Mine (Nikolai & Justine #2)

Nikolai: What's Left of Me (Nikolai & Justine #3)

Nikolai: Mine to Protect (Nikolai & Justine #4)

Asher: My Russian Revenge (Asher & Zariah)

Nikolai: Through the Devil's Eyes (Nikolai & Justine #5)

Trey (Trey & K)

The Italian Cartel

Dimitri

Roxanne

Reign

Maddox

Rocco

RomCom Standalones

Just Playin' (Elvis & Willow)

The Drop Zone (Colby & Jamie)

Ain't Happenin' (Lorenzo & Skylar)

Short Stories

Christmas Trio (Wesley, Andrew & Mallory -- short story)

Falling For A Stranger (Short Story)

K (A Trey Sequel)

Coming Soon

Skitzo

WANT TO STAY IN TOUCH?

Facebook: facebook.com/authorshandi

Instagram: instagram.com/authorshandi

Email: authorshandi@gmail.com

Reader's Group: bit.ly/ShandiBookBabes

Website: authorshandi.com

Newsletter: https://www.subscribepage.com/AuthorShandi

1

DIMITRI

Unsettled tension grips my throat as I stare at the rice-size tracking device in Rocco's hand. It's coated in as much blood as Rocco's hair, revealing the men who took Roxanne didn't just remove the device from her arm, they cut it out.

If the anxiety plaguing me is anything to go by, that's only the start of the torture they'll put her through. This is about more than money. Fien's low-ball ransoms already disclose this fact. If it were solely about the coin, as Roxanne said months ago, my daughter's ransoms would have been as extravagant as the one I placed on the table to keep Roxanne safe. They're playing me, and for once, I'm about ready to play back.

We play to play.

We kill to kill.

And we take down any fucker stupid enough to get in our way.

After licking my dry lips, I get down to business. Annoyance is bubbling under the surface of my skin. It's heard in my low tone when my snapped command leaves my mouth with a roar. "Send details of the van Roxanne was placed in to the teams located around Dr. Bates's practice. If they spot it, have them relay the information directly to me but maintain a safe distance. We don't want to spook them into doing something stupid."

The shit I'm spurting isn't anything new. This is how we planned to run our ruse. I'm merely implementing extra steps to ensure I reach Roxanne before any of the horrid thoughts in my head come true.

"Once that's done, bring up the surveillance before the blackout. I want to know the position of everyone in the clinic and a block each side of it before we were kicked in the guts." When Smith jerks up his chin, I lower my eyes to Rocco, who's peering up at the camera in the alleyway as if he can see me as clearly as I can him. "Anything?"

He reads the unease in my one word like no one else can. "I'm sorry, D, I had to take him down. He had a gun to my head and no intention of letting me leave the pharmacy once the command to move left your mouth."

He stuffs Roxanne's microchip into his pocket before dragging a man who'd weigh at least three hundred pounds into the frame. Since he's as worked up as me, he doesn't pay attention to the massive graze down one side of his skull I assume is the flesh wound of the bullet that was supposed to kill him while propping the man in front of the camera so Smith can log his face into his facial recognition software. The reason for the man's three bullet wounds to the chest makes sense when Smith gets an unhindered snapshot of his face. If Rocco had gone for a straight-up mafia kill, it would have made identification hard in this technology-dependent world.

With that in mind, I bring some old-school gangster tricks into play. Remembering where I came from and how I got here might finally have me one step ahead of my enemies. "Check his pockets.

His tats reveal he's a bottom dweller, so he may have been stupid enough to carry ID with him."

After pulling a face, disappointed he hadn't considered that, Rocco commences checking the buzz-cut man's pockets. A few seconds later, he pulls out a retro Velcro wallet. "Who the fuck carries around a tri-fold wallet these days?"

He answers his own question when he rips open the over-used Velcro with force to discover nothing but receipt after receipt after receipt. "Fuckers with no money, that's who."

My jaw has only worked through half a grind when Smith asks, "Do any of the receipts have payment details on them? Or was everything paid for with cash?" After raising his eyes to mine, he explains, "He might be lax on ID, but that doesn't mean we can't find out who he is quicker than facial recognition."

"Bing-fucking-o." After holding up a receipt for a purchase at a computer store in Ravenshoe to the camera for Smith to zoom in on, Rocco pops another bullet into the man who tried to kill him. This time, his bullet pierces his brain via a hole between his dark brows. He isn't just displaying he is pissed the wannabe gangster got a jump on him, he's sending a message. *The cartel is in town, and we want you to know it.*

"Where am I going, Smith?" Rocco asks, eager to move on to his next victim.

His hankering for a rampage hasn't been this perverse since a handful of my father's associates decided to test the authenticity of my threat. We went in hard and fast and without mercy. No one was spared.

As they won't be today, either.

"Give me a sec..." Smith punishes his keyboard as badly as I want to punish someone's face, pissed as fuck I made him work from Roxanne's family's ranch. Roxanne wasn't lying when she said the cell phone service here was shit.

My wish to kill is the highest it's ever been. It is brewing inside of me, warning that when it's finally unleashed, it will be explosive. I honestly don't know if I'll be able to control it. It has been building for years, so shouldn't it take just as long to dispel?

As the thirst for a bloodbath dries my mouth, another disturbing thought enters my mind. "How did they know Roxanne was wearing a tracker? No one knew she was wearing one. We kept it between the three of us..." My words trail off as pure rage takes their place. Although I have all my men on this case, one outsider was brought in. She left a couple of hours ago. "You fucking little snitch."

Smith appears lost to who I mean, but Rocco clicks on remarkably quick. While dragging his hand over his clipped hair, he growls out, "She's been under our nose the entire time."

"Don't remind me just how long, or I'll kill her before we get any information out of her." The roughness of my voice exposes I'm not joking. I am about to kill a friend I've known for years, and although her daughter's baby daddy isn't dead, the three consecutive life sentences he was handed down two years ago will make it seem as if she's an orphan. That messes with my head even more than wondering what's happening to Roxanne at this very moment. She's unconscious, naked, and in the back of a van with a doctor who sells babies for a living and a goon with an unrecognizable face. I could already be too late.

Rocco's deep timbre draws me from my dark thoughts. "Where am I meeting you, D? Harbortown Penitentiary or are we going directly to the source?"

My smirk tells him everything he needs to know.

"Directly to the source. I'll wait out back. Make sure the pool house is empty."

He waits for me to lift my chin in thanks before he hotfoots it to his ride, but not before laying his boot into the man now housing four of his personally selected bullets, though. He's pissed he got the jump on him. Not as much as me, but for now, I'll let it slide.

Time is critical in these matters. The verdict of me waiting until the deadline for Audrey's ransom exposes how dire things become when you leave them to chance. I took a risk my family's reputation would pull me out of the wreckage unscathed twenty-two months ago. I refuse to make the same mistake today. This entire operation falls on my shoulders. If I fail, it fails. I can't explain it any simpler than that.

"Have Rico keep a watch on my father. Until we find out exactly who has taken Roxanne, we can't assume anything. This could still be about the bounty on her head."

I know it isn't, but I'd rather be cautious, especially if it comes with less bloodshed on my side of the field. There can't be change without chaos, but can there be chaos without bloodshed? Up until a couple of weeks ago, I would have said there was no chance in hell you can't have one without the other. Now I'm not so sure.

I will protect Roxanne and Fien no matter what. I just don't want my victory to come at the ultimate price.

2

DIMITRI

With traffic light and my foot heavy, I make it to a ritzy family estate in a well-to-do area within a record-breaking thirty minutes. I want to say my blood cooled a smidge during the commute, but that would be a lie. If anything, it's more heated since the tail a secondary crew had on Roxanne was lost.

The van they transported her in has been dumped and burned, and the cameras in the area aren't controlled by me. They're owned by none other than Mr. Isaac Holt, and his security personnel isn't playing friendly. Smith has attempted to reach out to Hunter numerous times the past thirty minutes. He's yet to be successful. I'm tempted to ask Isaac what his problem is, but since that could cause more issues, I'm holding back the urge—barely!

Not wanting my guest to be aware of my arrival, I park at the side gate before using the secret entrance only a handful of people know about. I'm not surprised to spot a man guarding the door with a customized M4. Only a fool goes against a man with nothing to lose halfheartedly.

The guard slumps to the floor before he knows what's hit him. It isn't often a victim can respond to a bullet between the eyes. More times than not, they're dead before they hit the ground.

After pulling the security guard into an area he won't be seen by little eyes, I unlatch a set of keys from the waistband of his jeans, shove it into a retro-looking lock, twist, then wait for further instructions.

Smith is guiding me from above. Since this compound is wired to the hilt with surveillance, he has eyes in every room. "Target is in her office. She isn't alone. Halo is in the vicinity. Three guards are walking the hall. One is out back..." The hiss of a silencer whizzes out of the listening device in my ear a second before Smith corrects, "Pool house is clear. Rocco is on site."

As my lips curl into a smirk, I creep down the lit-up corridor like a real-life action hero. Despite my many wishes to be born to any family but the one I was, the adrenaline roaring through my veins bares reason to my birthright. Hate is strong in my bloodline, but so is vengeance. I live for this.

Pop. Pop. Pop.

Three guards are dead. Serves them right for standing together in an open arena. Regardless of what you've heard, there's no safety in numbers. If you want to stay alive, branch away from the group. You have a better chance of remaining hidden if the loud-mouth of the group is nowhere near you.

The faintest hum of a melody I've heard a handful of times buzzes into my ears when I lower the handle of the office door now housing the blood of three men. Their deaths were silent, but the smell of desecration is obvious. Unfortunately, it isn't solely coming from my side of the room.

Alice is standing in the corner of her home office. She has a gun butted under her quivering chin, and sweat is beading her brow. Her daughter, Lucy, sits at her left, oblivious to the fact her mother is moments away from blowing her brains out. She's immersed in a video game all kids seem to love these days.

Although shocked Alice has placed her life on the line with the very gun she bought to protect herself, it is understandable. She'd rather die via her own hands than be tortured like she was when she was seventeen. That's why Rocco is out back, waiting by the pool house. Alice's biggest fear in life is losing her daughter. Her second is being drowned like her father attempted to do when she told him she was pregnant with Lucy. Both Alice and Lucy survived his attempt to kill them. Alice's father didn't.

"I had no choice," Alice coughs out in a sputter as tears flow down her face. "They took Lucy. T-t-they wouldn't give her back until I helped them secure Roxanne. I didn't know she was *really* pregnant. I swear to God, Dimi, I had no idea."

Her blubbering response exposes holes in her defense. Roxanne let slip to her this morning that she didn't need free-flowing garments added to her wardrobe selection because her pregnancy was merely a ruse to fool Dr. Bates, so how is Alice aware Roxanne's test returned a positive result in Dr. Bates's office this morning? If all she did was inform my enemies Roxanne was wearing a tracker, she'd assume Roxanne's pregnancy was still part of our ruse.

Although pissed, news of Roxanne's positive test doesn't change anything. "Whether she's pregnant or not makes no difference. You went against me—"

"F-for L-Lucy," Alice defends, her words stuttering. "Only for Lucy. I couldn't let her be a part of that lifestyle, Dimitri. I couldn't only see her through a monitor like you do…" Her words trail off as her eyes widen in fear.

Bringing Fien into this won't do her any favors because not only is she reminding me just how far I'll go to protect my daughter, she's also reminding me that it's more than just Fien's life at stake now. Roxanne's is in my hands as well, and so is our unborn child's.

Too pumped with anger to stand still, I house my gun into the back of my trousers, then storm to Alice's side of the room, confident gamers these days are as ignorant as Rocco and I were anytime we played *Super Mario*.

I reach Alice before she even considers deflecting the barrel of her gun to me. She wouldn't fire at me even if I still had my gun in my hands because she knows as well as her ex-husband, it isn't an eye for an eye in this industry.

It's family for family.

Mine for hers.

Or better yet, hers for mine.

As I drag Alice toward the open French doors that lead to her patio, my anger gets the better of me. "They took my wife, they have my daughter, yet that still isn't enough for you. You want them to take everything away from me."

"No," she denies, shaking her head as she eyes the pool we're heading toward. "I was just protecting Lucy."

I've never laid my eyes on my daughter in person. That doesn't make me any less of a father, though, so I understand her objective, but I'm just too worked up with anger to absorb it. "Because your daughter's life is more valuable than mine?"

Fear leeches out of her pores before she once again shakes her head. This one is more hesitant than her earlier one.

"Then why did you do it? Why go against me knowing you could lose everything!"

As Alice's stilettos skitter across the pavers, she attempts to lodge them into the cracks, hopeful her fight to live will have me recalling the time I saved her from this exact scenario.

If my anger wasn't bubbling over, I might have, but it's too late for her now. I can't separate the past from the future any more now than I could when I was driving here. Roxanne is nowhere near as far along as Audrey was when she was taken. However, all I see when her face pops into my head is the horrific footage of Audrey going through a botched caesarian. My fucked-up head has replaced Audrey's face with Roxanne's, and it's messing with my mind even more than Lucy's frantic cries for me to stop holding her mother's head under the water in their half-a-million-dollar pool.

"Get her out of here!" I scream at Rocco a mere second before pulling Alice's head up so she can suck in the quickest breath. It isn't long enough to fill her screaming lungs with air, but it will warn her I'm not playing. I've played the game as taught the past two years. It got me nowhere, so it's time for a new set of rules.

As Lucy fights Rocco with more gusto than an eight-year-old should have, I bring Alice's drenched head to within an inch of mine. "Where are they taking her?"

"I don't kn—"

She's back under the water in an instant, gargling and screaming while her nails make a mess of my arms. She digs them in deep before dragging them to the hand wrapped around her throat. If the water doesn't suffocate her, the hold I have on her throat soon will.

With her eyes on the verge of sporting new blood vessels, I lift Alice's head for the final time. Her gasps as she struggles to fill her lungs with oxygen are barely heard over Lucy's frantic bangs on the window of her room. She's three floors above, but she thumps her fists on the glass as if breaking her window will magically save her mother.

I wish it were that easy, but sometimes, the heroes in stories need to be villains too, especially when the only person they looked up to disappointed them time and time again.

I'm waist-deep in freezing cold water, but my skin is so hot, it hisses as well as my words when I growl out, "Where. Are. They. Taking. Her."

"I..." when my hand moves for my gun, over the time waster Alice is being today, she talks faster, "... overheard them saying something about a ranch. T-t-that they had a bigger payday coming."

I instantly feel hopeful. "Roxanne's family's ranch?"

Tears mix with the saltwater coating her face when she shakes her head. "They were talking about a gala, something about a ransom drop."

When my hand raises in the air, Lucy screams my name in a mangled roar. It reminds me so much of Roxanne's endeavor to protect her mother. Even when she should have hated her, she still went in to bat for her.

"I'm telling you everything I know, Dimitri," Alice swears, her tone honest.

The truth in her eyes does little to calm me down. "You should have told me from the start. You should have warned me."

"Warned you about what?" she asks on a sob. "That your enemies were going to take Roxanne as planned *by you*? That she would be thrust into a world you should have done everything in your power to keep her away from? What was I supposed to tell you?"

I hold her under the water again, the truth of her statement too much for me to bear. Not only was this the outcome we were reaching for, I've known for years my enemies have always been one step ahead of me, so why did I expect today to be any different?

As Alice's crying comment rings in my ears on repeat, her thrashes become stiller and stiller. She's seconds from death, her fight honorable considering the circumstances. She gave all for her daughter, only to lose in front of her.

My grip on Alice's throat slackens when the frantic screams of a child in despair fills my ears. Lucy's bangs broke through the glass. She is cut up and bleeding, but her thoughts remain with her mother. "Stop, Uncle Dimitri, please stop."

Alice and I aren't related. I earned the privilege of being called Lucy's uncle when I saved her life. Now I'm taking away the only person she's ever cared about.

When Lucy's cries reach an area of my body I'm certain stopped functioning years ago, I fully uncinch my grip on Alice's throat. My unusual offer of mercy comes too late. Alice is floating in the pool. Her eyes are wide and unblinking. Her chest is still.

I killed her for doing exactly what I would have done in her situation.

I murdered her for putting her daughter first.

That makes me a fucking monster—just like my father.

3

ROXANNE

As the haze making my vision murky clears, I attempt to take in the area surrounding me. I'm lying on my side, a scratchy blanket the only thing responsible for my modesty. My throat burns with every swallow I take, and my head is thumping.

I don't know where I am, but I wish I could be here without being naked. This is as awkward as it gets for me. I'm not one of those women who are comfortable in their own skin. I'd rather be found in a hessian bag than have Dimitri's crew walk in on me stark naked when they track my location.

When I roll onto my side, keen to drink in something more than the rippled steel of an outdated van, pain shreds through my stomach. I don't know much about pregnancies, but I'm reasonably sure I shouldn't be cramping like this. I feel like the goon who grabbed me from behind punched me in the stomach before doing so.

If that is the case, what's their objective for taking me?

Aren't I more valuable if I'm carrying Dimitri's child?

Pregnant. Me. I still can't believe it. We were laid-back on protection, but I still would have thought it would take more than one time to get me up the duff. I guess my life could never be accused of being easy.

The roll of my eyes stops halfway when the groan I couldn't hold back announces to my captives that I'm awake. I don't know whether to laugh or glower when the knowledge has several guns aimed at the crinkle between my sweat-beaded brows. I'm pleased they see me as a threat, but I'd rather it occur without additional harm. Being chloroformed was worse than anticipated, so I'm happy to skip extra theatrics.

"Show me those hands, girlie," croons the goon at the front.

His shoulders are as wide as Clover's, his eyes almost as deadly, his voice is just missing an Arabian accent. That means nothing, though, because I swear the first voice I heard upon awakening was twanged with an Italian accent. It wasn't laced with maturity, so I don't believe it belongs to Dimitri's father, but it did have a familiarity about it.

"Don't make me ask you again." The stranger tosses his half-smoked cigarette on the drought-affected ground, stomps it out with his boot, then moves close enough to me the bright rays of the sun stop sheltering his face. He's handsome if mass murderers are your kink. "Your plaything the past nine weeks isn't the only man around here with no patience."

After absorbing the little nugget of information he unwittingly shared, I hold my hands out in front of myself, smug as fuck about his first stumble of the day.

I can't wait for him to have many more.

With his grin as shit-eating as mine, he lowers his pistol from my head to my almost exposed chest before grunting out, "Higher."

"If I raise them any higher, I'll lose the scarce bit of coverage I have. I will spit in your face before I'll ever let that happen."

The man with a sleeve full of tattoos grin turns gleaming. "Those there are fighting words for men like me. Are you sure you want to go down that road, girlie? It won't be as pretty as your face."

You don't scare me, I want to say, but hold back, mindful our ruse will be more effective if I play the damsel in distress. Only someone believing they're not in real danger would act nonchalant in this situation. This isn't the movies. Not even an imbecile would remain quiet when they're being led out of a packed restaurant with a knife jabbed under their ribs.

A montage of the footage I perused before drawing sketches of the people I saw at Joops the day Dimitri's wife was kidnapped halts playing in my head when something sharp jabs into my thigh. I was so deep into my thought process on Audrey's silence when she was led away by a stranger, I didn't notice the goon removing a needle from his bag of tricks at my side and stabbing it into my leg.

"What was that..." My woozy words answer my question on his behalf. I feel like I'm floating, like more than scratchy material is moving out from beneath me when he leans into the van to lift me out. Just like when I was carried through the hidden corridors of the office building shouldering Dr. Bates's practice, I'm fully exposed.

It's not all bad. My lack of clothing uncovers elements my dazed head wouldn't have noticed. Such as the warmth of the sun when I'm carried across the gravel-crunching ground and the direction the wind is blowing. It always howls in from the ocean. Since the gusts are nowhere near as strong as the ones that roll in from Bronte's Peak, I'm confident we've headed inland.

The shadow on the man's face and the lack of warmth from the sun exposes it's still early in the day. I either slept for an eternity, or we're still close to Hopeton. If my intuition is anything to go by, I'm leaning toward the latter.

The thought makes me smile. Dimitri is closer than I realized. Perhaps he's sitting in the dark sedan I spotted near the woodlands when my eyes were wrenched to the needle sticking out of my thigh. I only got the quickest glimpse of the vehicle before my eyelids grew weary, but I'm confident it wasn't my imagination. I have a knack for taking things in much deeper than an ordinary person would. It's a disturbing trait I developed from my father's wish to embarrass me. I gawk even when I shouldn't. Mercifully, I don't see it getting me in trouble this time around.

A second after the beep of an electronic lock sounds through my ears, I'm lowered onto a cool, bumpy surface. Although this metal doesn't feel as scratchy as the rusty bottom of the van, its distinct smell assures me I've been moved from one mode of transport to another. Regretfully, it isn't an elaborate private jet. The tire jack digging into my ribs assures me of this, much less the tight confines. I've been shoved into a trunk, the bend of my legs to fit adding to the gnawing pain in my stomach.

"Get comfy, sweetheart. You're in for an all-nighter," grunts the stranger with a chuckle before he slams down the trunk, trapping me inside.

Once again, I want to get smug, but once again, the reminder that Dimitri is only one step behind stops me.

We've created a storm.

Now we just need it to rain.

Fingers crossed it doesn't turn into a flood.

4

DIMITRI

"Call an ambulance!" I scream at Smith as if he's standing across from me instead of watching me via the security dome above my head.

With my earpiece bogged down by the water I'm wading through to reach Alice floating in the middle of her pool, Smith's response doesn't come out as crisp as normal. "Dimi—"

"Now!" My short reply doesn't weaken the severity of my warning. I didn't suggest for him to bring in the authorities. I told him to. That's a direct order. Ignoring it will see him on the receiving end of my wrath.

As Smith does as asked, I drag Alice's weighted body to the edge of her monstrous pool. Considering the fact my hands can circle her waist, she shouldn't feel as if she weighs a ton.

It takes all my strength to lift her onto the pool's edge, but it has nothing on the weight that slams down on me when Lucy suddenly falls at her mother's side a couple of seconds later.

She didn't escape Rocco's clutch. He freed her so he can help me fix the second injustice I made today. The first was letting

Roxanne out of my sight. "Dip her head back, you need to open up her airways."

As Lucy holds her mother's hand, crying for her to wake up, I rip open Alice's shirt and bra, cover her chest with my hands like I did almost nine years ago, then press down.

I do four compressions before Rocco uses her tilted chin to his advantage. He breathes into her mouth two times before raising his eyes to mine. "You were only supposed to scare her, D. You weren't meant to kill—."

I glare at him, cutting his scorn off halfway.

I'm riddled with guilt.

He doesn't need to make it worse.

Even confident I have nothing to answer for, the disdain in Rocco's eyes is too strong to discount. He's been angry at me many times and has wanted to rip my head off even more than that, but this is the first time he's been truly disappointed in me. "She helped them take Roxanne. She knew her pregnancy wasn't a hoax."

My confession sees me pumping Alice's chest more forcefully than needed. It can't be helped. I either take my aggression out on her chest or push her head back under the water until there's no chance she'll survive. This is the kinder of the two and only occurring because her daughter is kneeling across from me, ashen-faced and crying.

"She did it for…" I stop myself in just enough time. If anything Alice said was true, and I have a feeling it was, Lucy will already be traumatized. I don't need to add more angst to the bucketloads she has to tell her future therapists.

"Again."

Rocco barely forces half a breath into Alice's lungs when the gurgle of a woman clawing her way back from the brink of death sees him pulling back.

While Alice coughs up the water in her lungs, the sound of sirens is heard in the distance. She lives in a rich, leafy suburb that's so quiet, it's easy to distinguish the difference between a paramedic's wails and that of an unmarked police car.

"We need to go," Rocco says, stating the obvious. He rolls Alice on her side before re-tilting her head. It's clear from the rise and fall of her chest that she's breathing. She just hasn't fully come around yet—emotionally, not physically. "When she wakes up, keep her on her side, okay?" he says to Lucy. "She has lots of water in her lungs she needs to get out."

Like the brave girl she was born to be, Lucy wipes at the tears high on her cheeks before dipping her chin at Rocco's suggestion. She looks like she wants to gut me, but there's nothing but admiration in her eyes as she stares at Rocco.

"Send someone to collect her grandmother. Make sure she gets here before CPS. If she spends an hour with them, Smith, we'll have more than words."

He doesn't absorb my threat. He gets straight to work on locating Lucy's only surviving relative before updating us on how close the sirens we hear wailing in the distance are. "It's a single unit, but he isn't on payroll."

That means it can only be one man. Detective Ryan Carter.

While snagging a towel from a rack on my right to cushion Alice's head, I say, "Log a disturbance one block back. Ensure it mentions the words 'shots fired' and 'officer down.'"

Ryan can't help but be a hero. He was born to be one. Me, on the other hand, no matter what happens today, my credits won't ever include a synonym of the word. Every story needs a villain. It's just never anticipated for him to also be the leading man.

As Smith mimics the panicked voice of an officer in the middle of a furious gun battle, I shift my eyes to Lucy. It's stupid of me to do. All I can see in her big blue eyes is Fien in a couple of years. It has me convinced the carnage will never end. Whether right now or twenty years in the future, I will forever fight to keep my daughter safe. I just want the privilege of showing her how I'd go to the end of the world for her.

I also want to do the same for Roxanne. She put her life on the line for my daughter, and now she and our unborn child are at risk. I won't see her go through what Audrey did. I don't care what it takes, I will stop it before it has the chance to transpire. I'll keep her safe as I failed to do my wife. Then maybe, just maybe, the guilt I've felt the past two years will finally slacken enough I can secure an entire breath.

"I'm sorry, Luce," I whisper in a low, dull tone, the angst eating me alive too strong to discount.

My apology is barely audible, but the weight it lifts from my chest is phenomenal. It makes my steps to my car quick and buoyant like Lucy will forgive me as quickly as I'm hoping Alice will.

My lengthy strides freeze mid-pump when the faint voice of Lucy trickles into my ears not even a few seconds later. She called my name, undeserving salutation and all. It has me spinning to face her even faster than she dashes across the pavers lining the poolside to gather up her iPad she was mesmerized by when I arrived.

For the way her chubby cheeks bounce when she stops to stand in front of me, her words shouldn't be anywhere near as mature as they are. "Daddy always said it's too late to say you're sorry once you've done bad, but Mommy and I don't agree." Her lips quiver as she confesses, "She hasn't stopped crying all morning. She said it was because she was excited to see me after my sleepover. I didn't believe her. Look, she was even crying when she read me a bedtime story."

She twists her iPad around to show me a screenshot dated a

little after eight last night. It doesn't just show Alice's tear-stained face as she endeavors to put on a brave front for her daughter, it features Lucy's screen as well. Since she is holding her device far away from her face, several identifiable markers are seen behind her.

As it dawns on me what she's showing me, Lucy pushes her iPad into my hand, smiles in a way that reveals I'm still in her shit book, then she skips back to her mother's side.

I stare at her in awe for the next several minutes, stunned as fuck. If I hadn't spared her mother's life, I guarantee she wouldn't have shared this information with me. She's only doing it because she knows how this industry works. If she scratches my back, hers will never be itchy. She's a mastermind in the making, and she's only eight.

God save anyone who does her wrong when she reaches her prime.

Although the drone of a single police siren has been temporarily diverted, no amount of manipulation can alter the buzz of half a dozen. They're even howling above our heads, the big guns brought in for the sake of one of their own.

While a police helicopter circles above us, Rocco slides into the driver's seat of my car before firing up the ignition. I don't put up a protest. Not only does he drive faster and better than me, the change-up will give me time to peruse the image Lucy showed me.

"Can you see this?" I raise my voice to ensure Smith can hear me over the ruckus attempting to follow us out of Alice's gated community.

"Spikes on entry ramp 43, take Makers," Smith advises Rocco before shifting his focus to me. "I'm stripping Lucy's 'find my phone' app to trace the location the photo was taken from, but it would be quicker if you zoomed in."

My tailor-made pants slide across the leather interior of my car when Rocco takes Makers like a bat out of hell. We get airborne for a second, which increases the width of Rocco's grin.

Once our tires grip the asphalt, I get back to business. "On what?"

"Right on Lark." Smith's fingers tap out a million words a minute before he responds, "Top left. It appears to be some type of emblem. I'm certain I've seen it before."

As Rocco loses the last police cruiser tailing us by plowing through an intersection at a speed well above the designated signage, I double tap on the screen of Lucy's iPad. I don't need to angle it to ensure Smith gets a clear view of the poster in the camera hidden in my rearview mirror. I already know who it belongs to. It's a poster-size flyer of the ones I handed out the night of Ophelia's accident. The flyers Ophelia designed knowing our father would be more arrogant in front of an audience. He isn't one of those men who rain sunshine down on his family in front of others to portray the ideal husband and father. He preferred degrading us. Blood or not, if he could stand on you to make himself feel an inch taller, he would.

He still does.

With my jaw tight with annoyance, my voice is huskier than normal. "Have Clover meet us at the tunnel. We need to weapon-up before moving in." While Smith hums out an agreeing noise, I switch my eyes to Rocco. "We need to dump and burn."

He flashes me a cocky wink. "Already reported her as stolen." When I give him a look as if to ask when he had time to do that, he rubs his hands together like we're not sailing down the road at a speed well above the designated limit. "We all have our secrets, D. Even me."

If it were any day but today, I'd torture his secrets out of him. Since it isn't, they'll have to stay on the backburner. I want to finish my day strong, not burden it down with more stress.

5

DIMITRI

With the eyes of a dozen bloodthirsty men on me, I say, "The warehouse we're about to storm was once a Petretti stronghold. It isn't anymore. We would be fools to walk in blind."

Even while juggling a laptop like a circus clown, Smith jumps into the conversation with no hesitation in his voice. "We heat-scanned the warehouse. Readings are coming back with the imagery of a single occupant. Height, weight, and core body temperature reveals the target is most likely female—"

"Or he'll be wishing he was by the time we're done with him," Rocco interrupts, laughing. Humor is his go-to when he's feeling overwhelmed.

"She is also breathing."

I'm reasonably sure Smith's pause is to give me time to absorb the good in what he's saying, that Roxanne is alive and well. It's appreciated, but it doesn't lessen my itch to kill. I'm fired up and ready to go, only delayed by making sure the men about to follow me to battle know what they're fighting for.

They won't come out of today with a legacy. They will only be awarded my respect.

To some, that's as worthless as a piece of paper.

To me, it's the most valuable thing I own.

Smith's next set of words gobble up the last of the laughter from Rocco's witty comment. "The fact only one occupant has been noted should concern you. This is most likely an ambush."

He brings up imagery of the terrain surrounding the warehouse. Because it's an old industrial area that pumped out as much steel as drugs in the seventies, it is swamped by similar-sized buildings.

"As per Dimitri's request..." don't misconstrue Rocco's nicely worded statement, he's beyond pissed about my 'request,' "... while he enters the main warehouse from the front entrance *like a sitting fucking duck...*" he murmurs his last five words, "... we are to search the buildings on each side of it."

Eager to get back to the operation I'm helming, I add, "Smith has deployed drones. They will jam all signals, including ours. This isn't a seek-orders mission. If you must kill or be killed, always choose the former. If we can't get information out of them, we will find a way of getting it out of their corpse."

Needing to get things moving since we lost hours waiting for Smith to work his magic, I throw open the door of the van we're camped out in before making my way to the road's edge. Since we're back a good distance from the warehouse holding one occupant, I have to shield my eyes from the low-hanging sun to take it in.

I want to say my stare-down weakens the knot in my stomach, but that would be a lie. Smith wasn't deceitful when he said this is an ambush. My enemies are waiting for me to fall, but since I refuse to continue taking it up the ass as I have the past two years,

I'm rewriting the rules. It could get myself killed, but just like I'll never be a hero, I won't die a coward either.

"Let's go. The sooner we know who's in that warehouse, the better it will be for all involved." You didn't misread my tone. I'm doubtful the person holed up in the warehouse for the past two hours is Roxanne. An explosive personality like hers is felt for miles. Not even the slightest tickle is felt under my toes. My intuition is telling me I will get answers today. They just won't be answers to the questions I want answered.

After waiting for Rocco to slip into the Range Rover behind me, I slide into the driver's seat of the prototype vehicle we affectionally call The Tank. I'm not taking her for a spin because I'm afraid of a little bullet, I want to ensure if the warehouse doors are locked, I'll have no issues going through them.

With our group on radio silence, I have to hand signal for my men to move. There's an eeriness associated with our ghost-like approach. Hearing Smith's breaths in my ear has been such the norm the past two years, the ones raging in my chest sound foreign.

One by one, the vehicles following me peel off until I'm the lone soldier on a bumpy gravel road. While shifting down the gears, bringing The Tank's revs down to half of what they were, I scan my chest, anticipating the dots of a sniper's rifle to be lighting it up.

Unease melds through my veins when not a single speck is found. My chest remains clear of any visible markings when I pull The Tank up to the side of the cracked-open door, and not a dot highlights any part of my body when I make my way into the dusty space with my gun held high and my wish to kill even higher than it.

I jackknife to my left when a familiar voice says, "Has Smith always been this pedantic with protocol? Or did he become this way after we parted ways?"

My grip on my gun tightens when the pretty hazel eyes of Special Agent Ellie Gould lock with mine. She smiles like I won't kill her where she stands, unaware Smith has desired doing the same thing many times the past two years.

It isn't every day you find out your girlfriend is a federal agent, so I won't mention the fact he unearthed the truth while perusing tapes of her schmoozing with the enemy, or you might tempt me into killing her.

One less agent won't hurt anyone, except perhaps Smith. From what I've been told, you don't get over your first love. I've not yet had the chance to test the theory. That could change depending on the outcome of Ellie's resurrection. As the saying goes, 'stare at the dark so long, you'll eventually see what isn't there,' it fails to mention what you're striving not to see—a smile hidden under locks of bleached hair and a mascara-stained face. Nothing scares me, but the thought of never seeing them again is a nightmare I refuse to live.

I'll burn down this entire fucking hellhole before I ever let Rimi Castro beat me again, and I'll take Roxanne down with me because despite how many times I've told her otherwise, I want her. I want her more than anything, and I will have her. No fear.

6

ROXANNE

"Out, now. This one is out of gas."

The goon with thick biceps and a bad attitude doesn't wait for me to respond, he just yanks on my arm until I fall out of the trunk of a light-colored sedan for the fourth time today. I had wondered if the churns of my stomach the past couple of hours were from hunger or fear. From the low hang of the sun, I'm confident it's a bit of both.

I understand this is part of the plan, I'm playing my part of a kidnap victim well, but I'm also worried. We've been on the road for hours. I've not been given any water or food. Even my numerous kicks on the roof of the trunk advising I needed to pee went unanswered.

This man doesn't care about me *at all*. It honestly seems as if my pregnancy is more an annoyance to him than an incentive for a big cash bonus. Every time I use it with the hope it will see him issuing leniency, he becomes more aggressive.

Take now, for example. I barely murmur about the pain tearing me in two from his brutal yank on my arm, yet he acts as if

I asked him to purchase me a box of tampons. "Quit your grumbling. I told you we were in for a long trip."

The briefest moment of reprieve smacks into me when he tosses open the front passenger door of a truck parked in the middle of a road to nowhere. He has to be working with someone because cars aren't left in the middle of the boonies waiting to be hotwired. He drives each vehicle until the gas tank hits E, then we swap rides. That reveals our trip was methodically planned. It just seems as if my being pregnant didn't factor into the equation.

"Can I please have some water?" I ask half a mile down the dusty road.

The stranger with gleaming black eyes peers at me over the bottle he's guzzling down like he hasn't had a drink in hours before he shakes his head. The brutal crossing of my arms seems to humor him as much as my stink eye.

Although pissed he finds my dehydration entertaining, I'm glad it also sees him switching things up. "All right, I'm sure I can spare a couple of drops."

His tone already has me on the back foot, let alone the way he swishes the water around his mouth before he tilts his head to my side of the cabin.

"Open up," he talks through the slop in his mouth.

He almost chokes on the water he's gargling in the back of his throat when my eagerness to get away from him has my arm getting cozy with the steel panel of the door. It isn't just tender like every other region of my body. It's also bleeding.

What the hell?

As my head rolls through snippets of my first drugging, my hand shoots up to caress the implant site where Smith placed my tracker. It feels like the world closes in on me when my probing fingers fail to discover anything but a wound that appears to have been inflicted hours ago.

There's no bead-size device.

No implant.

Nothing.

I'm all alone, and Dimitri isn't one step behind me.

Fuck.

With my plan gone to shit, my mood soon follows it, but I refuse to walk into my death without a fight. I'll give as good as I'm getting. The odds aren't in my favor. My captive has a gun, and I've got nothing but determination, but I've fought with less for longer. My entire life has been a battle I was never meant to win, yet here I am, pregnant to the man I love and willing to do anything to ensure he sees his child's every milestone.

First smile.

First word.

First step.

I want Dimitri and his daughter to witness it all.

With that in mind, I batten down the hatches and settle in. The storm we created is coming. I can smell the rain on the horizon, feel the coolness of its imminent arrival in the air. It will be a beauty. I've just got to survive its wrath. If I do that, I'll have more than a rainbow to look forward to. I'll have the entire world at my feet.

7
DIMITRI

"I don't work for the Feds. I *use* them when it works in my favor." Acting as if my tone doesn't hold half the fury it does, Ellie moves to my side of the warehouse. My entire crew is here, including Smith, so I not only have to be conscious of what I say, I can't slit Ellie's throat to stop her speaking the insolent words she's been spurting the past forty minutes.

"We're chasing the same men, Dimitri. That puts us on the same team."

I laugh in her face. Both its pitch and length reveals how agitated I am. Out of all the days the Feds could reach out for my help, they chose today. I'm running out of time. Roxanne has been gone for hours. I don't even know if she's alive anymore, but I should stop my search because a 'friend' of Ellie's needs my contacts.

"I. Don't. Work. For. The. Feds." I speak extra slow, ensuring there's no way she can miss the fury in my tone this time around. "And if I need to tell you again, not even Smith will be able to save you. Do you understand me?"

Like a woman without a wish to live, she undoes the cuffs on her belt, unlocks them with a flick of her wrist, then brings them to within an inch of my hand. "Don't make me do this, Dimitri. I don't want to force your help, but if you leave me no choice, I will. This is a matter of national security. It ranks higher than your wish for revenge."

Wish for revenge? That snaps my last nerve.

After signaling for Clover to put Smith in lockdown, I grip Ellie's throat with everything I have. She struggles in an instant, her hands scratching at mine as her eyes bulge. A wish to live is seen all over her face when my brutal hold lifts her feet from the ground. It's almost as bright as the gleam on Smith's face as he fights against both Rocco and Clover to get to me.

He wants to kill me. I don't blame him. I'd do the same in his situation. Alas, I'm fighting for more than my girl right now. My entire existence is on the line.

"You enter my turf, waste *my* time, then threaten to arrest me. I should have killed you before Smith laid his eyes on you, then I would have gotten away with your murder without losing a valued member of my team. Now I might have to kill you both."

For the first time this afternoon, fright registers on Ellie's face. She's fearless when it comes to dying, but she doesn't feel the same way when Smith's life is on the line with hers.

"This also isn't a wish for revenge. If you weren't fucking the enemy, you'd know that." My last sentence calms Smith down. Not a lot, but it's better than nothing. "This goes *way* deeper than that."

Certain Ellie has gotten the point, I drop her from my hold, then spin around to face Smith. He's still being held back by Rocco and Clover, and he's red-faced and real fucking angry.

"Who do you work for, Smith?"

If he says anyone but Fien, he'll leave me no choice but to take this further. We've faced these issues before. Smith came out of it with both his life and job intact. I can't guarantee he'll be as lucky this time around. My enemies are always one step in front of me for a reason. Two years ago, we placed the blame for that on Ellie's shoulders. Now I'm wondering if I made a mistake.

"Who *the fuck* do you work for, Smith?"

"Fien. I work for fucking Fien!" he shouts back, his roar as loud as mine, his anger just as palpable.

After pushing Rocco and Clover away from him as if he is double their size, he storms my way. I slice my hand in the air, warning Clover if his index finger gets within an inch of his trigger, Smith won't be the only one letting off steam this afternoon. He answered how I wanted him to, and although a heap of fury was beaming from his eyes when he said it, it was barely seen through the honesty.

Smith stops an inch from my face before he growls out, "But once she's back, I'm done. I can't deal with your shit anymore. You're doing my fucking head in."

He misses the quickest dart of panic running through my eyes I couldn't shut down because his focus is no longer on me. He's staring at Ellie, torn between offering her a hand from the ground or adding to the red welts around her neck.

He goes for neither by shaking his head in disappointment before making his way to his beloved van, punching the steel door of the warehouse on his way by.

It's obvious from the noises rocking and rolling out of his van for the next several minutes that he isn't taking his anger out on a keyboard. He's demolishing equipment worth millions of dollars because he'd rather damage the irreplaceable things he loves than the one thing he can't replace, no matter how hard he tries. He loved Ellie, so her betrayal didn't just gut him, it changed him. He hasn't been the same man since.

Although the indent his rage will cause my hip pocket should be concerning, I'm not worried. We all have our ways of blowing off steam. Mine was a bender that saw me out of action for days. Smith's will barely last an hour.

Ask any underworld figure, they'll all tell you the same thing. A loss in revenue is preferred over a loss in production. If you're not productive, you are dead. Can't put it any simpler than that.

"Give him a few minutes to cool down, then roll out. We need to get a start on scanning traffic cameras on all routes out of Hopeton. Although they could still be local, until we learn otherwise, we should assume they're going to bounce Roxanne state to state like they did Fien the first few months."

Air whizzes out of Rocco's nose as he scrubs at the cropped beard on his chin. "With the van being dumped, what are we looking for?"

The panic roaring through my veins is heard in my reply. "Anything and everything. A snippet of red hair, a pricy car rolling down a dirt road... any suspicious activity."

Rocco's chin scarcely moves an inch when a husky voice cuts him off. "They headed south a couple of hours ago. Dark blue sedan. I got a partial plate."

I want to both kill and kiss Ellie. Kill her for holding back information that would have been useful hours ago, but kiss her for finally stepping up to the plate with something useful. "How many occupants?"

"One." After standing to her feet, she dusts off the dirt on her skirt-covered backside before digging a notepad out of the breast pocket of her jacket. Seeing her in a full agent get-up is shocking. I only ever saw her in ripped denim shorts, midriff tops, and her stark blonde hair pulled up in a messy bun. She was cruisy and laid-back, the very opposite of any agent I've ever met. "Approximately six-three, two hundred and sixty pounds. Had a cross tattoo above his—"

"Left eyebrow," interrupts a voice from the right, a stern, still unhinged voice.

After clambering over several mangled pieces of a computer, Smith jumps down from his van and re-enters the warehouse. He's still pissed. His scent is very telling, much less the tight grip he has on a single piece of paper. It almost rips when he thrusts it into my chest with no intention of letting it go.

After forcefully removing it from his grasp, I ask, "Who is he?"

"A military operative from Sicily," Ellie answers on Smith's behalf. "The Bureau has been tracking him for a while. This is the first sighting we've had in years. Where did you get it?" Her last question isn't for me. It's for Smith.

Ellie chokes on her spit when Smith answers, "From your laptop."

"You hacked into my computer?" Her question is barely heard over Rocco's laugh. He loves watching couples go to war. Why do you think he's been such a thorn in my ass the past nine weeks? "That's classified information."

Smith rakes his teeth over his bottom lip in an effort to half his smile. "Then you should have changed your password."

"But that wouldn't have stopped you, would it?" Ellie responds through a tight jaw.

When she attempts to snatch the document out of my hand, I hold it out of her reach. It isn't hard considering she's a short-ass. "You can finish your lovers' squabble later. For now, tell me how you don't know who he is if this was found on your computer?"

"That's what I'd like to know."

Ellie folds her arms in front of her chest to match the snappiness of Smith's question before replying, "I don't know how it got there. This is the first time I've seen an image of him."

A scoff vibrates Smith's lips. "It was sitting in a file on your desktop, plain as day for all to see."

"That doesn't mean I placed it there," Ellie fires back, her voice as vicious as Smith's glare.

"*Puh-leaze.* You're running that excuse again? I don't know how I got there. I just woke up in his bed."

Fighting not to tear my hair out, I step between the feuding couple. "Enough."

They continue arguing until the ricochet of a gun being fired shuts their mouths as quickly as it widens their pupils.

"I said *enough*! Fuck me, you two are worse than..." I freeze, out of the loop on any couple, either famous or an everyday regular couple.

Rocco doesn't face the same dilemma. "As Roxie and you?" He backhands Clover's chest, doubling the smirk he's struggling to hold back. "It's the make-up sex. It makes couples crazy."

"Kind of like a golden pussy?" Clover questions with an arched brow.

"Exactly," Rocco answers, completely ignoring my wrathful glare warning him not to.

He doesn't ignore my second directive. The bullet that whizzes through the minute gap between his and Clover's head is as effective as the one I fired into the air. "Get your heads into the fucking game. Roxanne's life is depending on it."

As Rocco's quiet apology trickles into my ears, I shift my focus back to Smith. "What else did you find on Ellie's laptop?" I shoosh Ellie by placing the barrel of my gun against her lips. I'm sure the heat of its recent firings will sting her lips, but it's got to be better than a bullet wound between the eyes. "I don't care about anything that doesn't relate to Fien and Roxanne. Even if it has the ability to take my father down, I don't care. I just want the information that will help bring my family back."

Smith balks, as shocked by the use of the word 'family' as me, but he keeps his head in game mode. "There's information on a possible new sanction popping up in the New York region. No names were mentioned, but a quick once-over makes it clear who it's about."

"Rimi Castro?"

When Smith jerks up his chin, Ellie gabbles out, "That can't be true. I'm not working Rimi's case. I don't have any of his files."

Aware federal agents never believe anything unless it's shown to them in black and white, Smith stomps back to his van, snatches up the only bit of equipment he didn't demolish in his tirade, then returns to my side. Although he's giving proof to Ellie, he keeps the screen tilted my way, ensuring he displays whose team he's on.

"They're not my files." Ellie lifts her eyes to mine, surprising me with the amount of wetness in them. "I swear to God, this is the first time I've seen those files." When Smith scoffs, as unbelieving as me, Ellie tries another angle. "Then, I'll swear on Jonathon's life." Jonathon is her little brother. He had an even rougher start to life than Fien. She would never place him in danger, not even if it could save her life. "They're not my files. Someone placed them there."

"Why would they do that?" I'm not saying I believe her. I'm merely ensuring I flip over every stone in my endeavor to find Roxanne and Fien.

Ellie shrugs. "I don't know." She freezes before her eyes widen. "Internal affairs is investigating our unit. They think we have a leak." The color drains from her face as her eyes bounce between Smith and me. "Do you think that's why I have those files? Is someone trying to set me up?"

"Perhaps." Smith's voice is more controlled than mine.

"But we don't have time to look." I shift my eyes to Rocco and Clover. "Let's move out."

My steps halt for the second time today when Smith's hand shoots out to grip my arm. His hold isn't what frustrates me. It's the desperation in his voice. "What if these cases are linked?"

"What if they're not, and we waste another six hours preparing for an ambush that isn't a fucking ambush!"

My roar doesn't harness his objective in the slightest. "Ellie was sent here for a reason, Dimi. If you find out what that was, you'll have more chance of finding Roxie."

I drift my eyes to Rocco. Don't ask me why. I don't seem to have control of anything today, much less my emotions.

When Rocco shrugs, leaving the decision up to me, I return my eyes to Smith. He's all but begging for me to listen to him. It isn't something I often do, and in all honesty, I sometimes wonder if that's where I've gone wrong.

Smith's exhale ruffles Ellie's hair when I ask, "Who sent you here?"

She hesitates. Not long enough for me to give my crew the signal to move, but long enough to take in the plea in Smith's eyes for her to cooperate. "Theresa Veneto."

A collective hiss rolls across the warehouse.

I should have known she was involved.

"Why?"

Ellie shrugs again before her brows join. "She didn't say. She mentioned something about a Megan..."

"Shroud," Smith and I fill in when she pauses to glance down at her notepad.

With her eyes wide and her jaw unhinged, she nods. "I was to wait here until you arrived, then bring you in. I assumed you had information on her death."

"Megan Shroud died over a year ago."

We know that's a lie. I'm merely testing Agent Gould. If she lies, our conversation is over. If she doesn't, I truly don't know where we'll go from here.

As the confusion in her eyes grows, Ellie informs, "Megan Shroud's disappearance was ruled a homicide late this afternoon." Not asking permission, she swivels Smith's laptop around to face herself, then clicks on a file on her desktop. Since Smith is already hacked in, it makes the process remarkably quick. "See." She brings up a police report oddly similar to the one Theresa forced through the system the first time Megan was 'killed.'

"Was there a body?" Rocco asks, jumping into the conversation.

Ellie immediately shakes her head. "A significant blood pool was found, and brain matter was embedded in the carpet, but no body."

I take a moment to consider Theresa's objective. It's clear she's running the same ruse she did on Maddox, but I have no fucking clue why.

Two seconds later, a lightbulb switches on inside of my head. "Who was arrested for Megan's murder?"

"An arrest warrant for a local woman is being drawn up. Her name is..." Ellie scrolls through the information on Smith's laptop, seeking a name. The wind in my lungs expels with a grunt when she discloses, "Isabelle Brahn."

Rocco sounds as uneased as I feel when he says, "That bitch is playing at something." He lowers his voice to ensure his next set of words are only for my ears. "Theresa didn't ask Ellie to wait here for no reason. She wanted both you and your time occupied."

I jerk up my chin, agreeing with him. "But for what reason? And how did she know I'd be out looking for..." Anger burns up my words.

She didn't pick this location for no reason.

She's fucking playing me.

"I'm going to kill her."

My arm is clutched for the third time today. It isn't Smith this time around. It's Rocco. "You'll never win the game if you keep letting your opposition blind you with false razzle and dazzle."

"She's playing me."

He doesn't deny what I'm saying because he knows it's the truth. "Because she needed you distracted. Find out why, and then you'll have all the pieces you need to win." When the groove between my brows doesn't budge, he chuckles out, "You're always running a million miles an hour, Dimi. Slow down, take a breath, and look at the entire picture."

He nudges his head to Ellie and Smith during his last sentence. They're no longer going to war with words. They are working together, side by side, their natural connection making it obvious they don't just make magic between the sheets. They could be just as explosive outside of them if I'm willing to give them a chance.

"If this backfires—"

"It won't," Rocco assures, slapping me on the shoulder. "Because firecrackers don't implode with despair. They make a starry night seem bland." In a rare show of affection, he pulls me into his side and whispers, "They'll come out of this, D. They're too strong not to."

8

ROXANNE

The dry throat I've been struggling to ignore the past seven or eight hours becomes unbearable when the dark-haired stranger pulls his car down a long, dusty driveway. I haven't seen a house in miles. There may have very well been ranches dotted along the many roads we traveled, but with winter arriving early, the sun commenced lowering over an hour ago. Farmers aren't a fan of burning the midnight oil, so I may have missed their ranches during our drive. Even the house we're approaching is scant on lighting. Only the flickers of a candle on a second story can be seen.

I swallow harshly when the black-haired man gleams a blinding grin. "It's not the Ritz, but compared to where you're going, it'll seem like it." He tosses a lint-riddled sweater into my chest before grunting for me to hurry up and get dressed. "If you walk in like that, you won't make it through the night untouched. Castro won't like that. He always gets first dibs."

The burn of my throat is horrendous. I've heard that name

before. It was mentioned by members of Dimitri's crew many times when they discussed the crew holding his daughter captive.

I'm grateful I am about to meet the little girl I haven't stopped thinking about since Dimitri showed me her photograph, but I'm also worried. This place is derelict and rundown. If my confines are worse than this, there's only one place I'm going. Straight to hell.

The stranger does a final glance at the shadows between my legs before he throws open the door of his truck and steps down. As he makes his way to my side of the retro-vehicle, I slip the sweater over my head, breathing easier when it falls to my knees. I'm not just grateful to have my modesty back, I am thankful for the warmth. It's a lot colder here than it was in Hopeton.

"Did this region have early snow as predicted over Thanksgiving?"

It's the fight of my life not to pout when he answers my question with a grunt. I was hoping he was as stupid as he looks. The fact he's going against a man as powerful as Dimitri reveals he's lax on smarts, he just doesn't want me to know that.

"Out." I fall out of the cabin of his truck too fast for my dead legs to keep up with when he tugs on my arm. My body isn't just sore from being motionless for hours. The press of my thighs as I've fought to hold back the screams of my bladder make it seem as if I have run a marathon.

"Can I please use the restroom?" I request from my station on the sloshy ground. "I can't hold it any longer."

"Soon." He hoists me from the ground by my arm. Although his reply wasn't what I was hoping, it's better than a straight-up no.

The reason for my unrequired deprivation of liberty is exposed when he guides me into a room on the lower level of the rundown ranch. The lights are switched off, but since my eyes have become accustomed to the dark, I can see the equipment in front of me as if it is daylight. A bed similar to the one in Dr. Bates's office sits squashed against the back wall, and an ultrasound monitor and paraphernalia is on its right.

"Get on the bed." I barely shake my head for a second when the goon rips my hair from my scalp with a brutal clutch. "I wasn't asking."

My eyes don't know which way to look when he drags me across the room by my hair—at the shadows above my head revealing there are people peering at me through the cracks in the floorboards, the shadow I hear snickering in the corner of the room, or the obvious ruckus of drunken men below me.

When I'm tossed onto the bed as if I'm weightless and tied down like a mental patient in a psychiatric hospital, I settle on the shadows dancing above my head. They're as silent as my frozen heart but somehow comforting. They wouldn't watch if this was about to be gory. Only horrible, vile people would stand by and watch someone be tortured.

A cool breeze wafts against my thighs when the man raises the waistband of the sweater, drawing my focus back to him. He bands the over-used material under my breasts before he squeezes a generous dollop of clear fluid onto the middle of my stomach.

"Lower," says a voice at the side, her tone very much feminine and unique. "If she's only a few weeks along, you need to scan just above her pubic bone."

Her knowledge of ultrasounds makes me sick.

This isn't the first time she's done something like this, guaranteed.

I stop seeking her features in the dark when the faintest movement in the corner of my eye captures my attention. With my bladder at the point of bursting, the man had no issue finding the unexpected bundle in the lower half of my stomach. I'm still a novice when it comes to all things pregnancy-related, but even someone as naïve as me has no trouble identifying the blob on the screen, even with its head appearing alien-like.

I'm so in awe at the smidge of black on the screen, I don't peer at the lady cloaking her face with darkness when she asks, "How far along?" I'm too interested in discovering the man's reply to pay the disgust in her tone any attention.

The dark-haired man twists his lips. "Not far. I'd guess around six or eight weeks."

"Good. That will make things easier." After waving her hand through the air like a regal princess, wordlessly granting the man permission to untie me, she exits the room via a hidden entrance on her left. It's just as dark in that part of the house as the room with my baby's image frozen on the screen, but the moonlight bouncing off her golden locks reveals she's as blonde as the reflection I saw in the mirror when Megan Shroud was admitted for a psych workup.

Endeavoring to keep my excitement on the down-low about the many pieces of the puzzle I've gathered today, I lower my sweater before accepting the hand the man is holding out to assist me off the sterile-looking bed.

Once my shuddering thighs are concealed by the low rise of the itchy material, I lift my eyes to the man and ask, "What will make things easier?"

I curse my inquisitiveness to hell when the man replies, "This will."

He grips the nape of my sweater, bends me in half to ensure my stomach feels the full impact of his fist, then hits me with everything he has. His punch knocks the wind right out of me. I fall back with a gasp, the pain tearing through me the worse I've ever experienced. It doubles the cramps I've been having all day and forces tears to spring into my eyes.

The only good that comes from so much pain is my body's natural instinct to curl into a ball. My new position protects my stomach from the man's boot when he kicks me over and over and over again, his onslaught only ending when the blackness seeping out of his heart overwhelms me, and my will to live gives up.

9

DIMITRI

I stare at the monitor on Smith's laptop with my blood boiling and my fists balled. The shoddy live broadcast shows Roxanne lying on a dirty floor. She's curled into a ball, unmoving and unspeaking. There's no physical indication as to why she isn't moving. If it weren't for the dried streams of wetness marking her cheeks, you could believe she's sleeping. She looks peaceful, almost angelic.

"There." Rocco points to the faintest rise and fall beneath the two-sizes too large sweater Roxanne is wearing. She's breathing, but it's shallow and irregular.

"Count them out to me," Smith requests after hacking into a 911 operator's program. "By counting her breaths, we'll get an indication of her heartrate. That will tell us whether she's sleeping or not."

"She isn't sleeping," I mutter out at the same time Rocco says, "Now."

"They didn't send me this for no reason. They want me to see what they're capable of. They want me to back down." When silence falls across my office, my determination grows. "I'm not doing that this time around. I'm Dimitri-fucking-Petretti. If you mess with me, you lose your life. Can't explain it any simpler than that."

I try to breathe out the anger eating me alive. I try to keep a rational head, but before even Rocco can predict what I'm about to do, I remove the gun from the back of my trousers, flick off the safety, then squash the barrel to the teeny tiny groove between Agent Ellie Gould's brows. "Give me something."

She's been here, working side by side with us for the past couple of hours, yet she's not shared one useful snippet of information. I don't like praising the Feds, but that is as irregular as me maintaining my cool when the itch to kill is skating through my veins. The Bureau doesn't hire solely on looks. They want the smarts as well. Ellie has both, and up until today, she used them to her advantage. She not once displayed the blonde bimbo she's been faking today.

When I inch back the trigger, Ellie's lips get waggling. "I don't know anything..." Her words are gobbled up by a big swallow when even Smith hears the deceit in her tone. He was on his feet in an instant, prepared to protect her as he had promised years ago. Now he's sinking away, certain he's being played for a fool.

"Smith..." She appears hurt by his reluctance, perhaps even heartbroken. "I-I-I swear, I don't know anything."

Her pupils dilate as wide as mine when Smith flicks on the communication mic next to his makeshift terminal before he speaks a set of words I never thought I'd hear him say. "Activate extermination orders for 8324 West Mulberry Lane, Ravenshoe. Shoot to kill. No survivors needed."

"No!" Ellie cries out with a sob, fighting me with more gusto than she's shown at any stage today. "Don't do this, Smith. Please."

She's so close to collapsing, I have to grip the front of her shirt as I did her throat only hours ago. Several buttons on her silky blouse pop, but it has nothing on the scream she releases when Smith lowers the projector screen at the side of my office to display Clover and a team of three men getting ready to storm Ellie's family's beachside residence.

I'm shocked. I thought I was the only one noticing Ellie's erratic behavior this evening. I had no clue Smith, Rocco, and Clover were aware of it too. Raids like this aren't something you set up in a couple of minutes. It takes time and preparation.

"No, no, no," Ellie screams on repeat when Clover screws a silencer onto the end of his weapon before he covers his tattooed cheek with a balaclava. "You can't do this. They're not a part of this. My career isn't on them."

Smith's accent is unrecognizable when he says, "You know what to say if you want it to stop. Tell Dimitri everything you know."

Ellie drifts her drenched eyes to Smith. "As I told them, I don't know anything. We broke up before Fien was taken."

The fact she knows my daughter's name is a slap in the face, but I keep my focus on the game I'm meant to be playing, not the one I already fielded. "Told who?"

Ellie's eyes return to mine. "I don't know who they are. They wanted information about your daughter. I told them I didn't know anything." Tears topple down her cheeks when she blurts out, "That's when they told me to go to the warehouse and await further instructions."

My brows join as confusion slices the tip off my anger. "I thought Theresa ordered you there?"

Since she's so worked-up, even her breathing crackles when she tattles, "They instructed me to tell you that if you showed up."

"And the plates we've been searching for the past four hours?" My voice is as hot as the anger roaring through my veins.

Ellie chokes back a sob before disclosing, "I did see a car when I arrived, but the tags and information on Megan's murder were patched through to my phone this morning."

I am tempted to crush her phone to death when she digs it out of her pocket to show us the messages she was sent. They're basic, but the prose is undeniable. She's being puppeteered by an outside source.

As the pieces of the puzzle slowly slot together, the truth smacks into me. "How did they get you to agree to do this? Not even an unbreakable bond could have you siding with the wrong side of the law."

Ellie doesn't need to answer my question. Her eyes tell me everything I need to know. They have the same petrified glint Roxanne's had when I used Estelle to force her to eat.

After stuffing my gun down the front of my pants, I snatch up the microphone Smith growled down a minute ago and press it to my lips. "This is a hostage situation. Exterminate the perpetrators. I repeat, *only* exterminate the perpetrators."

Clover peers at the body cam on Preacher's chest before he jerks up his chin, advising he understands my objective.

Once all four men are weaponed-up and ready to roll, they enter the Gould residence by a side entrance. The constant yap of a pair of chihuahuas exposes the perps are still in the vicinity. They don't pay Clover and his crew any attention. They're facing away from them, barking in the direction of the room Clover wordlessly instructs for his men to enter first.

The next thirty seconds is a blur of gunfire and wounded cries. The sobs aren't coming from my men. They don't murmur a peep during operations like this. They remain completely quiet, aware sneaky attacks are usually more deadly.

Within minutes of entering the premises, Clover unclips the body cam on his vest and swivels it around so I can see his face.

His brows are sweaty, and his grin is massive. He is in his element. "Perps have been exterminated. Hostages are uninjured and accounted for."

Ellie sucks in her first breath in what feels like minutes when he spins the camera around to show the remaining four members of her family bound and gagged but relatively unscathed.

"You owe me," I say before I can stop myself. "And I want payment in full, *today*."

I don't wait to see her nod because if it is slower than immediate, I'll order Clover to finish what Smith attempted to start. That's how worked up I am and how hollow my chest feels. Roxanne wasn't meant to get hurt, and although tears are usually painless, I have a feeling Roxanne isn't experiencing that tonight. She's hurting. I can feel it in my bones, and I'm going to make sure the people responsible for her pain pay with more than their lives.

I'm going to claim their souls as well.

10

DIMITRI

I scrub a hand over my tired eyes when Smith and Ellie enter my office at the same time. Since Smith's shoulders are almost as wide as mine, he has to take a step back to let Ellie enter first. It's cordial for him to do and expected since Ellie has kept her word the past several hours. She's left no stone unturned as she has endeavored to repay her debt. Just like she wouldn't fall on the knife for Smith, she won't for me either, but she's convinced she doesn't need to get her hands dirty to achieve a good outcome.

"I think we have a way of unearthing Rimi's location." Smith lays a set of official-looking documents onto my desk before pressing his palms to the battered material. "Although we have no intel Roxanne is with him—"

"We both know he is," I interrupt, confident I know him well enough to know what direction he's taking.

He lifts his chin. "Ellie contacted some friends in the Bureau about an operation that's being kept under wraps. When her inquiries didn't yield any results, she contacted less- attributed colleagues."

When I shift my eyes to Ellie, she faintly smiles. She isn't comfortable with the line she's crossed, but she'll wear the injustice if it has her name smudged from my tally board sooner rather than later.

"What I said earlier about Internal Affairs investigating my department wasn't a lie. We've been under scrutiny for a couple of months now." Ellie digs through the stack of papers Smith laid out until she finds a trio of two men and one woman. "With bureaucratic tape the thickest it's ever been, IA will never say who their main suspects are, but even rookie agents can smell a rat." She waits to see if Smith smiles about the wit in her tone. When he doesn't, she gets back to business. "These were the main runners for IA's investigation. I reached out to the first two with the hope a little bit of ego-stroking would entice them into an unethical conversation." She screws up her nose. "They didn't take the bait. However..." she places down a photo of a man I'd guess to be mid-thirties with a dramatic flair, "... he loved having his ego stroked. So much so, he wanted to exchange pictures."

My lips quirk. "You went in as an admirer instead of a colleague?"

Smith doesn't look happy when she nods. "Previous exchanges with him assured me it was the right route to take."

"Was it?"

Smith nods along with Ellie this time around. "They exchanged photos. He admired Ellie's *almost* nude photograph..." he overemphasizes the word 'almost' to ensure I understand she wasn't exposed "... long enough for me to poke around on his computer. He's the nark IA is seeking." After waving his hand over the official-looking Bureau documents, he adds, "This is only a handful of stuff he's shared with the men his team is chasing."

The extra beat of my heart is heard in my question. "Is Rimi's current location amongst this?"

Disappointment smacks into me hard and fast when Smith shakes his head. "But it unveiled a way we can find out where he is."

"How?"

Ellie takes over the reins. "You're not the only one chasing Castro. A specialist team has been on his tail for months. From what I've heard, it's a joint CIA/FBI operation, which makes no sense whatsoever since Castro is a US citizen." Realizing she's getting off track, she waves her hand through the air, shooing away her inquisitiveness before starting again. "Anyhow, the lead on the case discovered Castro is after a new mark."

"Roxanne?"

"No," Smith and Ellie say in sync. "This woman."

My brows join when Ellie sets down a photograph of Isabelle Brahn. "What does Isaac's girlfriend have to do with this?"

"Nothing," Ellie says with a grin, pleased by the confusion in my tone. "Castro merely thinks she's this woman."

She hands another photograph to me. Just like Isabelle's image, I immediately recognize the blonde in the photograph. When I told Brandon James I did some digging, I wasn't lying. Not only did Smith discover he's the son of the New York governor—who I happen to have ties with—we also unearthed his first love, mindful not even the ultimate betrayal can break a connection between soulmates. Take Smith and Ellie's joint operation as an example.

"Castro wants Melody Gregg so badly, he's willing to come out of hiding to get her. He purchased tickets to an event Isabelle was set to attend as Melody this weekend." Air whizzes from Ellie's nose when she exhales deeply. "Unfortunately, the stunt was siphoned down the gurgler a couple of minutes ago."

"Why?" I don't mean to be blunt. I'm merely lost as to why they'll build up my eagerness only to squash it like an ant a second later.

"Isabelle Brahn was just arrested," Smith informs, his tone low.

I shrug like it's no big deal. "Have a replacement brought in. Castro is like my father. He can't tell the difference between one blonde and another."

"We can't. It's too late," Ellie replies. "The lead on this case released Isabelle's image on a report she wrote up about Melody Gregg. Castro doesn't just have a name to go off on anymore, he has a face."

"She's a fucking woman not a priceless painting. Surely, you can find someone with similar features."

I know what I'm saying is wrong. I am just too filled with anguish to rope in my arrogance. This is the only solid lead we've had in hours, and it's for a function that's days away.

I can't wait days.

For every hour Roxanne is gone, her chances of survival greatly decrease. She's already been at Rimi's mercy for over twenty-four hours. I could already be too late.

Furthermore, I'm beginning to suspect her kidnapping isn't about money. Audrey's ransom landed in my inbox almost instantaneously with her kidnapping. That hasn't occurred this time around, making me believe Roxanne's captives want to drain my veins, not my bank accounts.

The best way for them to do that is to kill Roxanne.

I won't let that happen.

I'll become as vicious and relentless as my father before I'd ever let that happen.

With that in mind, I ask, "How can we get Isabelle to the event Castro will be at?"

Smith smiles as if I fell straight into the trap he set for me. "Simple. Get Isabelle out of lock-up."

I give him a look, warning him to dull down the antics before growling through clenched teeth, "She was arrested in Ravenshoe. I don't have jurisdiction there."

He completely ignores my threatening glare. "But you know the man who does."

I fall back into my chair with a laugh. It reveals how unhinged I am. "I'm not siding with Isaac."

"Why not?"

With my anger too perverse to hold back, I shout, "Because although he didn't hold a gun to my sister's head, he is the reason she's dead! If he had just forfeited the fight, Ophelia and CJ would still be here, and I wouldn't be left dealing with all my father's shit by myself."

I didn't mean to express my last sentence out loud, but I'm glad I couldn't hold back when it forces Ellie to use the non-agent side of her head. "Get Brandon to ask Isaac for help." She angles her body to face Smith. "You saw the way he protected Isabelle during her arrest. He cares for her, but—"

"He's still in love with his ex, so he'll always choose to place Isabelle into the fire over her," Smith fills in, gleaming. "Who were the arresting officers?"

They stop shuffling through papers when I mutter out, "You won't find them." I smirk at the shock on their faces before adding, "If Isabelle was my sister, and she needed someone to protect her during her arrest, you'd never find the officers responsible for it. The cartel doesn't leave evidence, and neither does the Russian mob."

Ellie gasps in a shocked breath. Smith's response is much more deviant than that. He smiles a grin I've only ever seen on his face once before. It was the night we bumped into Ellie as we exited a private jet. We were in New York to create havoc. Smith fell in love.

"What's your plan?" Smith asks, knowing me well enough to read the expression on my face as plotting.

After a few seconds of deliberation, I reply, "Brandon's father owes me a favor. Cash it in." After standing to my feet, I gather my suit jacket from the hanger in the corner of my office. "Her chariot won't be a pumpkin, and her footmen won't be knights, but we'll get Cinderella to the ball, even if I have to drag her there myself."

11

ROXANNE

A grunt involuntarily leaves my parched throat when my wrist is snagged in a firm clutch, and I'm yanked off the floor I've been cowering on the past several hours. I'm sore, on the verge of weeping, but still willing to fight. Even though he knocked me down, until my legs are broken, I will get back up, bigger, stronger, and meaner than ever.

My grunt this time around is well-timed. It adds to the fury of the fist I ram into the unnamed man's face and propels me so far out of his arms, I'm halfway out the door before he knows I'm running.

I don't race for the entrance he forced me through last night, I charge for the whispered voices that encouraged me to wake up when the blackness overwhelmed me. They want me to win as much as I want them to be free. We are in this together. I've just got to find where they're hiding to ensure them I am on their side.

I make it up four stairs before my ankle is gripped and pulled out from beneath me. While breathing through the windedness my collision with the wooden stairwell caused my lungs, I kick out like a madwoman. I smash my heel into the man's face that's already dribbling blood on repeat, determined to show him I'm not as weak and pathetic as he thinks.

It takes three solid stomps on his nose for him to release my ankle from his hold, and even longer than that for me to reach the peak of the stairwell. As I gasp in much-needed air, I take a moment to gather my bearings. The pain distorting my mind has me confused as to whether I took a left or right when I exited the room that had me gleaming with happiness and sobbing with sadness in under a minute. I think it was left, but I'm truly unsure.

When the heavy stomps of the man's boots boom into my ears, I dart to the left, praying I'm heading in the right direction. If the number of voices I heard overnight are anything to go by, just the volume of women in one space should conceal me until I work out my next plan of attack. I don't stand out in a crowd. I never have.

I send a quick thanks to my Nanna when she answers my silent prayer. The room I just barged into is brimming with women. There are ethnicities from across the globe—Americans, Asians, Europeans—they have every nationality covered.

There are children too.

Many of them.

Although I'm dying to seek a toddler with chubby cheeks, elf ears, and a dimple in the top of her lip, the furious breaths of the man hot on my tail stops me. I will find Fien, I've just got to survive this madman's wrath first.

"Thank you," I mutter in shock when several women switch out my sweat-drenched sweater with the Mormon-like clothes they're wearing.

Their nighties are white, cotton, and very bland considering how attractive their faces are. I thought they'd be glammed up to the hilt, ensuring they got top dollar from interested buyers. Instead, they're dressed as if they are in a convent.

"Sit, sit," says a blonde with a heavy accent as she tugs on my arm.

Once I'm on the floor, I am surrounded by over three dozen women. The fact they want to protect me springs tears to my eyes. They're living in horrible circumstances, and I don't want to think about how they've been treated, yet here they are, still willing to help someone in need.

Despite the circumstances, it is truly a beautiful thing to witness.

I tuck my chin in close to my chest when the man enters the door I left hanging open. The reason for his delay is unearthed when I spot the cleaver in his hand. He had to get reinforcements. The thought makes me smile.

"Where is she?" he asks a group of women on my right.

They don't answer him. They keep their heads bowed and their lips shut.

It angers him further. "I won't ask again! You know what happens when you don't listen to my first order."

My heart launches into my throat when he fists the nightgown of the smallest woman in the group. He's so much taller than her, her feet dangle inches from the grubby floor when he brings her close enough to him, the brutal crunch of his hand colliding with her cheek will ring in my ears for days.

"Where. Is. She?"

When he moves the cleaver toward her left breast, I almost vault out of my spot. The only reason I don't is because the blonde next to me curls her hand over my balled one before whispering in broken English, "He won't hurt. Not allowed. Slap okay. Further..." She makes a throat-cutting gesture. "Watch."

As promised, within seconds, the brute releases the brunette from his grip before he swings his eyes across the room. I'm confident he won't spot me in a crowd, so you can imagine my surprise when he mutters out a few moments later, "There you are."

The women rally around me when he grips my hair like he did before my ultrasound to drag me out of the room. They claw him, bite him, and whack into him as if their biggest fear is losing me. They give it their all, but it still isn't enough.

Before my head can register I'm the only one left fighting, I am tossed on a bed in a sterile, uninviting room, and the man tugs at his belt as unforgivingly as he did my hair. "If you don't want to get hurt more than you already are, I suggest you remain still."

I kick out with a scream when he suddenly dives for me. It does me no good. He pins me to the mattress in an instant, my small frame no match for his height and weight. My vision blurs with unshed tears when he uses his recently removed belt to bind my hands above my head. He isn't restraining me until I calm down, nor is he planning to mark me with his scent. He wants to take something from me I'm not willing to give. He wants the very thing I will fight to the death for.

"Get off." I fight him with everything I have, hating the disgusting slither of his hand when he slips it underneath the nightgown the women dressed me in. "He will kill you just for looking at me before setting his men onto your family. You'll die a death more painful than a thousand. He won't stop until your eyes cry blood and your entire lineage is extinct."

His voice is almost too composed for a maniac. "Not if we kill him first."

I don't get time to absorb the actuality in his tone. I'm too busy recoiling about the growl he releases when he notches a finger inside of me.

"Tight," he purrs on a moan before he swivels his finger around like he's testing the durability of my vaginal walls. I'm clenched so tight, I almost dismember him when he suddenly yanks his finger back out.

He stares down at his dry index finger like he's disappointed there isn't any residue for him to inspect. I realize that is the case when he swivels his torso to a mirrored door at the side of the room. He holds the finger he had inside of me in the air before briskly shaking his head.

Even with the spectator's sigh occurring after the *doink* of a microphone being switched on, I still heard it. It was as depressing as the dread that sludges through me when she says, "Do whatever is necessary to get rid of it." She spits out 'it' as if it scorched her throat.

Confident he will do as asked, the shadow under the door clears away a mere second before the goon yanks off a sheet from a silver tray next to the bed I'm tied to. It houses an assortment of instruments that are every woman's nightmare—a hospital-grade kidney dish, long skinny clamp-type instruments, a needle filled with a murky substance, and the most concerning, a rusty coat hanger that's been flattened so only the hook at the end remains.

"W-w-what do you need that for?" I hate the stutter of my first word, but it can't be helped. The coat hanger should be the least worrying of the instruments on his tray of horror. However, it isn't. I grew up in a region of America that didn't have the funds to handle unwanted pregnancies with dignity. I heard many horror stories during my two years at college. This isn't as brutal as the backyard cesarean Audrey was forced to endure, but the result will be so much worse.

Fien survived Audrey's ordeal. My baby doesn't stand a chance, even more so when the man uses my distraction to his advantage. He jabs the needle from the medical tray into my leg, paralyzing me from the waist down. Then, shortly after that, my vision blurs as blackness strives to overwhelm me for the second time in less than twenty-four hours.

12

DIMITRI

As I tap my tattooed-covered finger on my knee, Smith's voice comes down the earpiece in my ear. "The call has been made. Agent James should be out any minute."

I'm parked in front of Ravenshoe PD, awaiting Brandon's break for freedom. If the gleaming glare Detective Ryan Carter hit me with when he noticed Rocco's illegal park is anything to go by, he knows who we're here for. He was outside the restaurant when the Russians came to town for a visit, so he'd be aware of my impromptu meeting with a Federal Agent.

I could tell him things aren't as they seemed, but where's the fun in that? Ryan isn't my friend. He wasn't when he snagged the most attractive girl in junior high and won't be when he finally discovers where she's been hiding these past few months.

The restlessness keeping my stomach empty the past fourteen years ramps up when my cell phone suddenly buzzes in my pocket. With Smith in my ear, Clover on high alert a couple of blocks over, and Rocco acting as my driver, there's only one other person who has my private number—my father.

Since he's the last person I want to speak to, I slide my phone out of my pocket and hit the 'end call' button without peering at the screen. "Have my father's calls sent straight to my voicemail. I've got eyes on him. I don't want him in my ear as well."

Smith hums out a panicked murmur before he discloses he has footage of my father nowhere near a phone.

"Live feed?"

He gags. "From the pendant on the whore you sent over to keep him occupied this afternoon. Trust me, none of his fingers are able to dial right now."

While fighting the urge not to slit Rocco's throat over his chuckle about my disgruntled expression, I swipe my thumb across the screen of my phone and hit my phone app. The area code reveals my caller is in the New York region, but the number isn't familiar.

I'm about to ask Smith to commence a trace when a text message pops up on my screen.

Unknown number: *Please tell me she wasn't found on the Shroud ranch. I can't stand the thought of her being buried so close to home and not knowing. I thought I'd sense her presence. We were close like that.*

Against Smith's recommendation not to engage until he completes a trace, I type out a reply.

Dimitri: *Who is this?*

"Someone wanting to cover her tracks since she's bouncing her signal off multiple towers," Smith growls down my earpiece just as my caller's text pops up.

Unknown Number: *It's India. I thought you had my number stored. Was she there, Dimi? Did you finally find her?*

"What is she talking about?" I ask anyone listening, the twisting of my stomach too perverse to ignore.

Smith breathes out a curse word a mere second before Ellie's voice comes down the line. "I'm sending you a link. It isn't pretty."

Mine and Rocco's phone buzzes in sync. My eyes don't know which section of the article to absorb first. The fact multiple bodies were found on a ranch only a hundred miles from Hopeton, that they were buried beside enough hospital supplies to fill an antenatal ward with or the headline that the body of a toddler was found in the wall of the residence.

"How old was she?"

When nothing but silence resonates out of my earpiece for the next several seconds, my panic shifts to fury. "How fucking old was she!" I scream like my lungs don't need air to function. I thought the knot in my stomach centered around Roxanne. I had no fucking clue my focus should have been on Fien.

It should have always been on Fien.

If I had protected her mother as I'm endeavoring to protect Roxanne, I wouldn't be here, fiddling my thumbs while maniacs run my town to the ground.

Perhaps I am as bad as my father.

Maybe this is my penance for the wrongs I've done.

My self-reflection is held back for another time when Smith discloses, "The corpse was mummified. She had been in the wall for a while."

His tone is both sorrowed and angry, but it does little to ease my agitation. "That wasn't what I asked. You know you can alter the age of a corpse. You're aware you can manipulate it to fool forensic scientists. She could be Fien. She could be my daughter."

The pain clawing my chest gets a moment of reprieve when Rocco says, "She isn't Fien, Dimi." He swivels in his seat to face me before handing me a printout of the report Ellie just forwarded. The Tank isn't just a muscle car. She's a command station on wheels. "Not only do the dates on the newspaper clippings surrounding the little girl's corpse disclose this, so does your gut. You'd know if Fien was gone, D, because you live for her. You've not done a single thing the past two years that wouldn't benefit her in some way." His grin gets smug along with his comment. "Except Roxie, but she doesn't count because she improved your chances of getting your daughter back instead of reducing it."

Before I have the chance to reply to any part of his statement, the back entrance of Ravenshoe PD pops open, and a showdown between Ravenshoe PD's finest and the Bureau's golden boy gets underway.

It's clear Ryan and Brandon have had words before. The tension in the air is thick enough to cut with a knife, although it has nothing on the unease in the cabin of The Tank.

After slicing his hand across the front of his body, wordlessly sending Brandon off, Ryan locks his eyes with the back passenger window of The Tank. I store the report of the mass grave site at Shroud Family Ranch into the slot in my door before popping open the one opposite from me, more than happy for Ryan to know who I'm schmoozing. Perhaps if he knows my pull extends all the way to the Bureau, he might accept one of the many offers I've made him the past six years.

"Game face, Dimi," Smith mutters in my ear when Brandon's gawk at my open door sees him jogging down the stairs separating us. "He's smarter than his baby face implies."

I doubt Smith's assumption when confusion congeals Brandon's face a mere second after he slides into the back seat of The Tank. He walked into an ambush, smiling. A smart man doesn't do that.

He also doesn't test the durability of the locks the jaws of life couldn't budge.

"You'd have a better chance of shooting out the bulletproof

windows than getting its lock mechanisms to budge. I paid out the eye to make this thing a tank, but the quality of the product was worth its exorbitant price tag."

I hear his jaw go through a stern workover before he shifts his eyes to me. "What do you want, Dimi—"

"Information," I cut him off, eager to get things moving. My head is spinning. I don't have time for idle chit-chat.

Like a fool unaware of what happens to men who waste my time, Brandon's lips etch into a condescending smirk. "That isn't how things work. We ask you for information. If we find it beneficial, we help you. That's what being an informant entails."

"Informant?" Ignoring Smith's advice for me to take a chill pill, I spit out, "I'm *not* an informant for the FBI. They work for me, not the other way around."

It takes everything I have not to reach for my gun when Brandon replies, "That may have been how things worked with you and Tobias, but that won't fly with me."

"Reveal your hand, Dimitri," Ellie suggests, overtaking the reins from Smith. "I've never worked with Agent James, but if he's anything like the rumors I've heard, outsmarting him will work better than threatening him. He's all about brains over brawn."

After an inconspicuous nod, I shove the report Rocco gave to me into Brandon's chest. "Is this report accurate?"

The brutal bob of his Adam's apple reveals Ellie was on the money. He isn't stunned by the information he's reading on the reports, he is shocked I have them. I just wish suspicion wasn't also on his face. He doesn't realize I'm a victim of the trade he's investigating. He thinks I'm a part of it. I guess I shouldn't be surprised. My family name has been embroiled in controversy for longer than I've been born.

"Where did you get this? This hasn't even been logged with the Bureau yet."

I lower the angst in my tone before replying, "Where I got this information isn't important. I just need to know if it's true?"

He peers at me as if I have a second head before he mutters, "Yes, it's true."

"Are all the victims female?" I ball my hands together so tightly, my nails dig into my palm when I ask, "What's the average age of the women found?"

Brandon wets his dry lips before he sings like a canary. "Preliminary findings state the victims are between the ages of thirteen to late twenties."

The fact he doesn't mention the toddler found in the wall exposes he knows more than he's letting on. The knowledge he's holding back frustrates me to no end, but I do my best to maintain a rational head. "Had any of the victims recently given birth before their death?"

He shrugs. "We won't know that until the autopsies are completed."

"You would know." My voice comes out louder than intended. It even makes Rocco jump. "You'd know because she's eight months along..." I swallow the unease burning my throat before correcting, "She *was* eight months along."

With my head cloudy from the debilitating images in the report, I honestly feel like I've stepped back twenty-two months. Rocco is right, I'd know if Fien was hurt, I'm just struggling to get my logical-thinking head with the program. It's coded to see the worst in everything. Very rarely does it consider the silver lining.

Conscious our conversation may hit a stalemate, I remove the photograph of Audrey I placed into the breast pocket of my jacket, then pass it to Brandon. I hate the sympathy vote. More times than not, it makes me angrier than recalling how my enemies have played me for a fool the past two years.

I'm not feeling that sentiment today.

Brandon wears his heart on his sleeve. If I can play on it, I'll have him eating out of the palm of my hand even quicker than my daughter's upside-down grubby face stole my heart from my chest.

"I paid the ransom they requested." My jaw tightens to the point of cracking. "They didn't uphold their side of our agreement."

It dawns on me that Brandon was closer to Tobias than realized when he asks, "Was Tobias aware you paid the ransom?"

His expression remains neutral when I shake my head. "Tobias approached me a few days after the drop. He said there was a complication securing Audrey." I can't admit my wrongdoings in her ransom. If I do, guilt will eat me alive in an instant.

"I told you he's smarter than he looks," Smith says down the earpiece lodged in my ear when Brandon gabbles out, "You're not searching for Audrey. You're trying to find your child."

"Tobias was supposed to get her out. He assured me she was safe, and that it would be only a matter of time before she was returned to me." Those were the exact words Tobias spoke to me the night he called to say they were raiding the Castro compound within the hour. I begged him to wait until I got there. He said he couldn't. "Then—"

"Tobias was killed during the Castro raid?" Although Brandon sounds as if he's asking a question, I don't see it like that. He's summarizing.

After a couple of minutes of deliberation, he moves our conversation in a direction I never saw coming. "When was your daughter last seen?"

"I didn't get you out of lockup to investigate my daughter's disappearance." Although I appreciate his wish to help, the last time I got a federal agent involved in Fien's disappearance, I lost her for months on end. I won't let that happened again. "I did it so you can continue with your ruse to force Castro out of hiding."

Shock registers on Brandon's face. It's quickly swallowed by anger. "You can't use the Bureau to get revenge on Castro."

I smile an evil grin. "I'm not getting revenge on Castro. I'm going to kill him as he did my wife."

Roxanne's father may have held Fien by her feet after removing her from Audrey's stomach, but he wasn't the only man in the room. There were several of them, and I'm confident the ringleader was Rimi Castro.

"I can't legally help you with this, Dimitri."

With his resolve strong enough to know words won't crack it, I get inventive. "You'll do as I ask, or I'll release this to the hounds."

Blood drains from his face when I hand him a drafted bounty for his long-lost girlfriend, Melody Gregg. It hasn't been lodged, but all it will take is a single push of a button for her bounty to be activated. Unlike the payout on Roxanne's head, this one will be cashed in because men like Clover don't back down when they're on the hunt.

Brandon grips the single sheet of paper enough to crinkle it down the middle before he strays his eyes to mine. I had never really paid their hazel coloring any attention previously. I only switched things up today because they're filled with so much fury, they appear more green than brown. "How do I know you haven't already released this?"

"She's still alive, isn't she? Living it up in a fancy penthouse apartment in New York City with her billionaire boyfriend." I show him the video Smith and Ellie downloaded when they discovered Brandon's ruse to have Isabelle impersonate Melody at a function later this week. It doubles the blatant rage in his eyes. "Even with a wrong set of photographs attached to her file, the real Melody wasn't hard to find."

I don't mention the fact his father led a member of my New York chapter right to his ex. Vincent McGee only owed me one favor, but when you like your women young enough, you'll face consecutive life sentences if word gets out, you're a little more generous with your 'colleagues.'

Vincent's association with my family is being taken care of as we speak, but I'll have to save the details for another day since Brandon shifts our exchange from civil to prudishly fun in zero point eight seconds.

He grips the lapels of my jacket before dragging me to his side of the cabin. "If you hurt her—"

"You'll what? Kill me as I want to slay the man who murdered my wife. He cut our daughter out of her stomach, then left her to die! He treated her like fucking scum, so if I have to use your high school sweetheart as bait because your hero-complex wants to stop a war that started long before you joined the Bureau, I fucking will. I'll do anything it takes to gut Castro as he did me."

My rant started with Audrey in my thoughts, but it ended with Roxanne. I've told myself time and time again the past two hours that she was breathing in the footage I saw of her, and she looked unharmed, but my gut knows better. She's hurting. Deep down inside, there's no denying the truth.

Needing Brandon to go before I forget he isn't the man I'm chasing, I remember the reason I got him out of lockup. "Do what needs to be done to get Castro out of hiding, then leave the rest up to me." When I hear Rocco release the lock mechanisms on the door, I lean across Brandon to open his door for him. "And start here as he'll get your Honey Pot out of lockup even faster than your daddy's fancy title will."

Brandon misses my accidental slip-up. He's too busy staring at the entrance of Isaac Holt's nightclub, stunned as a mullet that I brought him here.

It takes him a handful of attempts to get his legs to follow the prompts of his brain. I assume because his knees are knocking about meeting the man who pipped him at the post but am proven wrong when he pops his head back into the cabin of The Tank. "If you do this, you'll be hunted as fiercely as you've been chasing Castro the past two years. What kind of life will that be for your daughter? Hasn't she been through enough? You're her father. You are supposed to protect her, not put her in more danger."

When he slams the door in my face, oblivious to the fact I'm seconds from removing his insides via his bellybutton, Rocco locks his eyes with mine in the rearview mirror. "We need him."

"We don't fucking need him." I want to add that I don't need anyone, but since Rocco will see straight through that lie, I keep my mouth shut.

Just like my pain is my motivation, so is my wish not to be alone. It takes courage to wage a battle by yourself, but it is even more courageous to admit you need help.

After climbing over the partition separating Rocco and me, I switch on the state-of-the-art GPS system. "Send through Rico's last known location to The Tank's mainframe." As Smith hums out an acknowledging murmur, I swing my eyes to Rocco. "It's better to fight for something than live for nothing, right?"

Rocco's smirk reveals he understands where I'm going with this, much less what he says next, "They say you should never interrupt your enemy when he's making a mistake. They don't say anything about helping them make it."

13

ROXANNE

"This will only take a couple of minutes, then you can rest up."

The drugs the dark-haired goon jabbed into my thigh must be top-shelf because he almost sounded sincere while assuring me I'll only be at his mercy for a few more minutes. Even the way he folds up the nightie the women upstairs lent me is gentle. He takes his time like he isn't in the process of stripping me of the only thing I've felt a part of wholeheartedly.

My ranch was my grandparents, my bed was bought on credit, even the shoes I was wearing earlier today weren't mine. They were from Alice's vast collection of pretty things. My child is the only thing I have of any value, and it's about to be taken away from me.

I don't know where my strength comes from when I gather it to shove the man away from me, but it's surprisingly robust. My push sends him crashing into the stainless-steel trolley he dragged closer to my bedside while waiting for me to succumb to his mind-numbing concoction. It reveals that only the lower half of my body is paralyzed. My arms, although heavy, can still protect my child and me.

"Now look what you've gone and done." His earlier niceties are now a thing of the past. He's back to the maniac who held me captive for hours on end without bathroom privileges.

While gabbling out about this being the reason he isn't nice, he bends down to gather up the instruments my push knocked to the floor. Forgetting my legs are numb, I use his distraction to my advantage. I fall to the floor with a clatter, bruising both my backside and my ego.

"Seriously?" the man chokes out, laughing. "Do you truly think you can crawl to safety? We're in the middle of nowhere, it will be below freezing as soon as the sun disappears, and you have nowhere to hide. You won't last five minutes out there."

When he folds his thick arms in front of his chest, it seems as if he wants to test his theory. He doesn't shadow my snail-like creep across the filthy floor. He watches my retreat with a smirk etched on his face and his brow arched, only jumping into action when I add a frantic scream into the mix.

"Help me! Please! I'm down here!" I bang and bang and bang my fists against the tiled floor when he hooks his arm around my waist and hoists me back, then I smack them into his chest. "He's going to kill my baby! Please help me!"

I fight him with everything I have—teeth, nails, and the brutal pounds of my fists. I whack into him on repeat, my fight only lessening when the violent crack of a skull being punished sounds through my ears.

I brace, anticipating impact.

The pain never comes because the man didn't strike me.

He was hit.

"Quickly."

A flurry of red and white circles me when my savior hoists me off the bed. With the drugs in my system finally displaying their full effect, my legs aren't the only things out of action. My head is as heavy as my limbs. I can barely see through the curtain of red in front of my eyes, and I'm not going to mention the slur of my words.

"I can't..." I stop, swallow, then try again. "I can't move my legs."

"It's okay, lean on me, we only have a few steps to take," whispers a soft female voice full of sorrow and distress.

With all my weight on her shoulders, she moves us through the residence still plunged into darkness even with it being late in the afternoon. She weaves us through narrow corridors like she intimately knows the floorplan, and within seconds, I'm once again at the bottom of the stairs.

"Help me, please," my rescuer begs to the shadows my cloudy head is confusing as demons dancing in the dark. They prance above my head, all impish and fiend-like. I'm so convinced they're Satan's urchins come to collect me for my transgressions when they finally relent to my savior's pleas, I pull back, undogged on my wish to live.

"No!" I scream at them as I did the man, certain they're destined to hurt me.

"It's okay. They will help you," assures the lady still glued to my side. "I promise."

When she strays her eyes to mine, assuring I can see the pledge in them, I'm certain my life is coming to an end.

My savior isn't an angel sent from above to protect me.

She is the very thing I'm scared about the most.

She is Dimitri's wife, Audrey.

14

DIMITRI

Rocco strays his eyes from Rico to me. "Do you think he'll tell her?"

His distrust is understandable. We just told a mobster the Feds are going to use his big sister as bait. If we shared the intel with anyone but Rico, worry would be the last thing we'd feel. Regretfully, Rico values his family more than his counterparts. It was risky of me to disclose my plans, but as I said days ago, as long as we continue working toward a common objective, I have no problem pretending we're on the same team.

"He wanted the man responsible for brutalizing Isabelle during her arrest. I handed them to him. It'll do him best to remember that, or we will no longer play nice."

Rocco waits for the tail lights of Rico's car to disappear out of the marina's lot before he slides into the driver's seat of The Tank. "What do you want to do about him?"

He nudges his head to the left. Agent Grayson Rogers doesn't even attempt to shield his face with the shadows of the night. He wants me to know he's watching, and I'm more than happy for him to do exactly that.

"Nothing. He isn't after me... *this time.*" Rocco chuckles at the slow deliverance of my last two words. Grayson has been hot on my tail for years. I only got him off when I proved I wasn't the one who sold Katie Bryne to Kirill Bobrov. He still hangs around every now and then, but not enough for me to respond to it. We played nice when we needed to. When we didn't, our work 'relationship' ended.

"Have you heard anything from Smith?"

Rocco didn't join Rico and me in blowing off steam on the three officers who tossed Isabelle around like she was a ragdoll. He's usually all about punishing men who use their size and strength against women but keeping tabs on Roxanne's disappearance was more important to him. It's mine too. I just needed to put steps into place to ensure I'm covered when I go in hard and brutal to get her and Fien out.

My last two hours with Rico were well spent. Although the Castros were once umbrellaed under an entity strangled by rules I've been forced to follow since birth, their 'protection' became null and void a few years back. Rico didn't go into details on what transpired, but the Popovs no longer work with the Castros. They're a completely separate entity, meaning the rules no longer apply. I can take down the king of their realm without the slightest fear of retaliation.

It's a glorious day to be a gangster.

Some of the air in my swollen chest deflates when Rocco shakes his head. "Not since you grabbed your bat out of the trunk. He's working on triangulating the location the video clip was sent from, but he said he had some bureaucratic tape to get through first."

"Isaac?" My jaw is so tight, my one word sounds like an entire sentence since it was strained through my clenched teeth.

Rocco fires up the engine before he once again shakes his head. "Not even Isaac has jurisdiction in this town, and from what I've heard, he's one of Henry's favorites."

"Henry Gottle is blocking Smith's inquiries?"

"Mm-hmm," Rocco murmurs in response to the shock in my tone. "He's making Smith real fuckin' twitchy."

He isn't the only one feeling tense. "Rico just disclosed the Castros aren't umbrellaed under the Popov entity anymore, so is Henry throwing up barriers because he took them under his wing?" When Rocco shrugs, truly unsure, I try another angle. "Smith..."

Like always, he chimes in with a hum.

"What else was on Agent Moses's computer when you hacked in?"

His voice is groggy when he replies, "You mean other than porn?"

Rocco laughs. My response to Smith's gall is nowhere near as polite. For a man who just spent two hours teaching insolent men what happens when you fuck with family, my growl is almost bloodthirsty.

After catching his breath with a quick gulp, Smith discloses, "There were some files about a money-laundering syndicate on the West Coast, a couple of borderline kiddie-porn write-ups, and an old home-invasion case from two decades ago. Why? What are you looking for?"

"A link between the Gottles and the Castros," I answer without pause.

Smith's fingers give his keyboard a workout before he sighs. "Up until a couple of years ago, there wasn't a link."

"But there is now?" I ask, my interests piqued.

Air whizzes from his nose, indicating I'm very much on the money. "It isn't close to the relationship Isaac has with Henry, but there are definite benefits being shared."

That's unusual. You've got to give Henry something big to be in his favor. He now runs the city my family built from the ground up, yet we're still not shared more than common courtesies for the past decade.

"Dig deeper into the files. There's something we're missing."

"On it," Smith replies before he disconnects our connection with a clank.

Rocco gives me a couple of minutes to shake off my confusion before asking, "Back to the compound?"

I shake my head without pause for thought. "Head to Roxanne's ranch. I want to grab a couple of her things for when she's back. She'll feel more comfortable being surrounded by her belongings."

I didn't mean to say my last sentence, but I'm glad I couldn't hold back when Rocco murmurs, "She doesn't need *things*, Dimi. She just needs you."

15

ROXANNE

I wake up startled and confused. I'm in a room similar to the one I escaped from yesterday afternoon, but the sky is no longer moody with a low-hanging sun and ominous clouds. Light is beaming through the cracks in the bordered-up windows, and its bright rays alert it is well past dawn.

As I cradle my thumping head, I try to recall what happened between yesterday afternoon and now. I remember my stepless dash through a rundown ranch, the scary shadows above my head, and my near coronary upon discovering Audrey is alive, but other than that, my mind is blank. I don't remember entering this room at all. It's as if a good sixteen hours of my life just up and vanished.

Was I drugged again? Is that why I feel hungover?

While I seek answers to my questions, I swish my tongue around my mouth. My throat is drier than a desert. I wish I could say the same thing about the area between my legs.

Even without my hand creeping across the bedding that's clinging to my sweat-beaded skin, I'm confident I am bleeding. Not only did my brief movement waft a coppery scent into the air, there's also a knot in my stomach that won't come undone no matter how long I strive to avoid the obvious.

After carefully dabbing my fingers over the dampness coating my thighs, I snap my eyes shut, then raise my shaky hand to my face. I'm not a religious person, but I pray for a miracle on repeat before I gingerly open my eyes to inspect the sticky goop on my fingertips.

No, I inwardly scream when I noticed the blood coating my fingers. It's red, bright, and spread from the apex of my thighs to the back of my knees.

As I scoot up the mattress, needing distance from the product ripping my heart to shreds, I suck in air, forcing down the sob bubbling in my chest. Nothing can fix the tears in my eyes, though. They stream down my cheeks unchecked before they're absorbed by the nightwear drenched with cups of blood.

I'd give anything to go back to yesterday, to feel the same numbness I felt when I was aided out of the stranger's room of horrors because the pain tearing through me now is worse than anything I've ever experienced. It's so bad, a bullet could pierce through me, and I wouldn't feel it. It hurts so much. It truly feels as if I'm dying, like more than my baby is being absorbed by a dirty set of sheets. My heart is there too.

I've barely brought my gut-wrenching sobs down to a whimper when the door to my room shoots open. With how brutal he was hit late yesterday afternoon, the last person I anticipate to walk into my room is my original captor.

Even with him being struck hours ago, his walk is staggered. Audrey's hit hurt him. I shouldn't smile at the thought, but I do. He's a murderer, he doesn't deserve my sympathy. I hope he rots in hell but not before Dimitri slowly drives him there. He didn't just hurt me when he killed my baby, he took something from Dimitri he can never return, and it will cost him more than his life.

When I say that to the goon, he has the hide to smile. "I've always believed in an heir and a spare." He rubs his hands together like he isn't wearing a thick coat, jeans, and boots. "Unfortunately for you, royals don't like tainting the bloodline with bastard children. You should ask Dimitri about it the next time you see him. *If you ever see him again.*"

"Oh, I'll see him," I snap out before I can stop myself. "You can place money on it. Just like I can guarantee you're on your last breaths."

His words are like a knife to my chest when he mutters, "At least I had the chance to breathe. It's more than your bastard child will ever get."

The amount of blood I lost overnight should make me weak. It should render me incapable of moving, much less retaliating. However, now Audrey's bewildering recovery makes sense. There's nothing more frightening than a momma bear defending her cub. I only knew of my child's existence for a little over twenty-four hours, but that doesn't lessen their significance to me. He or she meant something. *They still do.*

I drag my nails down the goon's face while he attempts to silence my campaign by shoving the barrel of a gun under my ribs. The fact he needs a weapon to defend himself humors me. He is double my weight, my head only reaches his shoulders, yet he's still scared of me.

Good. He should be scared because hell hath no fury like a woman scorned.

While grunting through the pain of my palm ramming into his sternum, the goon slams his boot into my right foot, then twists. Pain shreds through me, but I keep my howl on the down-low, refusing to give him the satisfaction of knowing he hurt me again.

Once he has me wrapped up in a bear hug I can't loosen, he lowers his lips to my ear. "I couldn't work out why you had them so worried.

Yeah, you're pretty, you've got a nice set of tits, an ass you could bounce a quarter off, and a tight cunt I don't see letting up for years to come, but so do a million other American women." He lowers his arm from the top of my chest to the curves of my breasts. "But now I get it. Oh, how I have seen the light. You've got spunk, charisma…" He gropes my breast for each word he speaks. "All the things his wife doesn't have." I think he's creeping his hand down my stomach to defile me some more. I have no clue he's stabbing a final nail into my heart. "It's a pity you don't have his kid anymore. You might have given her a run for her money if you had." I fall to my knees when he unexpectedly releases me. "Get yourself cleaned up. Wouldn't want you scaring the kids."

My brain tells me to stay down, but my heart demands the opposite. If Audrey is here, that means Fien is most likely here as well. My heart is breaking for both Dimitri and myself, but Fien's cute little chubby cheeks and eyes identical to her father's in every way could very well be the cure to my heartache.

With my back facing the coldblooded stranger, I peel my blood-soaked nightie off my body before replacing it with a fresh one folded at the end of my bed. My legs shudder when I slip them into the openings of a pair of panties only my nanna would think were fashionable. I'm not scared the man is watching me like a hawk. I'm horrified about the gigantic pad someone preloaded into my underwear.

Although I hate being reminded about what I've lost, the products surrounding me make sense of the cold, sterile room I awoke in. My baby wasn't the only one delivered here. The stack of maternity pads in the partially cracked-open closet is indicating enough, let alone the pediatric medical crib just outside the door.

"How many children have these women birthed?" I ask the man when he guides me out of the room with a firm grip on my arm.

He grunts, then continues shoving me toward the stairs.

My nanna always said my mouth would get me in trouble. If it's the good kind of trouble, I don't mind. "Are you not allowed to touch the women because your blood isn't royal? Are you a bastard like the rest of us?"

That stops him in his tracks. "My blood is more regal than any of the men here."

"Yet, here you are, nothing more than a paid goon."

His slap is brutal, but it doesn't weaken my smile. Only scared men act out with violence. Take Eddie's response to my 'betrayal,' for example. Real men prove otherwise.

"There's still time, you know?"

The grunting, red-faced goon drags me up the stairs like he has no interest in anything I'm saying. It's unfortunate for him, silence is a battle only the bravest can conjure.

"For what?" he asks with his hand resting on the door that leads to the room the women are in.

I crank my neck so I can peer into his eyes. "To save yourself. Tell Dimitri where I am, and I promise he will spare your life." I curse at my inability to lie when my eyes rapidly blink during the last half of my statement.

If Dimitri doesn't kill this man for what he did to me, I'll do it myself.

"Nice try," the stranger pushes out with a huff. "If you truly think he'll come all the way out here for you, you've got rocks in your head. He will never come here for you, he will never go anywhere for you because there's only one person Dimitri Petretti cares about, and that is himself. If you don't believe me, ask her." He throws open the door, nudges his head to Audrey in the corner of the jam-packed room, then tosses me into the quiet space. "She chipped away at his arrogance for months. She barely made an indent, so what chance would you fare since you were barely in his realm for weeks."

His smirk gets cocky when my attempt to shut down the worry on my face is two seconds too late. "What's the matter, girlie? Did you think we were only watching you the past couple of weeks?" He lowers the volume of his mocking tone to ensure his next set of words are only for my ears. "I would have gotten you off in the alleyway before running you over. Would have been more fun that way."

On that note, he shoves me into the room, slams the door shut, and twists a key into the lock, leaving me as defenseless as I am shocked.

16

DIMITRI

I slap my cheeks when Rocco walks into my office, waking myself up. I have a bag for Roxanne packed and sitting by the door, my guns loaded and ready to go, but I have no fucking clue which direction I should head. My intuition is leaning toward New York. That's where the gala is being held, and a tower just outside of New York was in Smith's report on the thirty-second footage we were sent of Roxanne, indicating it was triangulated in his search, but the last time Rimi made a move, he did it in my backyard. Who's to say he won't try and fuck with my head again this time around too?

"Did you sleep at all last night?"

I shake my head at Rocco's question. "You?" The weakness of his shake is more telling than the worry in his eyes. "How's Alice?"

He doesn't twist his chair around to straddle it backward like he usually does. He sinks onto it with a sigh before rolling his head around like his neck is giving him agony. "Docs say she will make a full recovery. Word is still out on Luce. She's giving her grandmother hell."

He drops his chin to his chest when I ask, "Anything I can do?"

After taking a moment to ponder my offer, he reluctantly shakes his head. "Might hold you to it once Fien and Roxie are back, though."

"So tonight?"

He smiles a grin I haven't seen on his face in years. "You're finally clicking on, D." Don't misconstrue. He isn't asking a question, he is stating a fact. "What's the plan?"

"Other than a merciless bloodbath, my head is telling me to stay put."

He twists his lips like he understands where I'm coming from. "And your gut?"

I drag my teeth over my lower lip to hide my ill-timed smile. I'm not smirking about the situation we're in, I am appreciating that Rocco trusts his intuition more than anything. It has gotten us out of some hairy situations in the past. I can only hope it will have the same effect this time around. "It was on a flight to New York five hours ago."

Rocco's grin doubles as he holds his hands out palm side up. "Then, what are we doing here?"

"I don't know," I reply, speaking the truth for the first time in forever, shocked enough about the rarity to laugh.

After chuckling along with me for the next thirty or so seconds, Rocco asks, "Can you feel her here?"

"Who?"

He gives me a look that says he knows I'm acting ignorant before he adds words into the mix. "Your girl."

He doesn't need to say Roxanne's name for me to know who he's referencing. I've never seen Fien in the flesh, so I've never experienced that stomach-tingling, nauseating, and somewhat infuriating sensation that hits me low in the stomach anytime

Roxanne is in my vicinity. I'm sure it will be there once we meet, but for now, it's an experience I've only ever felt with Roxanne.

"No, I don't feel her here," I reply, finally at the stage where I can stop denying Roxanne is my girl. She walked through Hell's gates for me. She has more than proven she's on my side, and now I will forever be on hers.

Rocco leaps up from his chair as if he isn't exhausted beyond belief. "Then, what are we doing here, D? Let's go to New York and get your girls. We play to play—"

"We kill to kill..." we say at the same time, "... and we take down any fucker stupid enough to get in our way."

After whacking me in the chest with the back of his hand, reminding me I'm not as old as my body feels, he scoops up my keys from my desk, then moves for Roxanne's bag by the door. His race down the hallway almost takes out Smith, who's coming in the opposite direction. He's balancing a laptop on his hand, the shadowing of gray under his eyes exposing his sleep was as lackluster as mine.

"You'll want to see this," Smith says after popping his head up from the screen of his first-of-its-kind laptop. When he spots Roxanne's bag in Dimitri's hand, his brows pinch. "Are we going somewhere?"

I jerk up my chin. "Can you tell me on the way?"

Nodding, he races back to his computer hub to grab chargers, another three laptops, and a gun. Rocco quirks his brow when he leans over a sleeping Ellie with his lips puckered. He almost kisses the tiny section of her forehead not covered by locks of shiny blonde hair but pulls back with barely a second to spare.

Instead of farewelling her as if the last two years never happened, Smith jots down a message on the notepad Ellie's cheek is squashed against before spinning around to face Rocco and me.

"What?" he asks, frustrated by our silence. "Old habits are hard to give up."

"It's been over two years, Smitty," Rocco says with a laugh.

Smith's eyes snap to Rocco. "Yeah, and your point?"

Rocco steps back with his hands in the air, acting as if the words cracked out of Smith's mouth were bullets. "I'm not sayin' nuffin."

I don't follow his lead. "She can come with us if you want?"

We don't know what we're walking toward. For all we know, having a female on our team could come with great benefits. I'm a father, but I am still clueless when it comes to things like pregnancy and birth, not to mention kids. As far as I'm aware, Ellie doesn't have any children, but with her little brother having the mind of a child, she understands them.

Smith takes a moment to consider my reply before shaking his head. "If this goes as deep as I'm thinking, I'd rather Ellie's career not be tainted by it."

"Are you sure, Smith?" Rocco questions, jumping back into the conversation. "If she gets booted from the Bureau, you'll have no reason not to be together."

His question is fair but only because he doesn't know their breakup goes deeper than Ellie's career choice.

"I'm sure." Smith's short reply reveals he doesn't want to go into details with Rocco right now. I doubt it's a conversation he wants to have in the next decade, he just won't have a choice. Rocco is like a bull in a China shop when it comes to any relationship he isn't a part of. "Do I need to organize transport, or is this another road-tripping adventure?"

The gargle the last half of his sentence arrived with reveals he's praying we're not taking the high road again. He'd rather hitchhike to where we're going than be stuck in the back of his van with Rocco for another three hours.

"Silas is on standby," I answer, slackening the groove between Smith's brows by a smidge. "Make sure he's ready to have wheels up in an hour." Before Rocco can grill me about the delay—the private airstrip we use is only ten minutes from here—I nudge my head to a recently approved court appearance date circled on a notepad brimming with handwritten notes. "We need to make a stopover first."

With his smile huge and his hands rubbing together like a crack dealer on payday, Rocco follows me out of the compound, aware who we're visiting and more than happy to update Smith all about it.

17

DIMITRI

"Where is he?" I ask no one, frustrated as fuck Agent James isn't upholding his side of our agreement.

Brandon will have no chance in hell of convincing Isabelle to unknowingly do his ruse if he doesn't support her during her arraignment for murder. It's the people who stick by you during the bad times you protect the most. If Brandon doesn't show up today, he'll be struck off Isabelle's friends' list without delay.

It would have been the same for Rocco and me when news of Fien's unkosher arrival circulated through my inner circle. He rocked up only hours later, drenching wet, furious, and ready to kill. I honestly don't know if I would have made it this far without him. Knowing your newborn daughter is being held captive by a madman is enough to make the most lucid man insane.

Rocco and Smith watch me like a hawk when I tap out a message on my phone. If I can't force Brandon to be at his 'friend's' side, I'll lose more than my cool. My agreement with Rico will be null and void as well.

Dimitri: *Should I follow your plan or make one of my own? If you're not here in thirty, the decision will be out of your hands.*

I don't mean minutes, I mean seconds. Brandon's apartment is only one block over. He can run here if he has no other option.

Once the screen of my phone advises my message has been read, I snap an image of the Ravenshoe Courthouse stairs then forward it to Brandon.

It feels as if not even ten seconds ticks by when I spot him racing up the stairs. I must have woken him. His hair is a mess, his face is crinkled, and I'm reasonably sure he's wearing the same suit he wore yesterday.

I'm about to slide out of the back seat of my Range Rover when Rocco grabs my arm. "Hold up. This looks like it could get interesting."

When I stray my eyes in the direction he's peering, I notice Brandon's race up the courthouse stairs has been thwarted by a blond man with wide shoulders and an arrogant mask slipped over his face.

"Who's that?"

"Agent Alex Rogers, Field Operations Supervisor for the Federal Bureau of Investigation." Smith isn't gloating. He sounds like he wants to rip off Alex's head as badly as Alex wants to tear into Brandon. "He was Brandon's supervisor."

"Was?" Rocco and I ask at the same time.

Smith lifts his chin. "Agent James was demoted last night. The FBI's golden boy isn't as shiny as he wants us to believe. His rap sheet is almost as long as mine."

"So, sweet fuck all?" Rocco asks with a laugh. "Or are you talking about the rap sheet you got expunged for sleeping with the enemy?"

Okay, perhaps he knows a little more than he let on.

Our interrogation shifts from Smith to Brandon when the crack of a fist colliding with a jaw silences a town not known for its quiet. Alex didn't hold anything back with his hit, and shockingly, Brandon takes it like a man. He gets up in Alex's face and says a few words, but he keeps his hands balled at his sides.

His response is nothing like mine would have been. I would have retaliated with more than my fists if I were in his predicament.

"Find out what that's about. If a war is about to begin, I want to know about it, especially if it involves the FBI."

"Already on it." Smith digs one of his laptops out of his satchel, then fires it up. Within seconds, he has a confidential report up on the screen.

"Who's the blonde?"

Smith double clicks on the trackpad on his laptop to zoom in on the image of a blonde in a towel. She's attractive—if you're into ball crushers. I swear I've seen her before, but I can't pinpoint where.

Smith alleviates my curiosity. "That's the infamous Regan Myers, Isaac Holt's lawyer..." *Ah, there's the connection.* "And Alex Roger's current squeeze."

I double back, certain I heard him wrong. The half grin he's wearing reveals I didn't, much less the tap of a revolver on the window next to my head. I don't know how I didn't put it together earlier. The Rogers' familiarities are almost on par with the Petrettis. There's no denying them when you drink them in at the same time.

Grayson Rogers, another one of Tobias's little minions, acts as if he doesn't have the scope of Rocco's M4 on his chest when he requests for me to roll down the window. I could drive off, but Roxanne's exasperating habit of nosy-parking has rubbed off on me. Furthermore, the last time I was in the same room as Grayson, I walked away with him owing me a favor. My assistance this time around will cost him much more than the gratitude I have no plan to cash in.

Rocco works his jaw through a thorough grind when I signal for him to lower his weapon. He has issues with law enforcement officers, most particularly, ones who are as cocky as Grayson.

After rolling down my window as requested, I say, "I'm shocked you're up. I didn't see you leave the front of the compound until well after four this morning."

I'm happy to let him know I realize he's watching me, just like I'm happy to watch his brutal swallow before he says, "Kirill—"

"Is not a part of my operation. I've told you that many times before." My interruption is snappy and to the point. I'm sick to death of having the same conversation with these people. Yes, I run drugs, and yes, my entity is part of the prostitution conglomerate but tell me one fucking cartel unit that isn't. If we weren't running it, corrupts fuckers like Ravenshoe PD would. I don't know about you, but I know who I'd rather deal with. It isn't the corrupt members of law enforcement who put away innocent men for murders they conjure on a whim.

Grayson acts as if I didn't speak. "Is the reason for Castro's resurrection." He shoves a set of documents through the crack in the window as if he's a bank robber, and I'm the teller he's demanding cash from. "He's stateside because of this."

I lower my eyes to the document to ensure he doesn't see the shock in them. From what Smith unearthed the past couple of weeks, Kirill hasn't been stateside since he purchased Katie from my father, so for him to be back, it must be for something big.

"You fucking idiot," I mutter under my breath when I realize what I'm looking at.

My father learned nothing from my grandfather's death, not a single fucking thing. I thought he squandered the massive payout he got for my mother's death on the business ventures I've tried to steer our entity away from the past eight years. I had no clue he used it to try and regain control of New York.

We built that city. The Italians, Greeks, and Albanians made it the mecca it is, but my father lost the ability to be king of that realm when he put his drug-fucked friend above our 'family.' He had no right to stake a claim, none whatsoever, and now Henry's lack of assistance the past few years makes sense.

"Consider your favor cashed in." Needing to end our conversation before I take my anger out on the wrong person, I commence sliding up my window.

Grayson blocks its climb by lodging his elbow between the tinted glass and the metal window channeling it. "That wasn't a favor. It was a warning. If you go into this with guns blazing, *as I'm reasonably sure you're planning*, you'll be up against more than Rimi Castro."

"I'm not worried."

Grayson laughs like Rocco's finger isn't itching to inch back his trigger. "Then that makes you a fucking idiot. There's more at stake here than your family's pride, Dimitri."

Something inside of me snaps. "*Pride?* You think this is about pride? Henry Gottle can have New York, he can have the entire fucking country as far as I'm concerned *when* I get my daughter back. *When* she's sleeping in the crib I built for her." I bang my chest during the last half of my statement. "And *when* I see her face for the first time in front of me instead of via a fucking monitor. That's *when* I'll let my *pride* slide. Not before. It most certainly won't happen before."

Grayson doesn't know how to reply. Nothing but silence resonates from both inside and outside of the cab for the next several long seconds. I want to say it eases my agitation. Regretfully, it doesn't. I'm more worked up now than I was when Rocco had to strain to see Roxanne's breaths to prove she was alive.

"How old is your girl?" Grayson's voice is as rough as the wiry hair on his chin.

Not interested in idle chit-chat, I signal for Preacher to go. He slots into the position of driver when Clover wants to catch up on missed sleep. He was on alert to move all night, so he's as tired as the rest of us.

"Hey, hold up." Grayson follows the Range Rover's slow creep down the road as Preacher seeks an opening in the traffic. "Do you want your girl back or not?"

"I don't need your help to do that."

Air puffs out of his mouth when he huffs out a laugh. "I wasn't offering my help. I'm *telling* you the job will be done quicker if we work together."

"I don't work with the Feds."

"Neither do I," Grayson fires back with a waggle of his brows. "Well, not when it concerns Kirill."

My lips involuntarily curl at the tips. I had wondered if my advice months ago worked. Grayson's disclosure reveals it most certainly did. "What are you proposing?"

When Preacher's eyes shift to the rearview mirror, seeking confirmation on if I want him to pull over, I shake my head. If Grayson wants to talk, he better do it quickly. We're almost on the open road.

The fact his words aren't chopped up from the clomps of his boots reveals he has maintained his fitness while undercover in Kirill's crew. "A mutual corroboration like the one you had with Tobias. Shared information on the agreement it isn't used for *any* outside influences."

My brow cocks. "A 'you scratch my back, I scratch yours'

situation."

"Yeah," Grayson answers, unaware I wasn't asking a question. I was merely validating his name got him into the academy more than his academics.

"Kind of like your arrangement with Rico."

I slice my hand through the air like I'm swatting a fly, not only wordlessly demanding for Preacher to stop, responding exactly as Grayson was hoping.

"Not as dumb as I look, hey?" He smirks a smug grin before straying his eyes to Smith. "You really should be careful which back doors you sneak through. When you leave it wide open, your footprints are easy to follow."

While grumbling several curse words under his breath, Smith attacks his keyboard with the malice of a savage. I can tell the exact moment it dawns on him that Grayson isn't lying. He not only initiates a lockdown on all our devices, he commences stripping information from Grayson's cell phone. How do I know this? A photo of Katie Bryne popped up on his laptop screen within seconds of him hacking in.

"You don't need to hack into my phone to understand my objective, Dimi." Rocco doesn't take kindly to Grayson using my nickname any more than me. "I'm more than happy to share it with you. We are, after all, on the same team."

Grayson's cockiness gets smacked into the next century when Smith barks out, "Katie Byrne was sold in a private auction when she was eighteen. Her handler was an up-and-coming prodigy your father had taken under his wing. He was supposed to prepare the mark for sale. Instead, he fell in love with her. That not only saw him falling out of favor with your father, it had his supervisor at the Bureau on the back foot as well." Smith raises his eyes to

Grayson, mouths *checkmate, motherfucker*, before he hits him with the motherlode. "Tobias did everything he could to help his rookie agent out of the pickle he got himself into, but despite both his stellar reputation and the rookie's dad's high standing in the Bureau, Katie was sold, shipped to another country, and was never seen again. Boo-*fucking*-hoo."

Ouch. I forgot how nasty Smith gets when someone tries to outsmart him.

Spit flies out of Grayson's mouth when he roars, "You punk-faced motherfucker." For a man with shoulders as wide as mine, I'm shocked how far he climbs into the car. He gets close enough to Smith to knock his laptop off his lap, but nowhere near close enough to wring his neck like he really wants to.

"Enough," I say a short time later, over the theatrics.

"Enough!" I roar for the second time when my first order is ignored. Grayson can get away with bypassing my directive, but Smith and Rocco can't. "Tell me what you have. If it is of interest to me, I'll return the favor."

Grayson's blue eyes shift to mine. They're not holding an ounce of the humor they had earlier. "That isn't how things work—"

"Then, we're done."

I signal for Preacher to go. I can tell Grayson wants to let me walk. It is in his eyes, slicking his skin. Hell, it's even readable in the way he holds his jaw. He hates negotiating, especially with men like me, but it just has nothing on the rage he felt hearing how the men who were supposed to have his back didn't.

After shaking his head in a way that exposes he thinks he's making a mistake, Grayson says, "Meet with me tomorrow morning."

"I'm going out of town for a couple of days."

"I know." He arches his brow, climbs back out the window, then taps on the roof of my Range Rover, signaling for Preacher that there's an opening before he adds, "I'll send the deets through your private network... *if* it's back up and operating by then."

On that note, he hits Smith with a cocky wink, spins on his heels, then stalks away.

18

ROXANNE

"Are you okay?"

I drift my eyes from the only window in a room to my questioner. I'm not surprised when I discover the kind eyes of Audrey glancing down at me. Not only has she checked up on me multiple times today, she has a very faint voice. Even if we were the only two people in a soundproof room, I'd struggle to hear her.

I don't know if her quiet stems from the other forty or so women crammed into the room with us treating her like a lecher or because her daughter isn't held in the same room as her.

From what I gathered from the women with broken English, Fien lives downstairs. I could be wrong, but I'm reasonably sure her living arrangements aren't recent. They kept saying 'no' while wiggling their fingers at Audrey. Although the rest of their sentences weren't in English, I have a feeling Audrey understood them. Anytime they guide me away from her, she cowers instead of standing up for herself.

I'm a bit disappointed her personality doesn't match her fiery hair coloring.

Redheads are usually hot-tempered. Audrey is as timid as they come.

When the worry in Audrey's eyes doubles, it dawns on me that I didn't answer her question. "Yeah. I'm okay. A little tender, but nothing I can't handle."

It seems as if a band is stretched across my mid-section, constantly tugging and pulling on my insides, but I can't help but wonder if that's because I can't sit still. I've clawed at the deadbolt on the only door in and out of this room, endeavored to pull up the hardwood floors that are stronger than they look, and have been working on the nails hammered into the window to keep it shut.

The women captive with me find my endeavor to escape amusing. I'm not sure how to respond to their smiles. I'm annoyed by their lack of assistance, but I also understand it. Perhaps they tried as hard as I did their first few days here and soon learned their efforts were a woeful waste of time. I've only been going at it for a couple of hours, and I already feel my optimism dithering.

The concern in Audrey's eyes shift to remorse before she asks, "Have you had any more bleeding?"

Her question is sincere, but it still stabs a knife into my chest. I've always believed you live the best life by leaving the past in the past. That's a little hard to do when I'm continuously reminded about what I've lost.

With words alluding me, I shake my head. Bar the initial big bleed I had overnight, I've only detected the occasional smear of blood while using the bucket in the corner of the room. The brown-tinged byproduct had me hopeful my baby stood a chance, but Audrey quickly snuffed out that flare of optimism. She wasn't cruel. She just knows how these things operate since she's been here so long.

In a way, her bluntness could be seen as a godsend. If I were still pregnant, the goon who tortured me yesterday wouldn't have left me alone today. He only has because he knows what my heart is trying to deny. I lost any chance of filling the memories Dimitri missed with Fien.

"You should eat something," Audrey whispers just as the group of women mending loose hems notice she's speaking to me. "You need to keep your strength up," she adds while slowly sinking into the corner she's been stationed at all day. "For when Dimitri comes, you need to be strong."

She glances at me as if Dimitri's sanity hinges more on me surviving this ordeal than her. Her gawk isn't callous. It's almost hopeful, which is odd considering it was her husband's unborn child they stole from me.

My focus shifts from striving to work out Audrey's peculiar personality when Fenna, the woman who hid me yesterday afternoon, runs her hand down my forearm. "Okay?" She nudges her head to Audrey. "She... no."

"Know or no?" I ask when her accented words sound more like a question than a statement.

When she peers at me lost, I try another angle. "Me and you..." I gesture my hand between us, "... are friends. We like each other."

"Like. Yes." Her smile is bright enough to make me forget the horrible things she's been through. It's too beautiful for such a dark, horrid world. "I like..."

My heart warms when she touches my chest, advising she likes me. It could have slotted into my second-most memorable moment if Dimitri had returned my declaration of love two nights ago. Since he didn't, it holds the top spot, and it may stay there when Dimitri learns the mother of his child isn't deceased as believed.

After giving my pity-party-for-one ten seconds more than it deserves, I get back to my conversation with Fenna. "We like each other. We're friends."

"Yes. Friends," she agrees, still smiling.

"You..." I touch her chest as she did mine, "... and Audrey. Are you friends?"

She glances in the direction I pointed when I said Audrey's name before she screws up her face. "No." She wiggles her finger in the air to get across her point. If I didn't know any better, I'd swear she was a teacher in a previous life. "No like. We no like."

"You don't like Audrey?" The shock on my face can't be missed in translation.

"No. No like. Stay away." She curls her arm around my shoulders as she has many times today before she leads me away from Audrey, her steps extra slow since my foot is blown up like a balloon. "Bad woman. Stay away."

Although the women across the room continue chatting while gawking at me, I know Audrey heard Fenna's comment. She wipes at the tears sliding down her face at the speed of lightning, but I still spot them.

If she's hurt about the women spreading vicious lies about her, why isn't she defending herself? I don't believe she needs to explain herself, but she as sure as hell doesn't need to take their crap lying down.

I shouldn't fight for her, some may say she's my competition, but for the life of me, I can't hold back. If she can't defend herself, how the hell will she defend her daughter when she reaches her age. "Say something to them. Tell them you're not who they think you are."

Audrey peers at me through the strands of auburn hair not covering her eyes before she shakes her head.

"Why not? You're a victim just like them. You didn't deserve what happened to you."

I shrug out of Fenna's hold more aggressively than I meant before I move to Audrey's half of the room, whimpering through the pain of a suspected broken foot.

"I saw the video. I saw what they did to you. That wasn't right, Audrey. What they did to you was wrong." I can tell my words are breaking her heart, but I continue on, confident a mended heart will work far better than an empty one. "Help me help them. Help me stop this from happening to anyone else." I'm getting through to her. However, my final set of words all but seal the deal. "Help me introduce a little girl to her father for the very first time. If you ever loved Dimitri, you'd want that just as much as me."

I level my breathing to make sure I don't mistake her whispered word, "Okay..."

"Yes? You'll help?" The shortness of my reply can't weaken the excitement bristling in it.

"Yes." The fire I've been seeking in her eyes for the past six hours finally shines brighter than her fear when she nods her head. "I will help."

Although I want to believe she's doing this solely for her child, a small part of me knows this isn't just about Fien. She wants Dimitri to know she is brave. She wants to show him she has the charisma and spark no one believes she has. She wants to prove she's worthy of him as much as I wish I couldn't see it in her eyes. They already have a connection that binds them together for life. Now she wants the commitment that comes along with it.

19

DIMITRI

Our arrival in New York doesn't occur unnoticed. No sirens, flashing lights, or armored trucks some law enforcement officers need to get their point across are seen. Just a single Maserati Quattroporte parked halfway out the hangar my private jet is crawling toward.

Our flight was scheduled to land in the middle of the night to ward off unwanted eyes. I should have realized that wouldn't fool Henry. He's been snuck up on too many times in the past to take the news the Italian Cartel is in town lying down.

From what Smith unearthed over the past twelve hours, the takeover bids Henry has faced during his thirty-year reign lost him more than revenue. It cost him the very thing I'm endeavoring not to lose—his family. There's just one difference in our stories.

Henry could see his son if Henry, Jr. would look past his twenty-nine-year absence. He doesn't understand his father gave him up to protect him, nor does he see the regrets and mistakes on Henry, Sr.'s face like I do.

He feels abandoned.

I could tell him he got lucky when it comes to cartel families but considering my father's endeavor to reclaim a kingdom he has no right to reign is the reason for his family's downfall, I doubt it would do much good.

I've just got to pray Henry, Sr. is more approachable than his son. His war is with my father, and although I bear his last name, I'm nothing like him. My daughter comes before anyone as does Roxanne.

When I hit Henry with the motherlode of information Smith's stumbled upon from returning Grayson's hack, he'll have no choice but to side with me. Gangsters don't play fair in general, but when it comes to family, just like me, Henry has no trouble laying all his cards on the table. He is fierce and impenetrable, and if I didn't believe he's governing a realm he didn't earn, I could see myself emulating him.

Alas, I can't reach the pinnacle of success without taking him down.

That alone means we will never be friends.

A smirk curls my lips when over half a dozen red dots line my chest as I commence walking down the stairs of my private jet. Henry's reputation usually sees him going without the fanfare, so I'm somewhat pleased I've rattled him enough for him to pay attention to my visit. He isn't a fan of mine, hasn't been since we bumped shoulders a mere second before I approached Isaac to fight in my father's underground fight tournament years ago. To be honest, I doubt we will ever be.

"Dimitri, to what do I owe this pleasure?" Henry's voice is a mix of accents. It's as unique as the cartel leaders who used to run this sanction. It's pitched with superiority, but there's a snippet of hesitation that reveals our industry has worn his patience thin.

He isn't the only one feeling a little overwhelmed. I feel so haggard, I often have to remind myself I'm not as old as believed.

Henry should have more wrinkles than he does. I've been chasing my tail for two years. He has notched up more than ten times that amount, so why the fuck hasn't he given up yet?

Because his family is safe, fuckface.

Yours isn't.

Not having the time nor the interest to work through the honesty of my inner monologue, I get to the point of my interstate visit. "I'm here regarding your brother, Liam Gregg, or as you knew him, Liam Gottle, the second." When Henry's jaw ticks like he's fighting not to signal for me to be taken down, I talk faster. "Rumors state my father was part of the operation to take him down—"

"It wasn't an order to take him down. His family was brutalized, and his wife and daughter were scared half to death."

I nod, agreeing with him. There's no denying the truth. I read the reports on the Gregg home invasion during our flight. The men who entered their house were paid for a standard hit. The fact Wren, Henry's sister-in-law, would spark an attraction out of them wasn't considered. Her looks changed their tactics in an instant. If it weren't for Liam, Wren would have faced more than a handful of scratches on her inner thighs and bruises to her breasts that night, and it would have occurred in front of her daughter.

The knowledge of their change-up is why my mood is so sour this morning. Roxanne has a spark men can't help but acknowledge. Her spunk is potent enough to feed the ego of a dozen men, so what will happen when they realize there's only one way to unleash her powers? Will she be attacked as Wren was but left defenseless since I'm not there to stop it?

The thought makes me sick. It honestly makes me the most unhinged I've ever been, and it's heard in my voice when I growl out, "You have every right to go after the men responsible for hurting your family, but you won't get anywhere if you continue chasing the wrong fucking sanction."

"Your father—"

"Paid more than his share to fund the *joint* operation to take you down!" My roar reveals more than half a dozen snipers are dying for Henry to make a hand signal, but I act ignorant over a two-decade-long injustice as much as I am my inability to find Roxanne and Fien without the help of my enemies. "But he felt your wrath, licked his wounds, then sat the fuck back down. He hasn't moved since, yet you're still facing the same issues you had when he wanted your throne."

My teeth grit when the last half of my sentence comes out with a jut from a gun being forcefully pressed to my head. I don't need to sling my eyes to know who has stepped up to the plate before Henry has finished swinging his bat. His big head causes enough of a shadow on Henry's face to know who he is, much less the flick of Rocco's safety switch when he returns Kwan's gamble with one of his own.

Rocco doesn't care if his retaliation will get him killed. He'd rather respond to an act of intimidation than take it up the ass like I have the past two years.

Following his lead, I say, "You're chasing the wrong crew."

Henry brushes off my statement with a wave of his hand. "Says the man too stupid to realize he's doing all the legwork of a man undeserving of his time."

"I don't work for my father." After a stern glare at Kwan, warning him we're seconds from a brutal bloodbath if he doesn't stop digging his gun into my head, I add, "Everything I've done the past two years has been for my daughter."

Henry tries to hide the shock of my confession, but the mask slips over his face too quickly for me to ignore. I've heard he isn't as hard as his fierce reputation. I would have never believed it if I hadn't seen it for myself.

"Her name is Fien. She was born here, of all places, exactly twenty-two months ago, forcefully delivered by the very man you've been sheltering for years." I hold up the first photograph taken of Fien. You could coo at how cute she is if it didn't also show a bloody and cut-open Audrey on a stained mattress in the background.

Once I'm certain Henry understands Fien's delivery was nothing close to ordinary, I show him an image taken only days earlier. Even though no fight whatsoever is seen on Audrey's face as she's led out of the back entrance of Slice of Salt, the family crest on both Rimi's ring and his neck are undeniable. "I've been paying to keep her safe ever since."

When I gesture for Smith to move forward, Henry signals for Kwan to stand down. The goon with a head the size of a watermelon hesitates for a second but eventually does as told. All good foot soldiers do. Although Kwan is like family to Henry, he's still aware of the repercussions if he ignores his direct order.

"We have information that leads us to believe Rimi's crew is relocating to the New York region." After opening up the laptop Smith hands me, I log into the event Rimi has tickets for. "He purchased tickets to this event."

"I am aware," Henry interrupts, his voice somewhat off. It isn't brimming with anger, but it is full of distrust. Can't say I blame him. I don't trust anyone, much less people with the same last name as me. "Permission was requested to attend. We have eyes on the proceedings." His eyes stray to Kwan during the last part of his comment, falling on a tattoo that looks oddly similar to the Castro family crest.

Although suspicious as to why Kwan is wearing a crest for an entity that isn't his, I continue with my endeavor to make Henry see sense through the madness, aware time isn't in my favor. "Permission I doubt you'd give if you understood the real reason Rimi is here."

I click on the only file on my desktop. Aware Henry never takes anything on faith, I had Smith install everything onto a device we don't plan to see again. Henry would hate for his fuck-up to be broadcasted to his enemies, so I'm confident Smith's prototype laptop will be destroyed by the end of tonight.

"Milo Bobrov ran down your brother and sister-in-law, but he wasn't acting alone—"

My teeth grit when Henry interrupts. "David Crombie orchestrated it. You're not telling me anything I don't already know."

He spins away from me, his steps slowing when I add, "Rimi Castro organized both the raids that terrorized your family *and* Liam and Wren's death. He's playing you for a fool." He looks like he wants to kill me, but I carry on, unfazed and unscared. I'm already living my nightmare. It can't get any worse than this. "Why do you think Kirill returned stateside after all this time? Even he has heard how much you love sucking Rimi's dick, and he wants in on the action."

For an old guy, Henry has a lot of strength in his hits. He punishes my ribs with an unrelenting left-right combination before he slams my back into my private jet's shell that feels as cold as ice.

I don't retaliate to his brutal clutch of my throat. I'm too busy laughing at the whitening of his gills when Smith plays a recording he found buried deep in the Bureau's database. It's a private conversation between David Crombie, a former associate of Rimi's, and an undercover agent, Phillipa Russell. It exposes just how long Rimi has been playing both sides of the field and exactly who he took down in the process.

After Henry releases me from his grip, too shocked to continue with his aggressive stance, I swallow down some saliva, hopeful it will ease out my next set of words. "Rimi nagged and nagged and nagged Milo to seek vengeance on Liam for the time he served in a state facility away from his family. When he finally got through to him, you thought you were safe from carnage." I shake my head like I am disappointed I'm not the only gangbanger one step behind his enemies the past decade. I'm not, but I am happy for Henry to believe I am. "You got slack. You thought it was over, then they hit you with everything they had."

"I took care of Crombie," he seethes through clenched teeth.

I nod, once again agreeing with him. Crombie was found dead in his cell within an hour of him being arrested. "But you left the main hitter out at the plate, unconcerned about your curveball."

When Henry tries to deny my claims, I hit him where it hurts. Unlike my father, it isn't his hip pocket. It's his niece, Melody Gottle, the only surviving member of the renamed Gregg family. "You did good. For years, your enemies thought she was dead. Then Crombie couldn't keep his mouth shut."

He snatches both the recent photo of Melody out of my hand along with a ransom drop the Feds are currently in the process of organizing. "Rimi doesn't even have Melody at his mercy, yet her billionaire fiancé is willing to pay one point five million dollars to ensure it never occurs."

This is what Alice meant when she said they had a big payout to collect. Rimi won't stop at one ransom. He'll continue demanding money until Melody's fiancé stops handing over the funds, then he'll kidnap her for real. Guaranteed. It's how I would handle this if it were my operation.

I think all my Christmases have come at once when Henry mutters, "If this information is legitimate, what do you want for it?"

Being owed a favor by Henry is priceless in this industry. You can't put a dollar amount on it. However, I can, because there's something I want a shit ton more than money.

I want my girls back, and right here, right now, it feels as if my wish is about to come true.

Good things take time.

Bad things bring justice.

With Henry's help, I'm about to serve Rimi Castro a little bit of both.

20

ROXANNE

"Does it have any charge?" I ask Audrey while peering at the cell phone she snuck in our room in the middle of the night.

I've been dying to see what she had up her sleeve for the past sixteen-plus hours, but with the man the women call 'Maestro' popping in and out of our room all day and night, now is the first chance I've had to speak to Audrey without an audience.

The women still watch us from afar, unmoved by my speech yesterday that an army has never won a war with only one soldier. They don't trust Audrey, and nothing I say will alter their opinion about that.

I can't say I blame them. If Audrey has had access to this device the entire time, why the hell didn't she use it to seek help?

My heart drums against my ribcage when Audrey nods. Its frantic wallops double when she slips the device out of my hand, fires it up, then shoves it back into my lap. Her hands are jittery like she's panicked out of her mind we're about to be killed.

If we're caught with this device, I'm confident we will be.

After gulping down a quick breath to settle my nerves, I log into her phone. It isn't one of those state-of-the-art ones with apps and gimmicks. It's retro, funky, and only has ten percent charge remaining. *Fuck it!*

Needing to hurry, I push out a little abruptly. "Where are your contacts?"

Audrey peers at me with her big eyes out in full force but remains as quiet as a church mouse.

"So I can look up Dimitri's number," I hurry her along.

Shock blankets Audrey's usually pretty face. "You don't know it?"

Her question shouldn't jab my heart with tiny knives, but it does. I don't even know the address of the compound I was held captive in, much less Dimitri's cell phone number. We didn't have that type of relationship. It was more fired by sexual attraction than communication, but since I can't tell Dimitri's wife that, I shrug instead.

Audrey does a quick sweep of the room to ensure we're without eyes before logging into the text message section of her phone. Dimitri's texts were the only ones received by this phone, so his number is easily distinguishable.

While endeavoring to work out how I can explain to Dimitri that his wife is still alive, I try not to look too deeply into how impersonal his messages to Audrey were during their marriage. They're stern and to the point like he was communicating with a member of his staff instead of his other half.

"Type something," I grumble to myself a short time later, frustrated I'm more concerned about how Dimitri will react to discovering Audrey is alive than getting out of the situation that caused the miscarriage of my child.

My hands shake as I type out a string of text. It's more a business-like contact for Smith to decipher than an attempt to clutch to the final hours I can pretend Dimitri is mine. I'd rather do that face to face than via the phone his wife owns.

Me: *Tracker disabled. Ruse still in effect. Send help to this location. Battery low. Act quickly. Roxie xx*

With the tiny gray device swamped by my hands, I move to the window I was peering out of earlier today before snapping a snapshot of the landscape. Although there isn't much to go off, I'm hopeful the preparation of the crops surrounding us will give Smith some clues to work with. It was amazing what he unearthed by looking at nothing but the satellite images of my grandparents' estate. If he can do that again here, we may be found sooner rather than later.

"Jesus."

I almost die a thousand deaths when Audrey's cell phone suddenly lets out a loud alert. I have no clue how to silence it, so I clench it with everything I have, hopeful my squeeze will suffocate its squeals without damaging it.

With my pulse beeping in my neck, and my eyes wide, I stray them to the door I'm anticipating for Maestro to shoot through at any moment.

When that doesn't occur within the next six seconds, I shift my eyes back to Audrey, wipe at the sweat on my brow, then drop my eyes to the screen of her phone. My only just receding panic gets a second wind when I discover the reason for the noise. My message couldn't be delivered to Dimitri's number since it is no longer in service.

Dammit!

After a couple of seconds of deliberation, I conjure up a new plan of attack. Although Audrey's phone is outdated, most social media sites were around when it was invented.

With my heart in my throat, I snap another picture of the landscape, save it, gingerly find my way to the internet browser, then log into my Instagram account. Smith mentioned he liked a handful of my drawings when he hacked into my Instagram account at the start of my 'arrangement' with Dimitri. He could have been lying to ease my panic when Dimitri was drugged, but that doesn't seem like something he would do. He's pretty truthful, even to the point of being brutally honest.

A ghost-like smile creeps across my face when I tap on the notifications on my Instagram page. Excluding clients, I don't get many interactions on my posts, so I'm certain the eight likes in a row are from Smith.

After following him, I prepare to send him a message. I could put the details in a post, but Maestro unknowingly mentioned two nights ago that I've been under surveillance for a while, so I don't want to run the risk of my social media accounts being monitored.

I have an almost identical message typed out when the faintest giggle steals my attention. It didn't come from inside the room. The women and children here have no reason to smile, so I don't see them releasing a giggle of pure joy. Furthermore, this was a babyish laugh, one I'm certain came from a toddler.

With my mind focused on anything but my freedom, I scoot toward the window before peering outside. It takes scanning the overgrown grass surrounding the ranch three times before I spot the cause of the extra flutter in my neck. Fien is sniffing wildflowers near the rickety verandah I was marched up three nights ago. Her giggles are from the petals tickling her button nose. She screws it up, tosses her head back, laughs, then goes back for another whiff.

I watch her for the next several minutes, totally mesmerized, my stalker gawk only ending when the quickest flurry of silver catches my eye in the distance. It could be anything, but considering there's nothing out here but fields and fields of crops, I pay it as much attention as the goon watching Fien's every move from his station on the corner at the verandah.

He stabs out his half-smoked cigarette into the sole of his boot before he moves to the very edge of the warped wood. My heart leaves my chest with a shocked gasp when he unexpectedly falls backward a second later. He didn't trip over the debris surrounding the rundown residence. He was taken out by a kill shot to the head. The still lifelessness of his body is a sure-fire sign of this, much less the bullet wound between his eyes.

He's coming.

Dimitri is here.

He found us.

The beaming smile on my face vanishes a microsecond later when a second man launches for Fien. While screaming that they're being ambushed, he holds Fien in front of himself, aware the only way he'll make it out of the carnage unscathed is by using her as a shield.

While my stomach decides which way it should flip, I track his race across the verandah holding the brain matter of his confidant. When he breaks through the front screen door under a halo of bullets, I charge for the only exit door of my room. The bullets flying past Fien didn't come from Dimitri's side of the arena. They were from the flood of men surging in the direction the silver flicker came from.

My throbbing foot screams with every step I take, but I don't slow down. Dimitri is so close to getting his daughter back, I can't stomach the idea of him losing her again. I don't think he'd survive it. The thread he's been clutching the past two years is extremely thin. One more fray could completely unravel it.

It takes me crashing into the paint-peeled door with enough force to burn my eyes with tears before it finally pops open under the strain.

I don't realize Audrey is following my race down the empty corridor until she says, "This way."

She throws open the bathroom door before jackknifing to her left. When she tosses a stack of towels out of a linen cupboard, my mouth falls open more in shock than to suck in much-needed breaths. The stack of scratchy material concealed a secret entrance. It leads to a concrete stairwell that goes to the basement.

After galloping down three flights of stairs, we enter a dark and dingy space at the very bottom of the ranch, sweaty and out of breath. It's cold down here, and the set-up makes it seem as if it housed an army in the hundreds the past week.

After taking in the multiple cots set up around the damp-smelling space, Audrey drifts her wide eyes to me. "There's a hidden garage on the fence line. If they're taking Dimitri's daughter, they'll go there."

"Where are you going?" I ask in shock when she heads in the direction opposite to the one she suggested I take.

She doesn't answer me. She just disappears through the underbelly of the ranch, her speed remarkably fast for how hard her thighs are shuddering.

I duck with a squeal when a bullet suddenly whizzes past my head a second later. Maestro stumbled upon my hiding spot during his sprint for the back exit. He isn't happy, and neither am I. He has Fien shoved under his arm. Even with her crying loud enough for two blocks over to hear, he acts oblivious to the fact his clutch is hurting her.

His rough handling of a child unleashes a side of me I didn't think I'd still have—my protective mother instincts.

With a roar, I charge to Maestro and Fien's side of the room, acting as if I am able to outrun a bullet. Maestro fires at me on repeat. I don't know if any of his bullets hit their target. I said the pain of losing my baby would be greater than the deadly pierce of a bullet, so I could be hit, I just refuse to give up.

The air in my lungs leaves with a grunt when Maestro loosens his grip on Fien's waist so he can backhand me. He has run out of bullets, meaning it is now just him versus me.

I shouldn't smile at the thought, but I do.

His hit has me seeing stars, but the howl he releases when I jab my thumb into his eye before kneeing him in the balls alerts numerous balaclava-clad men to our location. They surge into the basement two at a time, their approach more authentic than any action flick I've ever seen. Although their accents are foreign, they're not Italian, making me fretful I've been caught in the middle of a turf war that has nothing to do with Dimitri.

Maestro tries to suppress their surge like he's the Hulk, raging arms and legs go in all directions, but he's outnumbered within seconds, killed even quicker than that, and Fien and I are one measly step behind him.

21

DIMITRI

Sweat slips down my cheeks when I climb a rickety stairwell two steps at a time. I've killed a dozen men already this afternoon, watched another eight be slaughtered by Rocco directly in front of me, and saw Dr. Bates hung for his crimes in a practice not even chop-shop operations like the Castros could use without cringing, but I'm still thirsty for more. I don't just want every man responsible for the pained expression on Roxanne's face when she peered out of a top-story window twenty minutes ago to pay for their stupidity, I want them gutted for witnessing my daughter's happiness before me.

She was born into a world full of violence, ripped from her mother's stomach weeks too early, yet she still stops to smell the roses. She's a baby, barely a toddler, but Rocco was right, her eyes reveal she's strong enough to survive anything. I just don't want her to fight alone anymore. As I said, she's a baby. She shouldn't have faced the things she has, much less a brutal bloodbath with the intention of only taking one hostage.

I can't believe I agreed to Henry's request. I've been hunting

Rimi for years, so the thought of harnessing his punishment until the Feds are through with him has me wanting to take down Rimi's entire crew with my knife instead of my gun. It would be more painful that way, more vengeance fueled. Alas, I shook hands with the devil more than twice earlier today. Considering it got me here at a hidden compound Rimi is endeavoring to get off the ground, I'll swallow the injustice. Rimi will still be dead by the end of the day, just not until Grayson's team has drained him of information.

My heart races like it's about to go into coronary failure when I reach the landing at the top of the stairs. Although I've never handled them before, I'm reasonably sure nerves are also jittering in my stomach. Everything I've been working toward the past two years hinges on what I discover at the end of the hallway I'm creeping down. Roxanne was last seen in this location. Neither her nor Fien have been spotted since.

"Three... two... one..."

I kick down the door when Rocco reaches one, then we race inside shoulder to shoulder. My eyes go crazy while roaming over the four dozen pairs staring back at me. It's clear from the women's clothing and demure personalities that they're not a threat, not to mention them guiding Rocco and me to a bathroom partway down the hallway we just snuck down when they realize who we're seeking. Rocco showed them a picture of Roxanne he has stored in his phone—a photograph I was unaware he had until now. We will have words about it later, but for now, I'm happy to use his fondness of Roxanne to my favor.

"Fucking prick," Rocco grunts under his breath when his dip into a secret entrance sees a bullet ping off the concrete block next to his head.

A groan of a man taking his last breath rumbles up the stairwell a mere second before I pull Rocco back so I can take the lead. The stairwell isn't wide enough for us to go in side by side, so I will enter first. The suggestion to go in heavy was my idea, so if anyone is going to helm the charge, it will be me.

The scent of death teems into my nostrils when I step over the man Rocco took down from above. It isn't the secretion of his bodily fluids responsible for the rank smell in the air, it's the indent Henry's tactical team made to Rimi's crew when he stormed the lower level of his compound. Bodies line the floor. They stretch as far as the eye can see. The number alone reveals Rimi didn't walk into his new adventure lightly. He has almost all his men on deck for this.

Even himself.

He stands at the back of the room, smirking like the bodies of his crew aren't scattered around him.

When his eyes shift my way, and his smile doubles, my anger goes so white-hot, it could cause an aneurism.

With my eyes locked on the man responsible for years of torment, I shrug off my customized M6 machine gun, yank off the balaclava I requested the men of our joint raid wear so there'd be no mistaking the enemy, then pole-drive Rimi like several members of Henry's team aren't flanking him.

I know our agreement, I'm aware Henry only disclosed Rimi's whereabouts on the agreement Rimi would walk away from the carnage for a couple of hours, but that doesn't mean I can't fuck him over. He'll be more cooperative this way. More scared. I can rough him up how Grayson can't. I can make him bleed and not face any conflict about it. The rules changed when he orchestrated the death of Henry's brother. However, they were obliviated when he cut my daughter from my wife's stomach.

As the monster inside of me roars to life, I pound Rimi's face with my fists another two times before removing my switchblade knife from its pouch on my waist.

Rimi's scream will highlight my dreams for years to come

when I slice my knife across his stomach. I gut him like he gutted me all those months ago, unconfronted and without remorse. He tore my daughter out of my wife's stomach without anesthetics, not the least bit worried about how painful that would have been for her.

I bet he's regretting his decision now.

I bet he wishes he could take it all back.

It's a pity for him it is too late. I'm on a warpath, and I don't see anything slowing me down. Rage this hot can't be contained. It's uncontrollable. Brutal. Fucking all-consuming. Although it has nothing on the fervor that stops me in my tracks when my eyes lock in on a pair of gleaming green eyes in the corner of the room.

Half of Roxanne's face is hidden by the shadows of a wooden stairwell Clover and several members of my crew are stomping down. She's cradling my daughter in her arms, sheltering her eyes from the brutality she was born in with her chest while humming a melody to save Fien's ears from the slaughter as well.

As my knife falls to the ground with a clatter, so does Rimi. His head crashing into the boilermaker matches the frantic thump of my heart. Usually, I would find his attempt to hold his stomach together humorous. Today, I don't pay it an ounce of attention. My daughter is in front of me, in the flesh, breathing, and well, and she's with the woman I love.

That outranks anything in the world. Nothing could come close to the emotions bombarding me now. Not even my deceased wife stepping into the frame with a butchered stomach and an ashen face.

22

ROXANNE

Dimitri blinks several times in a row, certain he's dreaming but hopeful it won't turn into a nightmare. His daughter's messy dark brown hair is fanned across my chest, her thumb is stuck in her pouty mouth, and her eyes are puffy from her sobs, but since her mother is lying on the gurney separating them, fighting for her life, he hasn't had the chance to calculate just how many similarities they have.

I escaped injury in my endeavor to reach Fien, but Audrey wasn't as lucky. She suffered multiple stab wounds to her stomach. Her injuries would be fatal if it weren't for Dimitri's last-minute decision to bring Ollie onto the battlefield with him. He's doing everything in his power to save Audrey. He has since she collapsed into Dimitri's arms thirty minutes ago.

The back of a hotwired ambulance isn't the ideal spot for a reunion, but when news broke that the CIA was on the way, Dimitri had no choice but to bundle his crew into multiple transport vehicles and leave. I hated abandoning the women who had helped me beyond what I believed imaginable for what they had been through, but the elderly man leading the charge alongside Dimitri assured me it was the right thing to do. He said the CIA had contacts he didn't and that they would ensure every woman was returned to their families. That alone made the burden easier to swallow.

It's been a crazy thirty or so minutes since then, the haze growing more when Audrey murmurs Dimitri's name in her almost unconscious state. She barely saw him for a second before the wounds to her stomach overwhelmed her, but as I've said previously, it takes a lot to snuff the aura of a man as dominating as Dimitri. Audrey can sense his presence like I did moments before he took his wrath out on the man believed to be the head of the organization who kept his daughter captive.

I could have screamed for him to stop as I did when he tackled the police officer earlier this week, I could have shown him his daughter was safe and unharmed, but something held me back. I want to say it was because he was serving justice to the man responsible for killing our baby, but that would be a lie. I wanted Dimitri to get his revenge, to end the life of the insolent man who had caused him years of pain, then hopefully, when I reveal just how far the pain extends, he will handle the news better since the ringleader has already been executed for his crimes.

As Rocco races us through sloshy fields, Dimitri's eyes bounce between Fien and me, their springiness only slowing when I pull back the locks fanning Fien's face. It exposes more of her adorable rosy cheeks and plump lips, but it also reveals she's sleeping.

I'm not surprised. Crying is exhausting. The sob I released when I woke up in a pool of my blood had me napping for hours that day.

When Dimitri scoots to the edge of his chair, his face expressing his desire to run the back of his fingers down his daughter's chubby cheek, I nod my head, encouraging him. He can't come to our side of the ambulance since Audrey's gurney is wedged between us, and although I'd love nothing more than to hand him his daughter, the weapons strapped to his chest would make that awkward. Thankfully, the impressive reach of his arms won't throw up any obstacles for him to caress his daughter for the first time.

Dimitri's hand makes it to within a hair's breadth of Fien's blooming cheek when Audrey murmurs his name again. It's a groggy, pained wail that rips my heart out of my chest as effectively as it jerks Dimitri's hand away from Fien. He isn't retreating with remorse. Audrey conjured up the strength to slip her hand into the one she mistakenly believed was for her.

Her show of strength has me hopeful her injuries aren't as life-threatening as suspected, though I'd be lying if I said I also wasn't panicked. Dimitri appears as torn now as he was when he held a gun to my head in the woodlands outside of Hopeton. I don't believe he wants to kill me. He just has no clue how to process everything happening.

He isn't the only one lost. Fien is asleep now, but I had to fight her with everything I had to get her to settle. I'm not just the stranger who pulled her out of the line of fire, I'm also the woman who held her back when she attempted to race to a man she has mistaken as family. It broke my heart seeing her outstretch her arms for Rimi. I'm certain the cracks will heal when she learns to do the same for Dimitri, but for now, it still stings.

While Fien's daddy attempts to understand what her mother is saying beneath her oxygen mask, I carefully rake my fingers through her glossy hair. Audrey's voice is so frail, I can't hear the word she's speaking, but I'm confident it's only one. Her lips make the same weak movements on repeat, only stopping when an alarm overtakes the shrill of my pulse in my ears.

She's flatlining, and we're miles from nowhere.

With tears welling in my eyes, I watch the scene unfold. Ollie commences CPR while Dimitri tilts Audrey's head back, plugs her nose, then prepares to breathe air into her lungs. If I didn't know any better, I'd swear he's done this before. Saving lives isn't something the head of a cartel gang does. They usually take them, not fight for them.

Dimitri and Ollie continue compressions until the ambulance screeches to a stop at the front of a residence I've never seen before. I assumed we were going to Dimitri's New York compound, but I guess that was stupid of me to consider. Dimitri's crew just massacred over a hundred men. More than just local authorities will be chasing them.

The doors of the ambulance are tossed open by two large men flanking a petite blonde with big blue eyes. "Theater is prepped and ready. Take her through the double doors, into the elevator, then down one floor," instructs a lady I've never met before. She's only young, perhaps a year or two older than me. Blonde, regal-looking, and seemingly aware of who I am. Not only does the sweat beading on her forehead double when she spots my watch, fine lines crease the top of her lip. "I'll take care of Roxanne and Fien, you look after Audrey."

Although I appreciate Dimitri's quick glance my way to check I'm okay with the blonde's plan, it isn't necessary. He shouldn't feel torn between his wife and me. She's the mother of his child, and I no longer am. There's no competition. Fien needs both her mother *and* her father, and I refuse for my selfishness to steal that from her.

Besides, I rarely put myself first, so there's no chance of that changing today.

"Go," I whisper to Dimitri when his exit stalls long enough for the blonde's pencil-thin brows to join together. "I'm okay."

Dimitri lifts his chin, strays his eyes to Rocco for not even a second, then hotfoots it in the direction Ollie and a group of men dressed in white coats wheeled Audrey.

"You good?" Rocco's voice is full of suspicion, cautious of the hiss I involuntarily released while stepping down from the ambulance.

Since Fien is still cuddled in my chest, I placed our combined weight onto my sore foot to ensure my step down didn't wake her.

I shouldn't have bothered being vigilant. I've barely jerked my head up half an inch to assure Rocco I'm fine when Fien is ripped from my grasp.

"Hey!"

I'd say more if Fien responded to the woman's clutch with the devastation she displayed when I pulled her away from Maestro. She doesn't repel away from the lady like she did me. She startles, peers at her wide-eyed, then nuzzles back into her chest.

"While I get Fien settled, show Roxanne to the guest bedroom so she can get cleaned up." She spins away, takes one step, then whips back around. "The *downstairs* guest bedroom. I reserved the one on the second floor for Audrey and Dimitri." After dragging her crystal blue eyes down Rocco's blood-stained body, she purrs out, "You can stay down there too if you'd like. There are enough towels on the bed for both of you."

"Oh, we're not... we aren't..." I lose the chance to get out my stuttering reply that we're not a couple when she spins back around and stalks away, taking Fien with her.

Although my focus should remain solely on Fien, I kill two birds with one stone by asking, "Will Dimitri be okay with this?" I'm battered and bruised, but I am not so far down the rabbit hole I can't continue to fight to ensure Dimitri's wishes are being met. He has only just gotten his daughter back. I don't want her palmed from person to person like she was bounced state to state the past twenty-two months.

While rubbing at a kink in his neck, Rocco shrugs. "Dimitri isn't a fan of India's, but the fact she's Audrey's best friend means he has no choice but to put up with her."

"Oh." Now the disdain on India's face makes sense. She's defending her friend from the woman who kept her husband 'occupied' during her captivity.

Bearing in mind the circumstances, she's handling Dimitri's betrayal better than I would if it had occurred to Estelle. I wouldn't offer her husband's mistress to sleep in my guest room. If she was still breathing, she'd be in the doghouse.

Mistress. Yuck. The word alone makes me sick to my stomach, much less wondering if that's how I'm now viewed.

"No." Rocco adds a finger waggle to his abrupt reply to the question in my eyes. "I have some random dude's puke on my shirt and a ton of adrenaline to work through. I'm not up for an in-depth conversation on the uprising of deceased wives." He doesn't say how he usually expels his excessive energy after a raid, but his eyes most certainly do. "So how about we get cleaned up, fill our bellies with food, then tackle the shitstorm that comes with Audrey's rebirth?"

When I nod, cowardly bowing out of a fight I know will be the shitstorm Rocco is worried about, his lips curl at the ends. "Do you want a piggyback ride, or would you like me to carry you to your room wedding-night style?" His smile grows when confusion strains my features. "I know you're hurt, Princess P, you know you're hurt, and so the fuck does Dimitri. Why do you think he was so torn up about leaving you?"

I know what he's doing. He's trying to confirm that Dimitri cares about me in some weird, warped way, but in all honesty, his question cuts me up a little. I don't want Dimitri's attention because I'm hurt, I want it because he genuinely cares about me.

"Wedding style it is," Rocco says with a snicker when nothing but silence teems between us for the next several seconds. "It'll get more of a rile out of Dimitri, and we both know how much I like stirring that fucker."

Stealing my chance to reply, Rocco scoops me into his arms, gropes my butt in a way that isn't close to being appropriate, then charges down the hall like a groom dying to see what negligee his bride is wearing under her dress.

23

ROXANNE

"The faucet is as finicky as shit, but if you like your showers scalding, you'll be happy."

Rocco balances his drenched shoulder onto the doorjamb separating my room from the attached bathroom before running a towel over his wet head. For a woman unprepared for guests until ten minutes before we arrived, India laid out the welcome mat. My room is made up as if it's the presidential suite at a ritzy hotel, the bathroom is brimming with toiletries that took care of the gory scent bounding out of Rocco the past three hours in less than ten minutes, and we devoured a feast fit for a king.

I could almost pretend I was whisked away for a weekend of indulgence if the right man was humming in the shower the past five minutes.

Rocco hasn't let up on his endeavor to force a response out of Dimitri one bit the past three hours. He attempted to feed me strawberries dipped in chocolate, wipe away the dribble of a juicy steak from the bottom of my lip while chewing on his own, then sat so close to me, even if I wanted to forget I was only just freed from a baby-farming trade, I couldn't.

The only good that's come from his constant attention is not having the time to think about how much has changed in the past three days. I said to Dimitri I wouldn't walk away from him as the woman I once was, but even I didn't have a clue how honest my statement was.

I'm not close to the woman I used to be. I don't necessarily believe that's a bad thing. However, I'm confident walking away from Dimitri will hurt, nonetheless.

Ignoring the pain stretched from my heart to the lower half of my stomach, I maneuver out of the cross-legged position on the floor I've been huddled in the past hour, then pad to Rocco's half of the room. He watches me, forever on alert, but seemingly at a loss on which direction he should take this time around.

We haven't stumbled anywhere near the shitstorm we feel brewing on the horizon. We bunkered down instead, preferring to ride out the storm in a shelter instead of walking into it without fear as we suggested only hours ago. It's cowardly for us to do, but when you're facing a storm as brutal as this one, only a fool would pray for impact instead of doing everything possible to avoid it.

"I really wish you'd let someone take a look at your foot," Rocco says when I stop to stand in front of him. "The ice helped with the swelling, but for all we know, it could be a twisted wreck beneath the surface."

"It's fine," I assure him for the hundredth time this evening. I can barely feel its throb. Not only has the swelling settled, nothing can compare to the pain in my chest. It's as bad as it comes. "We iced and strapped it. What more could it need?"

"Oh, I don't know," Rocco answers, unaware I wasn't asking a question. "Perhaps a splint... or how about some pain medication? That might help, too."

"Truly. I'm fine. I swear to you." I run my hand down his arm, genuinely grateful for his company the past three hours but more than ready to have a few minutes of solitude. "While I shower, why don't you head down and release some of the excess energy that has you bouncing around like an Energizer Bunny."

He smiles before shaking his head. "I'm good. I like hanging out with you."

His reply warms my heart, but it does little to weaken my campaign. "I need some time to process everything." When his brows pinch as confused by the angst in my tone as me, I make out it isn't as big a deal as it is. "I need to use the bathroom... *in private.*"

"Oh..." His pupils dilate to the size of saucers before he adds a second, "Oooh," into the mix, this one longer than his first.

Even mortified, I nod my head to the humor-filled questions in his eyes. I'd rather he believe I'm about to stink up the place than continue my struggle to hold back the wetness in my eyes. Just like I don't stand out in a crowd, I'm not one of those girls who can pull off devastation without bloodshot corneas, scary suitcase-size bags under my eyes, and a heap of snot.

India's residence is gorgeous and regal—just like her—but its walls are paper-thin. Rocco and I hear her staff's incoming arrival long before they knock on the door of my room. The knowledge makes me grateful my room is in the equivalent of the basement. I'll be out of the loop with what's going on, but since that includes reuniting couples, my inquisitiveness is more than happy to face the injustice.

After tugging on a pair of gray sweatpants sans underwear and a crisp white tee from a bag one of India's staff brought down earlier, Rocco rejoins me next to the carved wooden door that leads to the bathroom. "If you need me, call out to Smith. He's always listening."

The realization that I'm being forever watched usually comforts me. Regretfully, this time around, it doesn't. It isn't that I believe Smith will tattle on me, I'd just rather our reunion occur without the awkwardness it is already going to be filled with.

In a last-ditch attempt to rile Dimitri, Rocco presses his lips to my temple. It isn't a quick half-a-second peck. His lips linger long enough for me to hear the gurgle of his stomach when nothing but heartbreak teems between us.

I appreciate what he's doing, and I love that he still has my back even with Dimitri's wife resurrecting from the grave, but I also hate it. Audrey is fighting for her life. Now is not the time to force her to glove-up for someone she never truly lost. At the end of the day, no matter what happens, she is Dimitri's wife and the mother of his child, and I am... *nobody*.

Incapable of holding back my devastation for a second longer, I briefly lean into Rocco's embrace to accept a comfort I don't deserve before I dash into the bathroom as fast as my quivering legs will take me, shutting the door behind me.

With my eyes shut and my heart in lockdown, I squash my back against the carved wood, my tears not permitted to fall until the squeak of a second set of hinges sounds through my ears. When that occurs, my sobs are devastating. I've been holding them in for days, so I expected nothing less than pure carnage when I finally permitted them to fall. They howl through me on repeat, not slowing even when the wetness flooding my cheeks becomes too much for my swiping hands to keep up with. I cry and cry and cry until the hottest water won't remove the red streaks from my cheeks, and I fall asleep on the tiled floor, alone and heartbroken.

I lost the man I love, our child, and my principles in one night. Nothing could have prepared me for this—not even falling in love with a notorious mobster so outrageously, I'd do it all again in a heartbeat just to see the light in his eyes shift for the final time.

Fien owns Dimitri's heart.

Before Audrey stepped into his path, I was responsible for its beats.

Now I don't know which way is up.

24

DIMITRI

I stop peering at my bloodstained hands when the voice of a man on the brink of exhaustion rolls through my ears. Ollie is wearing smocks like a real-life doctor. They're as blood-stained as my hands, and the knowledge it is the blood of my wife curtails my mood even more than not being given an update on her condition in hours.

I'm always a little unhinged after a raid. It causes a rush of adrenaline you can't get anywhere else—adrenaline I had planned to unleash on Roxanne until the wee hours of tomorrow morning. Instead, I'm sitting in the corridor that replicates a dungeon, waiting to see if a doctor kicked out of med school can fix the hack job someone did to the mother of my child.

I still can't believe Audrey is alive. She never showed the fight she displayed tonight once during our relationship. She was the meekest woman in the room, the one who forever shied away from controversy. I never suspected she would be able to survive the ordeal she was forced through. That's why I only ever searched for her body. I was convinced she was dead.

Shows what I know. Before Roxanne, I had never experienced the gut-tingling, ball-tightening, infuriating sensation I get when she enters the realm, but you'd think I would have felt a least a little bit of Audrey's gall. She's my wife, she carried my flesh and blood in her womb, so how could I not know she was alive, fighting to come back to me?

My frustrating debate is pushed back for another day when Ollie stops to stand in front of me. He called my name multiple times, but since I was so caught up in my thoughts, I didn't acknowledge his presence.

"Sorry, what did you say?" My voice is so rough, I don't recognize it. It's brimming with agitation and a heap of the adrenaline I've yet to disperse.

While raking his fingers through his shoulder-length hair, Ollie slots into the chair next to me. Considering we're in a residence, it should be odd acknowledging there's a fully functioning operating theater in the basement. However, since it's India, a freak in her own right, I'm not half as shocked as you'd expect.

We need to bunker down for a couple of days until the heat dies down. Although I would have preferred for that to occur anywhere but here, the realization that India has a house full of servants and access to every medical field there is had me changing tactics.

Supposedly India is in favor with an oil tycoon who has a hankering for the underworld. With the right amount of money, anyone can join some crews' ranks. That shit doesn't fly with me, though. I'd gut him just on the belief he can do what I do without earning it.

You don't get to where I am by throwing money at people. It's messy, gritty, and more fucked in the head than he'd ever understand. And more times than not, it occurs without the love of a good woman.

Perhaps that's why I can't sense Audrey as I can Roxanne? Audrey and I never shared those three little words I thought I would have to torture out of a woman before she'd ever give them to me voluntarily. Not even the day we wed saw them exchanged. We swapped rings, ate cake, then I fell into bed with a couple of hookers while Audrey went back to the honeymoon suite alone.

Fuck, I was an asshole. I still am. I just don't see Roxanne taking my shit. I was coked out of my head, but I still recall the way she ripped the blonde hooker away from me by the strands of her hair. She wanted to kill her, and in all honesty, if she had a weapon, I reckon she would have.

I scrub my hand across my mouth, hiding my inappropriately timed smirk before locking my eyes with Ollie. The way he stares at me reveals he knew my thoughts were elsewhere again, not to mention his shoulder bump. He did the same thing when he confirmed what Audrey's pregnancy test said, except back then, he was consoling me instead of livening me up.

"Is she going to make it?"

An unusual patter hits my chest when Ollie dips his chin. "She isn't out of the woods just yet, but I don't see her recovery having too many issues." As he balances on the edge of his chair, air whizzes from his nose. That's a telltale sign he's nervous. "We had to remove Audrey's uterus, ovaries, and part of her spleen. She won't be able to carry any more children."

I'm not stunned by his confession. Whoever got to Audrey made it clear if she survived the second time, she would be unable to bear children. They hacked up her uterus even more than they did when removing Fien from her stomach.

"Were there any signs she had... umm..." Who the fuck made me this whimpering, blubbering imbecile? I'm Dimitri-fucking-Petretti. I do *not* stutter.

"No," Ollie says with a shake of his head, saving me from

making a fool out of myself for the second time. "Excluding the scar from when she delivered Fien, there were no indicators that she had birthed other children."

His reply pleases me greatly. I don't want Fien to have half-siblings stretched across the globe like I had growing up. She'll only have one set. The children I'll have with Roxanne.

My cocky grin slips when Ollie discloses, "She's been asking to see you."

"She's awake?" I don't know why I sound shocked. My dead ass exposes how long I've been sitting on a hard, plastic chair, not to mention the annoying tick of my watch. I've been down here for over five hours. The delay feels as if it is slowly killing me. I don't just want to discover if Fien's cheeks are as soft as they look, I want to unearth the reason Roxanne limped when I loaded her in the ambulance Smith got onsite remarkably quick. She wordlessly assured me she was fine several times during our forty-minute ride, but I don't believe her. She's too brave to make a fuss and too fucking stubborn for her own good.

"Once you have things wrapped up here, can you take a look at Roxanne for me? I think she did something to her foot."

Ollie smiles before nodding, forever happy to please me. It makes sense when you see how much he charges for his services. "I'll stay with Audrey until she's out of recovery, then hand her over to India's crew."

After slapping him on the shoulder, issuing my praise without words, I stand to my feet.

"You coming?" I ask when he remains seated. I'm almost halfway down the corridor, yet, he hasn't walked a single stride.

My throat grows scratchy when he shakes his head. "Audrey asked to speak to you alone."

He smiles a beaming grin when my cheeks whiten. I was only married for a couple of months before Audrey was kidnapped, but even I know things aren't good when a wife requests to speak to her husband in private.

"She's pretty doped up. I doubt she'll be awake for long," Ollie says with a chuckle.

Needing to leave before I switch out his smile for a fat lip, I push through the doors he broke through a couple of minutes ago, then head toward the room Audrey was wheeled into when she was on the brink of death.

I won't lie. My footing wobbles a little when I spot her through the window of her room. She's a little pale, and she has oxygen prongs stuck in her nose, but she is as beautiful as the woman whose trek to the kitchen for a glass of water saved me from making a mistake with India I could never take back.

Audrey can turn the head of any man. She just can't make my gut tingle.

"Hey, none of that," I say when the dam in her eyes breaks upon seeing me. "You're okay. I won't let anything happen to you."

I don't know who's more shocked when I pull her into my chest so my shirt can dry her tears. I was never affectionate when we were married. Before I held Roxanne in my private jet, I had never comforted anyone.

Believing I know the reason behind her tears, I assure her, "Fien is safe. She's here, sleeping. I swear to you, she is safe."

"Fien?" Audrey's words are as weak as the bounce of her eyes. She appears truly stunned. "You named her Fien?"

"Yeah." I almost laugh at the crack of my one word. I hated the name Audrey had chosen, but now I couldn't imagine calling her anything else. "It wasn't my first choice, but you loved it, and so did your mother."

I thought my confession would lessen Audrey's sobs, not double them.

Shows how much I have to learn about women.

"Do you want me to call your parents? Tell them your safe?"

I can't believe I didn't do that instead of twiddling my thumbs the past five hours. It wouldn't have taken long to advise them their daughter is alive but organizing their flights and accommodation would have gobbled up some time.

I halt searching for my phone in my pocket when Audrey shakes her head. With how many drugs Ollie is pumping into her, it should be a weak, pathetic shake. It's nothing close to that. It was as determined as the clutch she has on my shirt and as resolute as the glint in her eyes. "I'll call them later. Once *this* all settles down."

The way she says 'this' has me suspicious she isn't solely referencing Fien, herself, and me. She was pretty out of it during our drive from Rimi's compound to here, but as Roxanne has said previously, the dead could feel the electricity brewing between us, so I'm confident a near unconscious woman would have.

Audrey will never call me out on it, though. I could go down on Roxanne in front of her, and she'd act as if I were doing something as innocent as eating breakfast.

I'm about to ask Audrey how much interaction she had with Roxanne the past three days, but the briefest tap on a window stops me. That gut-tingling sensation I mentioned missing earlier smacks into me full-pelt when my eyes stray to the noise. India is on the other side of the glass. She isn't responsible for the buzz surging my pulse with adrenaline more potent than a bloodbath. It is my daughter, who's being held in her arms.

Unlike when she was nuzzled in Roxanne's chest, Fien is wide awake, peering my way. Her eyes are more cobalt blue than I realized. Her photos failed to show the almost purple ring around her dark blue eyes. They make her eyes unique, as one of a kind as she will forever be.

When I gesture for India to join us in Audrey's room,

Audrey's hand shoots out to snatch my wrist. Once she has my focus, she adds a head shake to her firm clutch. "I don't want her to see me like this. It might scare her."

I curse under my breath, frustrated I hadn't thought about that. Fien witnessed enough bloodshed today to last her a lifetime. I don't want more horrific images added to the vault.

Relief engulfs Audrey's features when I say, "All right. Once you're set up in your room, I'll organize for someone to bring Fien to see you."

Audrey smiles. It isn't the blinding one she used to give when she felt Fien kick her hand. It's more subdued than happy. "Thank you."

She loosens her grip on my wrist for barely a second before she tightens it again. When she locks her eyes with mine, an unusual spark in them reveals the words she wants to speak, her mouth simply refuses to relinquish them. I don't mind. I've only heard those words from one woman before, and I'm more than happy to keep it that way.

"Get some rest. The sooner you're back on your feet, the better it will be for all involved."

I press my lips to Audrey's temple before exiting the room, my heart racing more with every step I take. I've waited for this day for months, but instead of it happening in front of the people responsible for its occurrence, it's being witnessed by two women who have always felt more like strangers to me instead of family.

"It's okay," India coos to Fien when I hold out my hands, hopeful a demure approach won't see her releasing the tears damming in her eyes. It will break my heart if she cries when I hold her for the first time. I saw how badly her tears affected Roxanne. I don't know if I'm strong enough to endure the same torture. "It's Dada, Fien. Do you want to go to your dada?"

Months of torment, years of carnage, and a lifetime of injustices are undone when my daughter reaches out for me as I'm reaching for her. It's all forgotten in an instant, but I will never forget the people responsible for this moment. No matter which side they were on, they will stay with me forever—Roxanne included.

25

ROXANNE

I wake up startled and confused. My foreign location isn't the sole cause of my bewilderment. My aching backside is responsible for the majority of it. My tailbone is screaming more than my foot. Serves me right for falling asleep on a tiled floor.

I truly didn't think I'd be left alone for hours on end, so I didn't put much thought into the location of my sob-fest. Don't get me wrong, I'm grateful for the privacy, but sometimes it's nice to have a shoulder to cry on.

Dimitri's was the first one I used. It was weird to be comforted by a man who had threatened to kill me only hours earlier. However, it displayed there was more to him than his dark and dangerous outer shell. He has a heart, a big one, and now that he has his daughter back, he has the chance to show it off.

Regretfully, it seems as if I've been shunted from the festivities again.

While grumbling about the pathetic woman I'm portraying, I clamber to my feet. Dimitri has been waiting for this moment for almost two years, so why am I annoyed he wants to relish it? I'd be mortified if he didn't at least ensure Fien settled in for the night.

Once I'm on my feet, I sway like a leaf in a summer's breeze, and white spots dance in front of my eyes. The dizziness bombarding me makes the removal of the nightgown Rocco handed me hours ago a little tedious. The one I was wearing when they rescued us was grubby and dotted with Maestro's blood, so I was more than eager to change into something fresh.

After peeling down the panties with a waistband that goes past my bellybutton, I suck in a fast breath before glancing down at the monstrous pad that should have offered more cushioning during my nap than it did.

My sigh is filled with both relief and devastation when I discover the pad is empty. I'm glad that stage of my life occurred quickly, but it will take more than a lifetime for tears not to prick my eyes when I remember the ebbs and flows of the past week.

I take a few moments drinking in my naked form in the vanity mirror. Usually, this is as uncomfortable as it gets for me. I'm not experiencing the same bother today. I look like a mess. My hair is knotted, my skin is mottled with marks, and my eyes are sunken from how much I cried, but I also look mature, strong, and undogged.

I fought, and although my victory can be accredited to the many men in Dimitri's crew, some of the credit also belongs to me. If I hadn't reached Maestro when I did, he might have left with Fien before the balaclava-clad men stormed the basement. He was mere feet from the exit. I stopped him from going through it.

That makes me proud.

That makes me strong.

And it has my chin rising instead of balancing on my chest as it has the past seven hours.

After giving my thanks to the warrior glancing back at me in the mirror, I enter the shower stall, twist on the tap until steam floats around me, then step into the heavenly hot stream of water.

I've barely drowned half the heaviness plaguing me when the heavenly gruff voice of Dimitri sends my head into a tailspin. "Eyes to the wall."

Certain I'm dreaming, I don't defy him this time around. I snap my eyes shut so fast, the scent my head is fabricating almost causes a tear to roll down my cheek. He smells so good. Dark and twisted, but oh so comforting.

My knees curve inward when the brisk scrub of a hand over a bristly chin is quickly chased by a second hand sliding around my waist. Even being afraid he might disappear won't stop me from leaning into his embrace. I'm dying to feel the heat of his skin against mine, and I am willing to risk falling out of the shower like a drunken fool to get it.

After setting my skin on fire with the briefest flutters of his fingertips over my midsection, Dimitri asks, "What did Ollie say about your foot?"

"Who?" I ask, purring. My mind is so wondrous, I don't just hear and smell Dimitri, I feel him thick and heavy behind me. He's hard like the only thing we lost the past three days was time. Our connection is as bristling as it's always been.

Dimitri peers down at me, smirking when he spots my groggy expression. "If I didn't know any better, I would have sworn you raided the liquor cabinet after dinner instead of sipping on the Sprite Rocco was adamant you must have."

I've barely gotten over the shock he's been spying on me when he stuns me for the second time. He doesn't just spin me around to face him head-on, he adds a heap of sexy words to the lusty glint in his eyes.

"Hook your sore foot around my waist. I don't want to hurt

you, but I need your cunt to squeeze my cock like I squeezed the light from Rimi's eyes an hour ago."

His confession that he just killed a man should weaken the intensity brewing between us. It doesn't. Not in the slightest. He knows as well as I do that men like Rimi Castro don't stop what they're doing with a warning. They must face whatever penalty Dimitri sees fit, and whether gutted, maimed, or killed, it will occur with haste.

Furthermore, I love how fearless he is when it comes to protecting his family. The knowledge he'd go to the ends of the earth to keep his daughter safe is the ultimate turn-on. It sees me kissing him with everything I have—teeth, tongue, hands—they all get in on the act. It's a possessive kiss, both claiming and owning. It tells him everything I'm afraid to say but would give anything to change—that I am his as long as he wants me.

My head lolls to the side with a moan when Dimitri cranks my neck a couple of minutes later so he can trail his nose down the throb in my throat. Even without his growl, I'm aware my scent has changed since the last time he smelled me. It isn't tarnished with the disaster of the past thirty-six hours, it's harmonized with hope, fortified with determination, and it has the faintest hint of his daughter's shampoo.

A shudder rolls up the length of my spine when he swipes the head of his cock across my clit. I'm buzzed all over and more than ready for the next stage of our exchange to occur.

Dimitri will never let that happen, though. He needs me wet enough to take him without pain because, for some reason, even loving the knowledge he's ruined me for any other man, he doesn't want to hurt me.

He hoists me up the shower like he did in the bathroom of my childhood home, inhales deeply, then growls when the scent of my aching sex teems into his nostrils. "You have no idea how much your smell brings me back from the brink. It can be so fucking dark, so fucking devastating, but your intoxicating scent is like a light at the end of the tunnel, forever encouraging me to find my way home."

Home? I almost choke on the word. It's the simplest phrase, but it has the biggest impact on my heart. I thought it had shattered beyond repair hours ago. Now it feels as if it is bigger than it was when it dawned on me that Dimitri had found us.

"Lean back, Roxanne. I'm about ready for a second helping of dessert."

After gripping my ass with his big hands, Dimitri buries his face between my legs and goes to town. He sucks my clit into his mouth, drags his tongue through the folds of my sex, and repeatedly pokes it inside of me.

He eats me for the next several minutes, his pace only slowing when the shudder wreaking havoc with my body requires him to resecure his grip on my backside.

"You better get a whole heap louder than that if you want to come, Roxie. I ain't taking no prisoners today."

He shoots his eyes to mine briefly before his head once again delves back between my legs. I call out, the sensation of him expertly eating me almost too much to bear. I was crazy to think things would ever be over between us. Our connection is too explosive to harness, too dynamic. If we tried to ignore something as destructive as the tension that forever bristles between us, it would be a catastrophe. I wouldn't be its only victim. The entire race would become extinct.

"Yes, Roxanne," Dimitri growls into my pussy when I'm blindsided by a ferocious orgasm.

His name falls from my lips over and over again as my tugs on his drenched hair turn violent. I'm screaming, shuddering, and on the verge of waking up the entire neighborhood with my begs for him not to stop.

With how crazy he makes me feel, I should be doing the exact opposite. I should beg for him to stop before getting on my knees and returning the favor, but for the life of me, I can't. The controls of my body are no longer mine to command. They've been relinquished, handed over. They're at the complete control of Dimitri, who takes what he wants, offers nothing in return, but continues to defy the dark, dangerous man he was raised to be.

He ravishes me until my orgasm stretches from one to two. It is a beautifully brutal few minutes, enhanced by the connection of our eyes when he makes his way from my throbbing, drenched sex to my face.

He licks my peaked nipples during his trek, but the hankering in my eyes exposes how badly I need his lips on mine. I want to kiss him. Possess him. Make him as wild as he makes me.

The crash of our lips is brutal. It blazes heat through me, making me grateful the water has switched from scalding to lukewarm. We kiss for several long minutes. It's an almost frantic, somewhat rough, and very much wild exchange. Hands go everywhere, and before I know it, one is guiding the head of Dimitri's impressive cock to the opening of my pussy.

"Look at me." I'm reminded just how tall he is when my elevated position means I don't have to crank my neck to look at him. Even with my head almost reaching the top of the tiles, he's right in front of me as dark and dangerous as ever.

It's the fight of my life to hold back my excitement for the third time when the collision of our eyes causes cum to erupt out of Dimitri's cock. He coats my pussy with his spawn, both inside and out, since he's too impatient to wait until he finishes coming before notching his cock inside me.

Once almost all his impressive shaft is stuffed inside of me, he darts his tongue between my lips, then kisses the living hell out of me. The pure possessiveness fueling his kiss doubles the wetness between my legs in an instant, and it has me on the brink of ecstasy even faster than that.

"That's better," Dimitri grunts with a steady rock of his hips. "Wet, screaming, and fucking relentless. The only way you should ever be seen."

He thrusts into me faster, stronger, and deeper with every pump he does. Within minutes, a familiar sensation tightens my muscles all over again. The thought of how fast he makes me come undone hazes my mind as quickly as it speeds up the rocks of his hips.

"I love the way your cunt tugs at my dick. Forever begging." He locks his eyes with mine. They have the memorable glint I'll never stop striving for. "Just like your eyes. So fucking greedy for more... but only from me. You don't want anyone but me."

After adjusting the span of my thighs, he drives into me like a madman, getting lost in the same uncontrollable ruckus overwhelming every inch of me. I saw the strong, impenetrable man he is earlier tonight, but this is the sexier version. The control he exerts in the bedroom is unbelievable. He uses every muscle in his body to please me, and even when I've been brought to climax multiple times, he continues his relentless pursuit until my legs either give out or we collapse from exhaustion.

I can see how tired he is, feel it in the weary muscles I cling to as he drives me to hysteria, but he doesn't give in. He never tires. He gives it his all until I'm quivering and convulsing like the water turned cold hours ago.

"Fuck, Roxie," Dimitri moans on a groan, his rocks unwavering. "You're so fucking beautiful when you come."

The volume of my moans jumps up a couple of decibels, inspired by his praise. I've been called cute, spunky, and sexy, but beautiful is new, and I fucking love it. It has another orgasm building inside of me. This feels more threatening than my earlier one. It spreads warmth through me, thickening my veins with the adrenaline Dimitri is trying to dimmish by pounding the living hell out of me.

He drives into me so deeply it feels as if his cock is poking more than my uterus. It's painful but crazily exciting. So much so, I succumb to my next orgasm even faster than I did my first.

As my nails dig into Dimitri's shoulders, his name falls from my lips over and over again. My screams are as uncontrollable as the orgasm rolling through me. It's almost too much, too overwhelming, too fucking good for me ever to believe this isn't a dream. It won't relent. No matter how loud I scream, it won't free me from the madness. It holds on firmly, gripping me as well as Dimitri's gaze spears my heart. He's staring straight at me, increasing the shards of pleasure shredding through me so much, I have no chance of holding back the words floating over my tongue the past hour. "I love you, Dimi. I love you so fucking much."

"There it is," he replies with a grunt, his pumps picking up like they had any more to give. "Now, let's see if I can work it out of you without another set of back-to-back orgasms."

With my legs curled around his waist and his smirk increasing the likelihood he will accomplish his objective before we reach the main part of my room, Dimitri shuts down the faucet, throws open the shower door, then walks me toward the turned-down bed.

His toss onto my mattress is playful this time around. It even arrives with a little giggle, which is pushed aside for a moan when he leans over to suck a budded nipple into his mouth.

Since the cold shower water has given my skin a blue tinge, the mottling of bruises on my thighs and hips are barely noticeable when Dimitri directs his focus a couple of inches lower. I was fortunate to get good genes from my nanna. Even when it's been put through the wringer, my skin heals rather decently.

Take the scar on my forehead, for example. Since the chemical peel Dimitri organized the first night of our arrangement, I haven't needed to cover it up with my bangs. I'm almost at a point I feel comfortable growing out my bangs. That might have more to do with how Dimitri lavishes every inch of me than anything, but it feels nice to have finally reached this stage.

When Dimitri's chin rests at the apex of my sex, I assume he's about to once again devour the feast growing more pungent with every nip, lick, and bite he does, so you can imagine my utter despair when he stops a couple of inches away from what I believe is his projected target.

There's no bump in my belly—even if I were still pregnant, there wouldn't be—but Dimitri cups it as if there is before he raises his eyes to me. My brain screams at me to tell him the truth, to expose that he didn't just right Audrey and Fien's injustices tonight, but I can't. There's too much life in his eyes for me to douse, too much happiness. I'm partly responsible for the misery they've held the past twenty-two months, so I refuse to steal the light from them for the second time.

I will tell him what happened, just not tonight, not when he finally feels capable of gulping in an entire breath. Instead, I tell him the only thing that matters, and since it is straight-up honest, not even the crackling of my words can take away from its authenticity.

"I love you, Dimitri Petretti. Your fierceness, your craziness, your protectiveness. I love it all... as will your children."

26

DIMITRI

I shoot Rocco a warning look, wordlessly suggesting he keep his riling comment in his mouth or risk losing some teeth. I'm not sneaking out of Roxanne's room at five in the morning because I'm ashamed we treated India's guest bedroom as if it's a brothel. I didn't unyieldingly pound my cock into Roxanne's mouth to lower her moans. I love how out of control she is in the bedroom. She forever puts everyone first, *except* when we're messing the sheets. There, nothing but chasing the next thrill is on her mind.

The same can be said for me, except I'm not seeking the quick, unenjoyable releases I sought before Roxanne stormed into my life. I want all the shit that comes before it. The flickers in her eyes, the scent of her sweat-slicked skin, her little declarations of love I had no clue I'd crave more than the drugs that regularly tracked through my veins as a teen. They thrill me even more than knowing Rimi finally got what was coming to him.

He chirped like a bird, tattled like the rat he is, yet, he's still dead. Killed by my hands under the watchful eye of Henry Gottle, the now rightful boss of all bosses. He came to the plate for me like no one else has in this industry. It earned him both my respect and my backing.

Forever willing to test my patience, Rocco ignores my unvoiced threat. "Your sneaking around is making me feel dirty." He shivers like someone just walked over his grave. "Do you mind if I borrow your shower again so I can wash off the funk? I promise to get undressed in the bathroom this time around."

I close Roxanne's door harder than intended before sliding out a key from my pocket and slotting it into the lock. I asked Rocco to come here so Roxanne wouldn't wake up alone in a foreign place, with her head still a little murky about what happened yesterday, not to make himself fucking comfortable.

I'd stay myself if I didn't want to offer Fien the same level of comfort. She didn't cry when I held her for the first time last night, but her wish to stay in my arms ended the instant India attempted to leave the room.

I'm keen to change that.

I don't want to be a hero, but I do want to be the man my daughter runs to when she's in trouble.

"Make sure Roxanne has something to eat when she wakes. She needs to recoup her energy."

I'm not bragging, Roxanne's moans could be heard two states over, I'm just—*all right, maybe I am bragging.* I'll fluff out my feathers and strut like a peacock if it gives Rocco the hint to fuck off. He played his hand. I won his chips. He isn't ready for round two.

"And stay out of her room." I thrust the key for Roxanne's room into Rocco's palm with more force than what is needed, hopeful it will get my message across. "Smith may not be watching, but he's always listening."

Like a perfectly-timed skit—or perhaps a sick fucking pervert—Smith's voice booms out of both Rocco and my cell phones not even a second later. "Fuckin' oath I am." His voice has the same springy edge Rocco and mine has.

Victory has a way of making the toughest men sound soft and the weakest men sound strong.

Once our joint laughter has settled, Smith clears the humor from his voice before adding, "When you've finished settling Fien, Ollie has been buzzing you most of the morning. I told him you didn't want to be disturbed, but he said it was important."

"Is it about Fien?" When a hum of rejection vibrates out of my cell, I ask, "Roxanne?"

"No." I can't tell if Smith's sigh is in frustration or humor. It may be a combination of both. "But she is the reason he didn't get a chance to assess Roxanne yesterday."

It takes me replaying what he said through my head three times before my brain finally clicks on. I'm so fucking high on the good shit money can't buy, I completely forgot my wife is holed up in a hospital bed downstairs, so unwell, she couldn't have any visitors last night. Not even our daughter.

"Tell Ollie I'll be down as soon as I can."

Acting ignorant to the regret in my tone, Smith replies, "On it," before he disconnects our connection.

"Don't bother," I say to Rocco when he attempts to tell me I have nothing to be regretful about.

Guilt is eating me alive, but it has nothing to do with Roxanne. She put her life on the line for a child she had never met—*my* child. I'll never feel guilty about relaying how much that meant to me, and don't get me started on the fact she loves me, or I may never leave this room.

"Just make sure she eats, okay? I'll handle the rest."

With my mood uneased, it takes me a little longer to reach Fien's room than my travels last night when I headed in the opposite direction. Once I was assured Fien was settled and safe, I practically sprinted for Roxanne's room, my race only slowing when I discovered someone had locked her door.

Rocco assured me it wasn't him, but he was determined to find out who it was.

It's fortunate the keys in this residence open *all* the locks, or my wish to join Roxanne in the shower would have been thwarted by me kicking down her door.

The guilt I was experiencing only minutes ago pummels back into me when the creak of Fien's door is gobbled up by someone singing a lullaby. I don't recognize the words since they're foreign, but their flow is oddly similar to "Hush Little Baby." It seems like the type of nursery rhyme you'd sing if a baby was upset.

My intuition is proven right when my glance into Fien's crib comes up empty. She isn't curled into the corner of the wooden crib she's a couple of months too big for, she's resting on India's chest, her breathing in sync to the gentle rocks India does in an antique rocking chair.

It takes everything I have to hold back my naturally engrained vicious tongue when India shakes her head at my silent approach. She glares at me like I have no right to look over my flesh and blood before she presses her finger to her lips.

Stupidly believing she's in control around here, she gestures for someone in the room next to Fien's to enter before she attempts to stand to her feet.

I work my jaw side to side when she shunts away my endeavor to assist her to her feet with another brisk shake of her head. It's clear she's pissed. I guarantee she isn't the only one. I basically skipped out of Roxanne's room since my mood was so carefree and light. Now I won't be able to take one fucking step without waking the entire continent.

"Can I speak with you outside." Anyone who doesn't know

India would assume she's asking a question. I don't face that issue—regretfully. She isn't asking for a quiet word. She's demanding.

I should tell her to fuck off before reminding her who's running the show around here, then I should put plans into play to change our hideout location to anywhere but here, but since India is Audrey's best friend, and Audrey will need her support when I advise her I don't believe couples need to stay together purely for their children, I hold back the urge—barely.

It's a fucking hard feat. The strain is heard in my voice when I ask, "What is this about?"

India splays her hands across her hips before arching a brow. "Seriously? You're going to act clueless as to why I've spent the last four hours comforting *your* daughter." I'm about to tell her to cut the theatrics before I do worse to her vocal cords, but she continues talking, stealing my gamble, "Your wife is in a hospital bed fighting for her life, your daughter just came out of a life-threatening ordeal, yet you spent the last four hours fucking your current side-dish whore of the month."

I try to keep a cool head. I tell myself time and time again that I don't give a fuck what India thinks, but I lose my cool when the word 'whore' rings on repeat in my ears.

Just like she did in the limousine all those months ago, India freezes like a statue when I pin her to the wall outside of Fien's room by her throat. "Who I fuck is none of your business." My words are as cold as ice, but as quiet as a wilted leaf blowing over a frozen pond. "It wasn't anytime you tried to weasel your way into my bed *after* I married your best friend, and it wasn't the many times you encouraged me to move on when you thought she was dead, so why the fuck do you care now?" I don't wait for her to answer me. I just hit her where it hurts. "Because you know Roxanne is more than a side-dish whore, and you're worried—"

"Of course, I am. Audrey is my best friend." She shouldn't be able to talk through the brutal clutch I have on her throat, but as Rocco has said previously, bitches don't stay down even when they should. "She deserves to be treated better than you're treating her, and so does Fien."

I compress her throat a little tighter, ensuring I get across my point before snarling out, "This has *nothing* to do with Fien."

I squeeze and squeeze and squeeze until her pulse is nearly nonexistent, and then I let her go.

A smart woman would shut the fuck up before licking her wounds in private.

India clearly isn't smart.

"She bludgeoned herself to secure your attention, but it still wasn't enough for you, was it? What will it take for you to pay her an ounce of attention, Dimi? Her life? Fien's?" My hands firm into tight balls during her last question. "She fought with the strength you said she'd never have, maintained it for almost two years, yet you still ignore her."

"You're lying." My short statement is an overall generalization of what she said.

I agree, Audrey is stronger, but I don't know what to think about the first half of her statement. Audrey is a meek, shy woman who'd prefer to die a painful death than face any type of angst head-on, so it seems odd for her to use brutality as a way of demanding attention. She didn't want my attention for the first few weeks of our 'courtship.' I had to show her otherwise.

India waits for our eyes to lock and hold before she shakes her head, assuring I see the truth in them. "That's why Ollie has been trying to reach you all night. Audrey's wounds were self-inflicted. She used the knife you dropped when you couldn't take your eyes off Roxanne because she knew *everything* she had strived for the past twenty-two months wasn't going to happen. You had moved on." When the honesty in her tone stumps me of a reply, she uses my unusual quiet to her advantage. "Prove her wrong, Dimi. Chase her like you did when she was the one rejecting you."

"It isn't that simple. Things have changed."

India pulls a 'duh' face. Considering the intensity of our situation, her response is ridiculous. "Yeah, they have. You have a daughter together. A family—"

"And I'm going to have a child with another woman." I almost say to a woman I love but realizing our raised voices have gained us an audience harnesses my reply. It's barely dawn, but India's home is brimming with people. Most are staff, but I don't give a fuck. I hate having my personal business aired. Why do you think I've been so quiet about Fien's birth? Most fathers shout their triumphs from the rooftop. I kept it under wraps because I knew it was the best way to keep her safe.

I plan to do the same now that she is freed. I'm not hiding her because I believe I am incapable of protecting her. I'm doing it so she can grow up without needing to prove she isn't as grubby as her surname. My father shrouded our family name with so much controversy, I can't even say it without tasting dirt.

My brows join together when India whispers, "She hasn't told you."

"Told me what?" I hate falling for her tricks, but I'm tired and overwhelmed, so my change-up can be easily excused.

After rising to her feet, India straightens out her nightwear before moving to stand in front of us. Her breath, which is awfully minty for the early hour, fans my lips when she says, "Roxanne isn't pregnant. She never was."

Now I know she is lying. I saw the test myself. From Roxanne peeing in the cup to Dr. Bates dipping the test into her urine, I saw every step—just as I did Audrey's.

"Spurting lies will get you killed," I spit out in warning. "It'll do you best to remember that."

I anticipate for India to come out swinging—she's worse than Theresa when it comes to retaliation, so you can imagine my shock when her eyes soften a mere second before she scoops my hand into hers. "The sedative Smith gave to numb the site of Roxanne's tracker had traces of the HGC hormone."

She's losing me with the technical talk. I'm a father, but I have no clue about anything related to pregnancy and hormones.

"An increase in the HCG hormone in both blood and urine usually indicates a pregnancy, but in Roxanne's case, that isn't what happened." She steps back, folds her arms in front of her chest, then adds, "If you don't believe me, ask Smith. Or better yet, the real mother of your child."

Smith's lack of interruption reveals he's listening in on our conversation, because the only time he goes quiet is when he's being proven wrong.

With my mood souring, my words get snappy. "Did the sedative you gave Roxanne have HCG in it?"

It takes Smith a couple of seconds to reply, "Yes, but the amount was small."

"Enough to make a pregnancy test positive?" When nothing but silence resonates out of my phone for the next several seconds, my last nerve is obliviated. "Smith..."

He huffs, hating that I'm listening to a single thing India has to say. He doesn't dislike her as much as Rocco, but he isn't friendly with her either. "I doubt it."

"Doubt it or *know*. Those are two entirely different things."

He punishes his keyboard long enough to notch my annoyance from a five to an eight before he replies, "Her sedative could have *possibly* resulted in a false positive."

Disappointment is the last thing I expected to feel, but it is *all* I'm feeling. I liked the idea of Roxanne being knocked up with my baby, not to mention having the chance to experience all the things

I missed with Fien. Her first word, the horrendous teething India harped on about yesterday, her first steps. There are so many things I can't get back but had planned to replicate with my child with Roxanne.

I guess I'll just have to get her knocked up again.

I can't pretend I'm disappointed by the prospect.

"Where are you going?" India asks, shocked.

Smith's frustration is a thing of the past when he snickers about my reply, "To fix an injustice."

Since my steps are thumping, India has to shout to ensure I hear her scorn, "You are seriously delusional! Your mistress fakes a pregnancy, then lies about it, but instead of killing her as you would have any other woman, you encourage her lies."

She should be glad I walked away because if I was within touching distance of her, I would finish what I started only moments ago. "Roxanne didn't lie about anything. She *thought* she was pregnant. She still does." My last three words don't come out as irritable as my first couple.

I'm a prick, have always been a prick, and will forever be a prick, but I'm not looking forward to breaking Roxanne's heart when I tell her she isn't pregnant with my kid just yet. I'll make it right. It may just take a couple of attempts.

Once again, I'm not disappointed at the prospect.

India throws her hands into the air, her nostrils flaring as she gets lost in her anger. "She doesn't *think* she's pregnant. She *knows* she isn't. Audrey said she had her period the first night at the ranch."

When I jackknife back, certain she's lying, the smugness on her face is almost her undoing. I've wanted an excuse to kill her for years, and her self-righteous expression may very well be her undoing.

Clueless as to how close to death she is, India steps closer to me. "Let me guess, she didn't tell you that either, did she?"

It's weaselly for me to shake my head, but I'm too stunned to think up another response. Roxanne acted odd when I cupped her stomach last night, but I figured she was still in shock she was about to become a mother.

Now I'm not so sure.

"If you're lying..." I don't finalize my threat. I take a deep breath and exhale before letting my glare take care of it on my behalf.

"I'm not lying, Dimi," India assures, as cool as a cucumber. "And I have the means to prove it if you can't trust the word of your mistress."

Ignoring Rocco's warning glance behind India's shoulder, I lift my chin, accepting her offer. I've only just stopped being fucked in the ass by my enemies. I'm nowhere near ready for round two, so if what India is saying is true, someone is about to die. I just have no clue who it will be. Should I kill the people responsible for unearthing the truth so my reputation remains intact, or the person lying to me? Thirty seconds ago, I would have swayed toward the former. Now I have no fucking clue which way is up.

27

ROXANNE

Yesterday, I awoke with exhaustive, tired muscles. Today, I woke in the same manner, except this time, it wasn't the horrid, my-world-has-been-ripped-out-from-beneath-me feeling. It was filled with euphoria, adrenaline, and a happy little buzz in the bottom of my stomach I assumed I'd never experience again.

Dimitri can be thanked for that.

Last night went above and beyond anything we've ever done. He was attentive and sweet. He truly rocked my world. I've been on cloud nine for the past two hours, and if the scent mingling in the air is anything to go by, it is onward and upward from here. We still have a lot to discuss and a heap of issues to work through, but the cloud above my head doesn't seem anywhere near as dense as it did only yesterday.

"Good morning," I breathe groggily in the direction I sense Dimitri's presence.

I like my water scalding hot, and with my mood being extra diva-like this morning, I've gone over my allotted four-minute time slot. I've also glammed myself up, hopeful silky-smooth legs and gleaming skin will add to the seductive sparkle in my eyes.

"Would you care to join me for a mid-morning shower?"

After opening the shower door, releasing the fog making my head extra woozy, I lock my eyes with Dimitri. He has his shoulder propped up on the doorjamb. Unlike when he left our room in the early hours of this morning, his jaw is tight, and the veins in his hands are bulging like he's open and closed them multiple times since we parted.

"Is everything okay?"

Concerned by his quiet, I shut down the faucet, shove my arms into my hideous Fran Drescher-inspired dressing gown Dimitri packed for me, knot the cord into place, then float to his side of the room.

Well, I really shouldn't say float. I stumble like a newborn foul, suddenly fretful by his glare. He's only stared at me like this twice before. The first time was when he had a gun held at my head, and the second time was mere minutes before he forced me to hold a gun to my mother's head.

"What did my mother do?" If it's anything close to the horrid thoughts in my head, I don't know if I can pardon her again. She killed her own flesh and blood. She should have never come back from that. The only reason she has so far is because I'm too much of a chicken to make her pay for her injustices. I agree with Dimitri, insolent people should be punished, but it's hard when the person deserving of your fury is your parent.

I stop seeking answers from Dimitri's eyes when he says, "I need you to get dressed and come with me."

The dread his words were soaked in scorches the back of my throat. It has me more worried than the anger pumping out of him. "Can we please not do this again. If you believe my mother needs to be punished, punish her. I won't hold it against you, I swear."

"Your mother isn't the issue," Dimitri replies in a cool, calculated bark.

Even with his vacillating anger wanting me to call a timeout, I can't help but ask, "Then who is?"

It feels as if more than water circles the drain when Dimitri mutters, "You are."

"Me?" I touch my chest like I'm five. "What did I do?" I swallow to soothe my dry throat before confessing to something that's been burning a hole in my heart the past sixteen-plus hours. "If this is about the mark on Fien's arm, that wasn't from me." I cringe, hating my inability to lie. "Well, it could have been me, but it wasn't on purpose. I had to get her away from Maestro before he fell on her." When confusion crosses his features, I try to settle it. "Maestro is what the women called one of the head guys in Rimi's crew. He was taken down while he had Fien clutched under his arm. I had to grab her to pull her out of the line of fire. I never meant to hurt her, Dimi. I swear to God."

My confession soothes the deep groove between his brows, but it doesn't fully eradicate it. "I still need you to come with me. I'm out of my depth, and I have no fucking clue who's holding my head beneath the surface." His voice comes out composed but with a hint of anger.

Happy he's endeavoring to curb his dominance and eager to have him forgetting the worry his comment etched his face with, I nod before making a beeline for the bag resting by the door. I selected an outfit before I entered the bathroom, but Dimitri's wavering personalities ensures I'll need a jacket. He truly is one of the hardest people to read. For all I know, my lips could be about to turn a shade of blue.

Once I've dressed under Dimitri's watchful gaze, I follow his somber walk up a glamorous staircase. I'm hopeful his dour mood is because he kept his distance while I was getting dressed, but something tells me it's much bigger than his inability to keep his hands to himself.

It's obvious he isn't in the mood for chit-chat, but my Nanna always said my inquisitiveness would get me in trouble. "Did you see Fien this morning?"

Dimitri hums out an agreeing murmur before gesturing for me to enter a corridor before him. Since it's lined with exquisite antiques, we can't walk side by side. Dimitri's shoulders are too wide for that.

"And what about Audrey? Have you seen her today?" The jealousy in my voice can't be helped. Audrey is a beautiful woman, she is also the mother of Dimitri's child, so I have a lot to be jealous about. Dimitri spent the night with me, in my bed, but he snuck out in the wee hours of this morning like he didn't want anyone to know where he was.

That stings. Not a lot, but enough to make me feel a little sick to the stomach.

I can't tell if his murmur is a yes or a no this time around. It appeared more a growl than a hum like he's more frustrated than pleased his wife was resurrected from the dead.

With his moods a little hard for me to read, this is the last thing I should say. "If you have time today, I'd like to sit down and discuss what happened at Dr. Bates's office... T-t-the pregnancy test." I bite the inside of my cheek, loathing the stutter of my words.

I wish I could keep our conversation on the back burner for months, but that would be wrong for me to do. He has a right to know what happened to our child as much as he has the right to mourn the loss with me.

A tangy copper taste fills my mouth when Dimitri replies, "We can do that now."

"Oh... okay." I follow him into a room at the end of the hallway, grateful our talk will be in private.

I barely make it two steps into the dimly lit space when I'm tempted to walk right back out of it. We're not alone as first thought. Smith and Rocco are here as is Audrey's best friend, India. Then there's a man in a white doctor's coat standing next to an identical lot of equipment that soared me too great heights four nights ago before it all came crashing down.

"What's going on?" I choke out, almost stuttering.

When my question falls on deaf ears, I shift on my feet to face Dimitri. His expression is as cold as his icy blue eyes. He knows I'm keeping something from him, but instead of asking me what it is, he's gone down his usual route.

He wants to torture the truth from me one painful memory at a time.

Although my anger is brewing, I try to keep things amicable. "Can I please speak with you alone? This is a conversation that needs to occur between us."

My neck cranks to my left when India mumbles under her breath, "So you can fill his head with more lies?"

Even having no reason to defend myself to her, I snap out, "I haven't lied."

"So, you told him you're *not* pregnant?" India asks with a raised brow and a stern glare. "He knows you're no longer carrying his child?"

"No." For one word, it shouldn't crack my voice the way it did. It was almost as fragile as my heart feels. This isn't a conversation I wanted to have with spectators. It could only be more uncomfortable if it were happening while I was naked. "But that's because I haven't had the chance." I spin back around to face Dimitri. My fast movements cause a rush of dizziness to bombard my head, but I continue on, preferring to face an interrogation head-on than cower like a coward. "I lost our baby the first night I was taken. Maestro did an ultrasound on a machine just like that—"

"*Puh-leaze*. Like a hired goon would know how to turn on a sonograph machine, much less use it."

I continue talking as if India never interrupted me, "After discovering I was around six to eight weeks along, he hit me in the stomach, then kicked me over and over again." Tears spring in my eyes just recalling what happened. "When he couldn't kill our baby with brutality, he tried another way." Big salty blobs roll down my cheeks when Dimitri cups my jaw. His hands are so large, they take up almost all my face, and the callouses on his fingers scratch my cheek when he wipes away my tears. "They had hospital-like rooms on the lower level of the ranch. There was medical equipment, pads, and a whole heap of other things I don't want to remember."

India huffs again, but I don't care. Dimitri seems to believe me, and that's all that matters.

"He was going to..." I make a hand gesture that shouldn't speak on my behalf, but it somehow does. "... but Audrey stopped him. She hit him over the head, then helped me get away."

Now I feel bad about what Dimitri and I did last night. I thought it was the start of something magical, where in reality, it was the commencement of me being his mistress. He's married, and the woman he is married to did her best to save our child. I owe her more credit than I'm giving her.

After sucking down a nerve-cleansing breath, I finish my story on a somber note, "Unfortunately, it was too late. I miscarried our baby the following morning." I step closer to Dimitri, not wanting the slightest snippet of air between us when I say, "I wanted to tell you last night, but you were riding the high of your victory. I didn't want to steal the glory from you." I stray my eyes around the room, noting the remorse on both Smith and Rocco's faces. India's is nowhere near as repentant as theirs. "I'm sorry I had to tell you like this, with an audience, but I didn't lie. I just omitted the truth for a more appropriate time."

"Please tell me you're not believing her sob story," India gabbles out when Dimitri's thumb switches from wiping away my tears to tracking the curve of my kiss-swollen lips. "I doubt she was pregnant to begin with. Who has a miscarriage and only bleeds for an hour or two?" I feel both sorry and angry when India mutters, "It doesn't work that way. I know because I've had plenty of miscarriages." She races to the doctor's side I had forgotten was in the room. "Tell them. Tell him how unlikely her story is."

The gentleman I'd guess to be mid-sixties coughs to clear his throat before saying, "It is unlikely to only bleed for a couple of hours."

"But possible?" Smith jumps in like he too knows how it feels to be put on the spot when predicting medical anomalies.

The doctor lowers his chin, his head-bob somewhat cowardice. "But possible."

After glaring at the doctor with a stare as woeful as Satan, India locks her eyes with mine, then snaps out, "Fine. If they want to believe your sob act, prove you were really pregnant."

"How can I prove it?" The hesitation in my question is understandable. I'm still new to all of this. "Maestro didn't print out memory keepsakes for me."

India steps closer to me, her hips swinging like she's on a runway instead of a warpath. "Dr. Klein can do a quick ultrasound of your uterus. If you recently lost a baby..." she air quotes her last word like she doesn't believe a single thing I said, "... he will be able to tell."

"Is that true?" Dimitri's tone is a mixture of annoyed and hopeful. I thought he was on my side, so the unease in his voice is a little off-putting.

The doctor dips his chin. This one is more headstrong than his earlier one. "Yes. Pockets inside the uterine wall can indicate if a pregnancy was recently dissolved." The way he mutters 'dissolved' makes me sick to my stomach. I didn't dissolve my pregnancy. Our child was taken away from me against my will. I didn't do anything wrong. I am not at fault. I fought with everything I had.

As I will again now. "Okay. I agree to do your sonograph."

"You don't need to do this, Roxanne."

Although I appreciate Dimitri's sudden return to the plate with a bigger bat, it comes too late. The ugly head of doubt has already been raised.

I whip around to face Dr. Klein so quickly, my hair slaps my face. "Where do you want me?"

When he places a pillow on the opposite end of the bed, I sidestep him, shrug off my coat, then lay down. I don't peer at the monitor every set of eyes in the room arrow in on when he lifts my shirt and squirts gel onto my stomach. I scan Dimitri's face, knowing there's only seconds before the distrust in his eyes switches to remorse.

I hate that he needs to bring in outsiders to trust me, but I also understand it. He can't even trust family, so why did I stupidly believe I ever stood a chance?

I renege on my wish to watch Dimitri's every expression when he asks a few seconds later, "What's that?"

My eyes shoot to the monitor so fast, my head grows woozy. I scan the black and white image like a crazy woman, seeking anything similar to the jelly-bean shape blob I saw days ago.

I don't find a single thing close to a baby. I discover why when Dr. Klein says, "That's Roxanne's ovary. It's badly damaged."

"Because she miscarried?" Dimitri asks before I can.

Sprinkles of salt and pepper hair fall into Dr. Klein's eyes when he shakes his head. "No. Excluding miscarriages in the fallopian tube, they don't affect the female reproductive system. Roxanne has what we call PCOS. Polycystic ovary syndrome. It is a hormone disorder commonly found in women of reproductive age."

"Which can cause long-term infertility issues," India jumps in, her tone smug. "So not only are Roxanne's chances of becoming pregnant again extremely low, *if she was even pregnant to begin with*, she couldn't have conceived without help."

I return her glare before requesting for Dr. Klein to check the pockets he mentioned earlier, dying to hit that smug bitch where it hurts.

Dr. Klein once again clears his throat before going to work. He taps and clicks on his sonogram machine numerous times before he pushes his glasses up his nose and says matter-of-factly, "I can't see any indication Roxanne was ever pregnant."

"What?" I blurt out at the same time a collection of hisses roll across the room. "Check again. You must not be seeing things right. Maestro said I was six to eight weeks along." I lift my shirt to my bra before tugging my pants down so they're low on my hips. "You're not far enough down. He scanned right above my pubic bone."

India tells me to stop being ridiculous, Smith and Rocco back up my request for Dr. Klein to check again, and Dimitri stares at my stomach for three painfully long seconds before he pivots on his heels and races out of the room, knocking over the freestanding sonogram machine on his way out.

Both my head and my heart scream for me to go after him, but for the life of me, I can't get my legs to move. I've seen firsthand what he does to people who betray him, and considering it feels as if my life is just getting started, I don't want it ended just yet.

28

DIMITRI

A roar rips from my throat when I throw my fist into the concrete pillar holding up the top story of India's residence. It sends pain shooting up my arm and down my spine, but I don't hold back. I punch and punch and punch until my fists are bloody, my heart is colliding with my ribs just as dangerously, and my wish to kill is only ramping up.

A million phrases played through my head this morning. Little snippets of all the conversations I've had the past couple of days have been on a nonstop loop. India's sworn testimony that Roxanne is playing me for a fool. Smith presenting evidence on sedatives causing false positive pregnancy tests, and just now, Roxanne's heartbreaking confession on how she was treated the first night under Rimi's care. They rolled through my head on repeat, only stopping when I hinged every belief I've ever had on a simple sonogram.

It should have cleared everything up.

Science has a way of making liars truthful and the truthful dead.

That didn't happen today. Roxanne's ultrasound raised more doubt than it gave answers. Not because I believe what Dr. Klein said but because not only has Roxanne given me no reason to doubt her, she has evidence to back up her claims. Bruises I somehow missed, nicks I brushed off as grazes because I was too busy basking in the glory of my win to make sure she had made it out of the carnage without a scratch, and the faintest bruise on her hip that looks like the imprint of a man's boot.

Roxanne has said time and time again that the person responsible for Fien's captivity was a woman. Although it's clear Rimi was the ringleader behind the organization who staged my daughter's captivity, I agree with Roxanne.

Furthermore, if Roxanne's abduction was purely about money, they wouldn't have harmed our child. Fien's captivity netted the Castro entity millions of dollars each year, so imagine how much I would have paid to guarantee the safety of two of my children, not to mention the woman I love.

The fact they forced Roxanne through every woman's worst nightmare exposes my fatal flaw.

I gloated a victory I've yet to win.

Basked in an ambiance that isn't mine to savor.

I let Roxanne down in a way I never thought possible, and I've threatened to kill her more than once.

I've said it before, and I'll say it again, I'm a fucking asshole.

That stops today.

I can't change what happened to Roxanne. I can't undo the hurt she endured, but I can ensure it won't happen again. I've just got to play the game as I've been taught, show my enemies I'm not to be messed with, and I must do it without Roxanne by my side because, as far as my enemies are concerned, the only way you can teach a bird how to fly is by pushing her out of the nest.

29

ROXANNE

"It isn't as it seems. I swear to God, I have no clue what happened back there."

"It's okay," Rocco assures me, his pace lowering so he can rub my arm reassuringly. "I don't give a fuck what the Doc said. We know the truth."

I want to believe his 'we' is referring to him and Dimitri, but regretfully, the knot in my gut won't allow me to portray a brainless bimbo. He was referencing Smith, who has done everything in his power to discredit Dr. Klein's integrity for the past two hours. He combed through decades of records, sought any insurance claims that may have been settled out of court, and he even reached out to his ex-wife. All avenues were extinguished without the slightest spark being ignited. Unlike Dr. Bates, Dr. Klein's records are as clean as a whistle.

Smith said he would continue scouring for evidence. Fien is back, so he has nothing else to fill his time, but I told him not to bother. There's only one person I want to believe me, and he's been ignoring Rocco's calls as often as he would mine if I knew his cell phone number.

"Do you know how long we're planning to camp out here for?" I ask Rocco just as we reach my room.

He scrubs at the fine hairs on his chin. "First plan was for three or four days. That's about how quickly the media would move on to another story. When the public interest shifts, so do the Feds."

It sucks to agree with him, but I do.

"But things are a little muddled now." He opens my door before gesturing for me to enter before him. "No one was expecting to find Audrey alive." I'm surprised he sounds more annoyed than relieved. Although he works for Dimitri, he is also his best friend, so shouldn't he be happy he got his little family back? "Since she's not fit to fly, we could be here a little longer."

"Great."

After flopping onto the mattress, I throw a hand over my eyes. I'm not tired, I just want to hide the tears the ruffling of Dimitri and my combined scents caused my eyes.

I'm so damn emotional lately. Take my exchange with India when Dimitri raced out of the room like his ass was on fire. She called me a homewrecking whore, and I just stood there and took it. I didn't slap her. I didn't put her in her place. I just stared at her with enough fire in my eyes, the tears welling in them didn't have a chance in hell of falling.

That killed me. I wouldn't hold back my retaliation if Audrey called me that, so a stranger who doesn't know me has no right to speak to me in such a manner. Yet, I let her.

I scold myself for a couple of minutes before I roll onto my hip to face Rocco. I'm not surprised to spot his unhidden watch. He has barely taken his eyes off me since Dimitri rocketed out of the room like he had a jetpack strapped to his back. "What's the story with India? I get she's standing up for her best friend, but something about her rubs me the wrong way."

"You're not the only one," Rocco mutters under his breath before he joins me in lying on his side. He stares at me for a couple of moments, pondering on what to say before he comes right out with it. "Dimitri and India were almost a thing a couple of years ago."

I hate thinking about Dimitri with anyone but me, but as they say, curiosity killed the cat. "Almost?"

Rocco *boinks* my nose, wordlessly advising he heard the jealousy in my one word. "*Almost.* They had a handful of dates. One night, they were heading back to her apartment to... you know—"

"I get it. You don't need to spell it out for me," I interrupt, fighting the urge not to gag.

He throws his head back and laughs, says something about Princess Peach being extra cute when she's jealous, then gets back to his story. "They didn't get past a rough game of tonsil hockey when Dimitri spotted Audrey. Despite India's best efforts, Dimi wanted Audrey then and there." This hurts to hear, but I love his honesty. "She wasn't having a bit of it, though."

I balk like he jabbed a knife under my ribs. "Audrey turned Dimitri down?"

Don't mistake the shock in my tone. Audrey is beautiful, and I can imagine the number of men she had clambering for her attention, but still, I'm shocked. I couldn't turn Dimitri down when he had the blood of my father on his shirt. I don't think he could do anything that would see me rejecting him. Even now, believing he isn't on my side hasn't changed my objective. I would stupidly sign on to be his mistress if it's the only way I could be a part of his life.

"Yeah," Rocco responds with a laugh. "Then the chase pursued. I honestly didn't think she'd ever give in, then all of a sudden, she arrived on his doorstep."

My eyes pop out of my head. "Audrey went to Hopeton?"

Rocco nods. "She spent a couple of weeks there, then moved back to her hometown two weeks before she found out she was pregnant with Fien." He shrugs like he isn't cut about the gap in his friendship with Dimitri. "The rest is a little hazy for me from there. I stepped back as Dimitri stepped up."

"You came back when he needed you, Rocco." I'm not trying to weaken his guilt. I'm being straight-up honest.

"Yeah, but I can't help but wonder if things would have been different if I had hung around." He peers at nothing while muttering, "I might have noticed something fishy, or watched Audrey while Dimitri was watching you. There's more I could have done."

"And no guarantee any of them would have made any difference. Everything happens for a reason."

Rocco scoffs, then peers at me as if I'm an idiot. "You don't really believe that, do you?"

I push him on the shoulder, unappreciative of the candor in his tone. "Of course I do."

This is outrageous for me to say, but if Audrey hadn't been kidnapped, perhaps Dimitri and I would never have crossed paths. His watch wouldn't have made me climax, Eddie wouldn't have needed to retaliate to my 'deceit,' and Dimitri wouldn't have killed him for hurting me. If none of that had happened, I'd still be in the town I hate, unemployed without two nickels to rub together, and most likely looking for a cheap thrill somewhere I'd end up either dead or a drug addict like my parents.

Or worse, I could have been sold to a baby-farming syndicate.

My voice has an unusual twang to it when I ask, "Do you think Dr. Klein's diagnosis is why my mother changed her mind?"

Rocco tries to shut down his surprise at the quick change of our conversation, but he isn't quite fast enough for this little black duck. "I'm unfamiliar with girlie shit, but I'm reasonably sure you can't diagnose PCOS by looking at someone."

"You can't, but you can via an ultrasound, which I had the week before my meeting with my father." Confusion crosses his features, but he doesn't get the chance to seek clarification for it. "For years, I had horrible periods. Cramping, clots, and—"

"I get it. You don't need to spell it out for me." Rocco grins to ensure I know there's no malice in his reply. He's mortified I'm discussing my cycle with him, but he'll handle the injustice if it helps unjumble some of his confusion.

"I went to a local women's clinic. They usually just stuffed condoms in my hand and sent me on my merry way, but there was a doctor on that day who specialized in reproductive organs. He sent me for a sonogram. Since I was young and under the impression I didn't want to have kids any time in the next century, I—"

"Didn't go back for the results," Rocco fills in, clicking on. "Sounds like something you'd do. I'm beginning to wonder if you are allergic to doctors with how hard you try to avoid them." After scrambling to a half-seated position, he digs his cell phone out of his pocket. "Smith..."

I take a mental note to remember any conversations I have with Rocco are never private when Smith replies, "I'm hacking into the clinic's mainframe now. They're as lax on security as you."

Rocco laughs before replying, "If you get anything, come back to us."

My inclusion in Smith and Rocco's duo is appreciated, but I just realized how foolish I'm being. Instead of discrediting India's claims I was never pregnant, I'm feeding the hype. This won't help me convince Dimitri I was telling the truth. It could do the exact opposite.

It dawns on me that Rocco has mindreading abilities when he

says, "Although this won't aid in smoothing things over with Dimitri, it could give us a lead on the people playing him."

"He got the people playing him." I speak slowly as if he is deaf. In reality, I need time to process my words since I'm so damn confused. "Rimi is dead."

Loving the uncertainty in my voice, Rocco hits me with a frisky wink before he heads for the door. My heart is a twisted mess, but since my head is still screwed on straight, I race him for the door, slamming it before he gets close to exiting. "Tell me everything you know."

"I don't—"

I cut off his lie with a glare before adding words into the mix. "You asked me to jump. I sailed over the edge without fear. That makes me a part of this..." I wave my hand around my room as if Dimitri, Fien, and Smith are with us, "... and I don't care what Dimitri says, I'm going to be a part of it until the end."

Rocco leans so close to me, I smell what he ate for breakfast in his shallow breaths. "Some would say the curtains are already closed, Roxie. That the show is over."

I return his lean without the slightest bit of fear knocking my knees together. "And I'd say they're full of shit because even gangsters know the show isn't over until the lights go out."

I saw the light in Dimitri's eyes when he glanced down at me partway through my story, felt it heating my skin. It isn't close to being snuffed, so that not only means I need to keep fighting, I must do everything in my power to keep it lit.

I am, after all, the reason for its glow.

Rocco licks his lips before cracking them into a smile. "Are you sure you want to go down this road, Princess P? Your castle is mighty enticing, but everyone knows mushrooms grow in fungi."

I'm a little lost to what he means, but I figuratively roll up my sleeves, preparing for battle. "You shouldn't underestimate mushrooms. They're all edible, but some you will only nip at once."

30

DIMITRI

I spot Roxanne's race past the downstairs sitting room I'm using as an office before she pivots back around and charges into my room. Considering her foot is still a little bunged-up from her time under Rimi's watch, she moves quickly.

I'm not surprised. Her firecracker personality suits her hair coloring. I don't see anything slowing her down. Not even my rejection the past three days has made an indent to her fiery personality. That's why I upped the ante today.

Unlike India's numerous staff, Roxanne doesn't knock and wait for permission to enter. She steamrolls into the room at the speed of sound, her steps so fast, the smell I've fought like hell to ignore the past three days whips up around me, tightening the front of my pants even more than her beautiful face.

"Can you please tell this *lady*..." She spits out her last word like she's doubtful India's head of housekeeping is a woman. Sofia is standing outside of the door, clutching the bag I asked her to pack for Roxanne in her hand. "That I do *not* have a flight to

Hopeton scheduled for tonight. She's packing my things like I'm—"

"Leaving?" She closes her mouth, pinches her brows, then nods. "You *are* leaving. That's why Sofia is packing your belongings."

My jaw tightens to the point of cracking when Roxanne steps closer to my desk. My hands itch to touch her, but I ball them at my sides instead. The past three days have been pure torture, but the threads I stupidly stopped seeking days ago are popping back up everywhere. There is almost enough of them to ruin an entire outfit, and if the person who killed my baby with Roxanne is wearing it when I hit it with my wrath, I'm all for shredding every last piece of it.

With her eyes locked on mine, seeking any deceit in them, Roxanne says, "Rocco only said this morning that we need to lay low for a couple more days."

What she's saying is true. Although pissed I didn't hold back and wait as agreed upon, the Feds aren't the only one chasing my tail. The CIA is right there with them. I'd gloat if it didn't mean I have to maintain an amicable relationship with India. She's more demanding than Audrey, and I'm not even married to her.

With the annoyance on my face believable, I use it to my advantage. "Yes, we need to lay low for a few more days. Since the men Officer Daniel was working with have been taken care of, you are no longer included in that equation."

Roxanne scoffs, huffs, then scoffs again, truly unsure how to respond. Her shock is understandable. I'm a neurotic, jealous prick when it comes to her, but to play this game right, I have to live up to the hype of my last name. Shipping Roxanne off is the next logical step. Then, not only will the woman I'm chasing lose her scent, she'll shift her focus back to her original target—my wife.

Do I feel like an absolute cunt drawing the focus of a deranged woman back to Audrey? Yes, I do. But the knot in my gut is nowhere near as tight as it is when I consider what could happen if I don't. Roxanne put her life on the line for me, she lost our child in the process. I owe her this level of protection.

Some may say Audrey deserves to be safeguarded the same way. I agree, for the most part. There's just a niggle in my gut that won't quit warning me to remain cautious when it comes to anything to do with Audrey. It feels like there's more at play here than just my marriage, and when I find out what it is, there will be hell to pay.

Once Roxanne settles her emotions, she folds her arms in front of her chest. I really wish she wouldn't. I sustained from sexual activities for almost two years, but that was my choice. This, however, is not. "We're not doing this again, Dimitri. You're not sending me away to see if I'll come back. We've done that, we moved past it, now can we please get onto the real issue here. I can help you. You've just got to let me in."

My mask almost slips when her voice cracks at the end, but I suit back up, forever ready for battle. Her departure won't be forever. If I play my cards right, she could be back in my bed, where she belongs, by the end of the week.

But, if I don't play my hand with the viciousness it deserves, I won't have any cards left to place down. They will be burned, scorched, left wilted without purpose, and they'd still make it out of the carnage better than Roxanne.

I refuse to let that happen.

I'll kill every fucking person in this godforsaken kingdom before I will ever let Roxanne be hurt like the numerous scenarios that have played out in my head over the past three days. That's how much she means to me. That's how much it is gutting me knowing I failed her.

I promised to protect her. I'm only upholding my end of our

agreement now. Some may say it is too late, but it's better than not at all.

My hostile mood is heard in my voice. "I'm not sending you away to see if you'll come back. Our agreement is over. My daughter is home, so there's no reason for you to stay anymore."

The shock on Roxanne's face switches to frustration. "You don't believe what we had was an agreement."

"I do," I reply matter-of-factly, halving the fiery glint in her eyes. "That's why you've spent the past three nights alone." *And why I've slept in my daughter's room each night because she's the only person capable of stealing your devotion, and even then, it's a struggle.* But since that isn't something I can say, I keep my mouth shut.

I should have realized she'd see straight through my ruse. She isn't just attractive, she's smart as well. "You've been with Fien?" Since she's unsure about the authenticity of her statement, it comes out sounding like a question. "Right?"

"Wrong." I lower my eyes to the paperwork in front of me, acting as if the pain in her eyes isn't affecting me. "If you want a rundown on my activities of late, perhaps I can get Smith to clip together some footage for you. Would you like it with or without sound?" I feel like a complete and utter prick when I lock my hooded eyes with hers and mutter, "I'm sure you understand how vocal some women are when they're being fed a healthy dose of dick."

Roxanne looks set to blow her top. She's red-faced, her fists are clenched, and steam is almost billowing out of her ears, but she keeps her cool—mostly. "You can order someone to pack my bags, you can march me onto a plane on the shoulder of one of your goons, but you will never be rid of me..." she tightens her arms under her chest, all sassy like, "... because I'm unforgettable."

"My wife said that once too. She soon learned otherwise. I can only hope it won't take my mistress quite as long."

That was a low blow. I know it, and so the fuck does Roxanne.

"You... you... ugh!"

On her way out, she slams the door shut so hard, it knocks a priceless painting from the wall. I could pick it up, but it's broken frame and shattered glass adds to my ruse that I'm done with her. Not even a woman known for her theatrics can hold back the urge to drink in a daily dose of drama. "Someone isn't happy. Did she misread the fine print that discloses the Petrettis don't do monogamy?"

Knowing Theresa will never fall for the sweet-guy act, I bring out the asshole gene I was gifted from my father. "Or perhaps she also doesn't appreciate walking in on her understudy giving me head."

Air whizzes out of her thin nose as her eyes slit. "You invite me to some Hicksville mansion on the guise you want to talk shop, then insult me within a second of arrival. If I wanted to be treated like scum, I would have accepted your father's many offers to become your step-mommy."

"I like the way you said that as if you haven't had my father's withered dick between your legs. It was very authentic." I stand from my chair, button my suit jacket, then gesture for her to join me for a late-afternoon drink at a crystal bar set up next to two leather couches. "I have a business proposal for you. An easy exchange. Shouldn't take you any longer than thirty minutes."

Theresa paces to my side of the room with her hips swinging and her eyes brimming with hope. "Is this the real reason you invited me here, to discuss business?"

I work the disappointment in her voice through my ears three times before benefiting from it. "For the most part." After placing a whiskey decanter onto a round table, I track the back of my finger down Theresa's cheek before moving my hand to the throb in her throat. I'm not surprised when the vein in her neck doubles its beeps when my touch switches from gentle to dominant. She is as kinky as she is corrupt. "But I've also been recalling the fun we had before my girlfriend's pregnancy forced her to become my wife."

"You're married?" She plays the scorned victim well, but I'm not buying her act. The grip I have on her throat relayed the increase in her pulse from my confession, not to mention the cruel curve of her lips. "Is she still in the picture?"

"She is." I release her from my grip, then push her away from me with a demoralizing shove, smirking when she almost tumbles to the floor. "For now. I'm not sure how much longer I can put up with her nagging, though."

I swallow down a double whiskey faster than intended when Theresa mutters, "Perhaps if you didn't sleep around, she'd quit nagging." I feel a little dirty when she rights herself before she runs her nails across my pecs. "What do you need from me, Dimi? A public fuck? A shakedown? I could order one of my cousins to pay her a visit."

I pretend to consider her options for a couple of seconds before saying, "I need her to go away for a little while. Not permanently. Just until her voice stops ringing in my ears. I heard you might know of a place." While I shift on my feet to face her, I make sure my face is showcasing the infamous half-smirk she's obsessed with. "Somewhere like the *establishment* you sent Megan to."

"I didn't send Megan anywhere..." Her smile would have you believing you're looking at an angel. She's attractive, she just has repulsively ugly insides. "This time. My lips are sealed pertaining to other matters. I never discuss business, even when it's with the man who ordered it." She either truly believes I set Maddox up to take the fall for Megan's murder, or she's a damn good actor. It could be a combination of both.

Needing to keep my focus on a present injustice instead of an old one, I ask, "Did you at least use an alias this time around? Shroud may be a common name, but you'd have to be a complete fucking idiot to hide her in plain sight for the second time."

"Your worry is unneeded, Dimi. I know what I'm doing." Her use of my nickname for the second time already has my mood nosediving, so I won't mention my response to her hands lowering to the buckle of my belt.

I've fucked women for less information than the underhanded easter eggs she scattered throughout our brief conversation many times in my life, but that isn't the way I operate anymore. I just can't let Theresa know that right now. I need her scratching my back, then when the timing is right, I'll drag mine down hers so brutally, she won't have time to secure a final breath.

"Nuh-uh," I force out with a fake moan while scooping up her hands. "There isn't the time nor the instruments in this room to satisfy a woman as deviate as you. I need hours, *many of them*." Her purr makes me fucking sick. "So why don't you go freshen up in preparation for a night out, and I'll come find you when it's time to go."

"Okay." She does a childish tiptoe up my chest with her fingers before she presses two fingers to my lips. "Don't keep me waiting long. Your family already has me burning the candle at both ends, my fire might burn out while waiting."

"We only work you to the bone because we know how much you love a good workout." Imagine a sick prick stroking one out on a sandy dune in the middle of the day, then you'll have an idea how sexually suggestive my voice was.

After biting Theresa's fingers, ensuring she feels the sting of my teeth, I spank her ass before guiding her out the door she entered only minutes ago. "Wear something sexy. You never know who may end up seeing you in your little number tonight." *Fingers crossed, it's a coroner.*

She yelps about my spank, purrs like a kitty at my comment, then saunters down the corridor with her hips sashaying back and forth.

I've barely scrubbed the horrid taste of her skin from my mouth when a faint voice trickles into the room from the other side. "Was that Theresa?"

Since Audrey is still weak, she more leans on the doorjamb for support than in the casual I-want-to-beat-your-face-in stance Rocco used it for earlier today. Her folded arms, though, they're new.

Perhaps she does have more of a backbone than believed.

I scrub the back of my hand over my mouth for the third time before answering, "Yes, it was. I invited her here to discuss business." That was the exact line I gave her when she walked in on Theresa and me fooling around in my office weeks into our 'courtship.'

No longer smiling, Audrey enters my office. "Business?"

I jerk up my chin, my ability to lie not lost by the hope in my wife's eyes that I will one day be an honorable man.

"Okay." She takes another two frail steps. "Can you tell her I said hello?"

Hello? She wants me to pass on a friendly greeting to the woman she saw sucking my dick.

What the fuck?

Roxanne would kill Theresa just for the thought.

It would be an exchange I'd pay money to see.

After ensuring my smirk is hidden, I reply, "Perhaps you can tell her yourself. She will be at the function tonight."

I don't mean to be a prick. That's a trait I only reserve for

Roxanne these days. I am merely being optimistic that if I push Audrey as hard as I pushed Roxanne, she'll gain half her gall. Then maybe she'll have enough valor to see our daughter graduate middle school.

It seems to work when Audrey mutters out snappily, "I would have to be invited first."

"You're invited," I respond like it was always my plan to have her in attendance. "I'll have Smith forward you another invitation since yours got lost."

The event is invitation only. If you don't have one, you won't make it past my security personnel. I did that not only to ensure Roxanne wasn't in the same room as the many women I've fucked, but so I could concentrate on anything but her and Fien for a couple of hours.

My businesses ran like oil through an engine while searching for Fien, but now that she's home, everything has gone to shit. My Arabian event for this month was rescheduled, a massive drug shipment is stuck in customs in Africa since my bribe was a day late, and even with Petrettis Restaurant being raided only last month, it was hit again two days ago. It is as if the universe saw I was getting slack, so they hit me with back-to-back losses to ensure I know no matter how weary I am, the Cartel never sleeps.

After tossing back a second whiskey, I place the glass down, then spin to face Audrey. "I'm about to see Fien. You can join me if you like." I don't know why I made my demand sound like it was an offer when it wasn't.

Fien has warmed to me greatly the past three days, but it would be a smoother transition if our exchanges weren't occurring with two strangers in the room with her. It's always India and me instead of Audrey and me.

Even though India drives me bat-shit crazy, I can admit her assistance this week has been a godsend. Fien has taken a real liking to her, and since India involves me in Fien's day-to-day activities, that fondness is slowly being transitioned to me. But, once again, I believe that would be an easier process if Audrey would step up to the plate to parent our child as she deserves.

"Fien is about to have dinner. I'm certain Rosa made enough for everyone."

My clutch around Audrey's waist could be classified as cruel, considering she underwent surgery only five days ago, but it makes the dismissive shake of her head less obvious.

"Here he is. Dada has arrived to eat spaghetti." India's head pops up from the clips of Fien's highchair to the entrance of the kitchen, her eyelids fluttering when she spots Audrey tucked into my side. "And he brought Mommy with him. Aren't you a lucky girl?"

I'm a hard-ass gangster in every meaning of the word, but I'd also be a lying prick if I said Fien's giggles didn't do weird things to my chest. Even with them being produced from India tickling her tummy, they're still such a rarity, I drink in every one of them as if she released them solely for me.

The scent of someone in love with their perfume smacks into me when Audrey arrives at my side of the kitchen. Her eyes are on me, but her words are for Audrey. "How are you feeling? I'm a little concerned you are already up and about."

While India guides Audrey to the other side of the garlic-and-tomato-scented space to discuss her worries in-depth, I slot onto the dining chair directly next to Fien's highchair. "What have you got there? Spaghetti. Yum." When I rub my stomach, she peers at me like I'm an idiot. Today, it doesn't make me want to go on a murderous rampage. "Can I have some?"

She watches me with a slanted head and a twinkle in her eyes for a couple of seconds before she digs her hand into a bowl of mucky redness, then slams her grubby hand into my face.

I'm not the only one laughing about the mess coating my lips. The faintest chuckle sounds through the door I forced Audrey through only moments ago.

Roxanne's giggles do a weird thing to my chest as well, but they also make me want to go on a murderous rampage. Not just because she has to watch my interactions with my daughter from afar, but because I have to be an asshole to ensure she maintains her distance.

It feels wrong using Fien to strengthen my objection, but I don't have a choice. I'm still being fucked in the ass. My enemies are just using Roxanne against me now instead of my daughter. "How about we feed Mommy some spaghetti too?"

Fien's eyes brighten like she understood every word I said before she holds her grubby hands in the air. She claps them together while saying, "Mama."

I assume she's reaching out for Audrey. Alas, it isn't just my businesses being siphoned down the gurgler this week. Audrey is no longer in the kitchen, and India is tiptoeing across the room like she has the ability to ease both Fien's and my disappointment.

"I'm sorry, sweetie, Mama had to lie down. She was feeling dizzy," India says before she playfully chews on Fien's outstretched hands, sending her girlie shrills bouncing around the kitchen. "Yummo, that's the most delicious sauce I've ever tasted." She rubs her belly before she shifts on her feet to face me. A devious grin is stretched across her face, and her eyes are gleaming with a sparkle I've never seen before. "Do you think we should feed Dada some more spaghetti?"

Before I can object, or at the very least, request they use a fork this time around, India scoops up a handful of spaghetti in her hand, then splats it down one side of my face.

My first thought is to reach for my gun, but the clapping cheer of my daughter stops me. She isn't giggling about India's unexpected gall, she's clapping her hands while cooing 'Dada' on repeat. It's the sweetest fucking noise in the world and has me responding in a way my crew would never expect.

"Oh. My. God. That's warmer than I realized," India says on a squeal when I upend my untouched bowl of spaghetti onto her white blouse. "Tastes good, though."

Laughing, she flings half the spaghetti on her chest into my face before playfully rubbing the other half into Fien's hair. Like all toddlers, Fien loves the mess. She adds to the sticky goop flattening her already dead-straight hair before she tosses strands of pasta off her highchair, joining the food fight India instigated.

We go at it for the next several minutes, laughing, cheering, and making a mess. Before we know it, a week's worth of spaghetti is on the floor, India's sauced-coated body is being cradled in my arms, her lips are an inch from mine, and Roxanne is racing for the closest exit.

31

ROXANNE

They have no connection.
 No spark.
No chemistry whatsoever, so why the hell am I pacing the floor of my room like Dimitri's 'mistress' comment was accurate?

Because it isn't the fire brewing between him and his wife you're worried about.

Ugh! I can't believe I stood by and watched India fawn over Dimitri like a freak. They weren't kissing, but they may as well have been. The intensity between them was ferocious enough to overcook the spaghetti they were tossing around, fully aware their mutual hierarchy would mean they'd never have to clean up the mess.

My heart, on the other hand, can't be passed onto a member of Dimitri's staff. He made it the mess it is, so it's up to him to fix it.

If that's what I still want.

I truly don't know anymore. The past three days have sucked. I was called a liar by the very woman Dimitri is playing house with, had my child's life discredited by a doctor the community believes is morally ethical, and found out even if I could somehow forge a way back into Dimitri's life as weirdly encouraged by Audrey the past three days, I could never give him what he so desperately craves—his missed months with Fien.

It appears as if my mother didn't have a change of heart. She merely knew handing me over to Rimi would have cost her more than my life. Rumors are he didn't take kindly to people who deceived him.

For future reference, selling a woman incapable of breeding to a baby-farming entrepreneur isn't recommended if you're fond of breathing.

I won't lie. It hurt discovering the real reason I was spared that day. I thought my mother had finally protected me, that she had saved me from the harm my father tried to inflict on me since I was three.

Sadly, Rimi wasn't the only person she fooled.

Rocco assured me I have the means to fix the injustices she made. I just have to work out how far I want to take it. At the moment, that isn't something I can do. My head is too muddled trying to work out what the fuck is going on with Dimitri to add more shit into the mix.

Audrey swapped seats with me twice the past three days to ensure I was seated across from Dimitri at dinner. She hasn't worn the wedding ring found amongst the carnage of Rimi's crew once, and she's been nothing but genuinely kind to me.

Even with her having every right to hate me, she truly doesn't.

Dimitri, in contrast, hasn't followed her lead. He's been avoiding me like I have the plague, and it's killing me more than I care to admit.

After flopping onto my bed and throwing an arm over my eyes, I take a moment to deliberate. Perhaps I should let India's head housekeeper pack my belongings? I can't give Dimitri what he wants, so letting him go may be the nicest thing I could ever give him.

That's what I do.

I forever place everyone's needs before my own.

My inability to place myself first is the only reason I didn't replace the sauce stains on India's blouse with blood. Believe me, it was hard walking away. It took all my strength.

Do I feel like the better person? No, I don't. But at least I didn't force Fien to witness more violence than she already has in her short life.

My deliberation gets a much-needed intermission when a tiny gust of air trickles into my ears. My door isn't locked. Excluding Rocco, no one comes down here. I usually hear the clumps of his boots long before he knocks on my door. That didn't happen this time around. My greeter's steps sounded as weightless as a feather.

Curious, I prop myself onto my elbows before I stray my eyes to the door. My heart pitter-patters in my chest when I spot an envelope on the floor mere inches from the carved wooden door. It isn't overly fancy, but the gilded cardboard inside of it most certainly is.

I creep toward the envelope like it could explode at any moment. When it fails to detonate, I scoop down and gather it up, breathing easier when I notice it is minus a single smear of spaghetti sauce.

Although my inquisitiveness is demanding for me to open the envelope this very instant, a much higher, much more willful stubbornness sees me opening the door to my room instead.

"Audrey..." I call out, certain she is the owner of the red locks swishing around the corner. Her hair is beautiful and healthy since she never chemically bleached it to change its natural coloring. I often envy it when I need a moment of reprieve from Dimitri's glaring stare across the dining room table. He wanted me uncomfortable enough not to eat. I refused to give him the satisfaction. I gobbled down my meals like my stomach wasn't bulging against the zipper in my pants, begging for some room. Then, when it produced the infamous half-smirk Dimitri would give anything to remove from his face, I tackled dessert as well.

When Audrey fails to hear my shout, I re-enter my room, close the door, then rip open the envelope like a savage. If my deliverer is who I think it was, something major must be happening. I haven't had many interactions with Audrey the past three days, but everyone we've had has involved Dimitri in some way.

The twinge of rejection I've been struggling to ignore the past four days gets a boost when my eyes scan a handwritten invitation. There's no indication it was meant to be addressed to me, and its prose indicates it's for an event way above my level of sophistication, but I act ignorant.

The event at an exclusive nightclub commences two hours before I'm due to fly out.

Its timing couldn't be more perfect.

My value hasn't decreased because Dimitri no longer sees my worth. If anything, it has increased because he helped me find the strength to believe I'm worth more than nothing, and now I have the chance to expose exactly how valuable I am.

A smirk etches onto my mouth when Rocco takes a staggering step back. "What the fuck, Princess P? I thought I was driving you to the airport?" As he chews on the corner of his lower lip, he rakes his eyes over my body-hugging strapless top, skintight leather pants, and pumps that would make most men cream their pants just at the thought of having them curled around their sweaty hips. It killed me trying to squeeze my ballooned foot into the tiny opening of my stiletto, but I made it work, determined it added to the authenticity of my ruse. "That outfit is *not* flight appropriate. I'm not even sure it's club-worthy." I realize I hit the bullseye when he grabs his crotch, wordlessly begging for it to calm down. "It's gonna give D a heart attack."

"Good." I snatch up my denim jacket and clutch purse from a set of drawers next to the door, then bump Rocco with my hip to barge him into the corridor so I can latch the lock into place. "Because that is the *exact* look I was aiming for."

Rocco's smile has me convinced even if my plan backfires, I will survive it. It won't be an all-encompassing life full of light-altering moments with wickedly deviate spankings, but I will still be breathing. "We're not going to the airport, are we?"

I hit him with a frisky wink. "No. We're going to a special *invitation-only* event."

"Hold up, Roxie." He reduces the length of my stride by grabbing my arm. "You need an invitation for an *invitation-only* event."

The fact he assumes I don't have an invite makes it obvious the one slipped under my door four hours ago wasn't for me. It doesn't weaken my objective, though. Tonight is my last opportunity to prove to Dimitri that this war was started with lies, so it can't end until the truth is revealed.

"Where the fuck did you get that?" Rocco asks when I slide a gold-gilded slip of cardboard out of my clutch purse.

"Where I got it from doesn't matter. It's how *we* use it that counts," I reply before making a beeline for the exit like butterflies aren't fluttering a million miles an hour in my stomach.

I hear Rocco say something to Smith before he joins me at the end of the corridor. I grow panicked I misunderstood his wish to stir Dimitri at every opportunity when he snatches up my wrist before I break into the main part of India's house—the lit section.

My worry is unfounded. He isn't foiling my endeavor to show

Dimitri I'm still on his side. He's strengthening it. "Put this away before we head out. Smith isn't the only one watching."

While shoving the invitation he returned to me into my purse with enough force to crease it, I drift my eyes in the direction he nudged his head. Unlike days ago when we entered this residence, a camera sits in the corner of the spotlessly clean space. It is clear it's new because not only has the pricy wallpaper been peeled away from the wall to accommodate a set of shiny screws, the domes housing them were only invented by Smith two months ago. He showed me his drawings of their designs when Dimitri was drugged. He was hoping Dimitri would integrate them into his security system within the year. I'm glad Dimitri hasn't shunted all his teams' ideas.

"If you want Dimitri to believe you're following orders, you might want to quit smiling." Rocco licks his lips before doing another quick sweep of my body. "And you should probably change."

With my mood as sassy as the glint in his eyes, I reply, "There's no time for that."

Once I'm certain my face represents a scorned woman, I march across the foyer of India's home, struggling not to whimper at the pain in both my foot and my stomach. Forever willing to push the boundaries when it comes to Dimitri, Rocco snatches up a random set of suitcases before he shadows my walk, his demeanor as moody as mine. Even with my room being on the lower level of the compound, I still heard the words he exchanged with Dimitri when news of my departure reached his ears. He called Dimitri a heap of names, his tirade only ending when I assured him I was happy to leave.

Shame filled Rocco's face. He thought I was giving up without a fight, unaware if you have to fight another woman for your man, you've already lost him.

Tonight isn't solely about showing Dimitri what he gave up. It's baring my strengths, displaying that I may have been knocked down, but I still got back up, and that I'm not just a force to be reckoned with. Come hell or high water, I'll be your judge, jury, and executioner if you do me wrong.

Killing my unborn baby is as low as it gets. Despite what Dr. Klein says, I was pregnant with Dimitri's child, and the woman determined to hurt him killed our baby.

Now, I'm going to kill her.

I just have to find her first.

32

DIMITRI

"Married?" I pull on the collar of my shirt, acting as if I'm a naughty boy for openly flirting with a taken woman, even with me doing exactly that multiple times in my early twenties. "How long ago did that happened?"

Aria, a once-in-a-blue-moon bed companion from around the time Audrey was kidnapped, fans her flushed cheeks with a napkin. The pigheaded side of my brain wants to say she's heating up because of my trademark half smirk, but the logical side won't allow it. She was petrified about how I'd respond to her turning down an unvoiced invitation to my bed. I'm not known for my appreciation of the word 'no.'

"Almost a year and a half ago." She rubs her stomach before pivoting away from the bar, exposing her protruding midsection. "We had to rush things along when we had an unexpected intruder."

"You're pregnant." I have no clue why that came out sounding as disgusted as it did. I'm just relaying to you what's happening.

"This is baby number two," Aria exposes, giggling about the shock on my face. "Quade turned one last summer." She must move quickly as her bump looks an easy seven or so months along. "Would you like to see a picture?"

She misses the shake of my head since she's rummaging through her overloaded handbag. It should have been the first indication that I could scratch her off my suspect list. She's so accustomed to packing diapers and baby wipes, even without her kid in tow, she still carries the necessary 'mommy' supplies.

After snagging my whiskey from the glistening bar, I swivel away from Aria. "Why didn't we cross mothers and wives from the guest list?"

I hear Smith's chair creak into place before he replies to my mumbled comment, "Because some of the women you bedded were wives and mothers *before* you slept with them."

I growl, wordlessly warning him to keep his attitude in check. He's as pissed as Rocco has been the past five days. Not even requesting him to send live footage of Roxanne from India's residence saw him giving me any leeway. I guess that could have something to do with the fact it was around the time Rocco was set to drive Roxanne to the airport, but that isn't the fucking point. They're not the only ones struggling. I feel like I'm drowning. I have been since Roxanne told me what happened to her.

I want to maim.

I want to kill.

But more than anything, I want Roxanne to know I took down the people responsible for her pain. When she looks at me, I want to return her stare knowing justice was served. I feel it when I tuck Fien into bed every night, but it's only at half its strength since the person responsible for giving me that joy isn't a part of the picture.

With Roxanne incapable of leaving my thoughts for even a second, I ask, "Have they arrived at the airport yet?"

I stop scrubbing the back of my hand over my eyes when Smith says, "They?"

He isn't stupid, so why the fuck is he acting as if he is?

"Roxanne and Rocco?"

Air whistles between his teeth when he struggles for a reply. "Uh... no. They haven't arrived yet."

Pretending his delay has nothing to do with him being deceitful, I ask, "How far out are they?"

"Ah..." Another pause adds another tick to my jaw. "Around forty or so minutes."

I check my watch, noting that Roxanne's flight is due to leave within the hour. "What caused the delay? They left over an hour ago..." My words fade to silence when the answer I'm seeking waltzes into my peripheral vision.

Roxanne isn't on her way to the airport. She's mingling with the women she made me forget existed. She isn't alone. Rocco is holding the purse Alice said was a perfect match for the final outfit I gifted Roxanne before I released her into the wild.

Because it would look mighty suspicious to host a party with only female invitees. Roxanne's provocative curves aren't solely being eyed by the long list of women I've fucked, she's caught the attention of men who'll take without asking, mark without permission, and fuck without fear of prosecution.

You don't fear the law when you're one of them.

"Smith..."

He coughs to clear his throat before answering, "Yeah."

Nothing but honesty rings in my tone when I mutter, "Rocco's death is on your hands."

I throw back a double shot of whiskey, slam my glass down, then make a beeline for Roxanne, signaling for the valet to bring my car around on the way.

I barely make it three steps away from the bar when I'm

bumped into by a stumbling and somewhat drunk blonde. "Dimi, I thought our get-together was a single-invitee gathering." Theresa pouts like a child before tiptoeing her fingers up my chest. "I don't mind. I just wish you would have told me." Her childish voice shreds my eardrums almost as Roxanne's narrowed glance across the room cuts me to pieces. She isn't a fan of Theresa's. She's not the only one, but since admitting that would underhand my ruse tonight, I pretend I'm not tempted to cut off Theresa's fingers when they lower from my pecs to the crotch of my trousers. "I would have packed something more enticing if I knew I had competition. These women may know how to fuck, but that isn't what you do, is it, Dimi? You completely devour."

Her scarce friendly demeanor is explained when Smith mumbles down my earpiece, "Just like you did the little concoction Preacher slipped into your drink." When my eyes stray to a camera in the corner of the room seeking answers for his riddle, he explains, "Loose lips sink big ships, but I figured you'd rather loosen hers with some Molly instead of your cock. Despite the shit you've been spurting the past three days, there's only one set of lips you want wrapped around your cock. They don't belong to Theresa."

Neither the honesty of his statement nor his unusual mix-up will strike his name out of my shit book, but what Theresa says next improves the odds of it happening within the week. While peering at a man I'll forever hate more than I will emulate, she asks, "Do you think it's weird your father spared Megan's life twice, but he wouldn't piss on you if you were on fire?"

While laughing like her scold has no sting, she stumbles forward at a rate too fast for her hazy head to keep up with. I love carnage, my ego feeds off it, so normally, I'd step back and watch her fall.

This time, I can't because not only does her next confession have me dying to keep her awake, it knocks me on my ass even quicker than the drugs Preacher slipped into her drink. "I get she's a little kooky, and you pissed him off by keeping your daughter a secret, but still, shouldn't he treat all his kin the same?"

33

ROXANNE

"Ouch!" I snap my eyes to Rocco, peeved as fuck he pinched me. I'm already dealing with horrific cramps and a sweaty body that has me dying for a shower. He didn't need to up the ante. "What was that for?"

He hits me with a stern glare someone as playful as him shouldn't be able to pull off before he scrubs a hand across his wiry beard. "Believe me, you'll rather my torture than the one you're about to subject yourself to."

I act as if I have no clue what he's talking about. "Whatever do you mean?"

Fighting the urge not the pinch me again, he spits out through a tight jaw, "The headcount the green-headed monster on your shoulder *thinks* you're doing in your head."

His reply all but answers my suspicion. It also doubles the painful churns of my stomach. I had wondered if the women in the nightclub were previous 'associates' of Dimitri's. Now I know without a doubt.

I won't give you an indication of how many women are in this room, or you'll think I'm crazy when I update you on the horrifying amount of jealousy brewing in my stomach.

When I arrived hours ago, my eyes locked with Dimitri's across the room in less than a nanosecond. The look on his face assured me he was about to have me marched out, or at the very least, do it himself, so you can imagine my shock when neither of those things occurred. He hasn't glanced my way once, much less scowled at Rocco.

I tried to use the time to my advantage. I've spoken to almost every woman in attendance without the slightest bit of disdain in my voice.

It was no easy feat.

Only one lone wolf has slipped my net. Her evasion has more to do with the fact she's hanging off Dimitri like a leach than anything else. Just watching her rub her breasts against Dimitri's arm to whisper in his ear has me wanting to heave, and I've kept my distance, so I'm not so sure I should test my tolerance up close.

My ruse to act unaffected by their closeness will end as disastrously as it did when I wretched a hooker from Dimitri's crotch by the strands of her faultless hair. Guaranteed. I'm already on the cusp of slaughter now, and they're still fully clothed, although I don't see that being the case if the blonde has her way. She isn't just tiptoeing her fingers along Dimitri's chest anymore, she's undoing the buttons keeping his tattooed pecs hidden.

After a couple of minutes trying to talk myself out of it, I give in to the temptation burning me alive. My nanna always said I got my rebellious streak from her. I'd hate to stain her legacy by standing back and watching my man be mauled by another woman directly in front of me.

Don't misunderstand. I won't fight her for Dimitri.

I'm merely going to make him come to me.

"You're really going to do this?" Rocco asks with a laugh before he downs his drink with one big gulp then follows me across the room.

The nightclub Dimitri hired has a moody, underground sex club feel to it, it is just minus multiple sex pods and a viewing chamber for those who like to watch. High-back booths take up a majority of the space, and a handful of sunken privacy-roped areas give it a risqué, sophisticated edge.

If the women dotted throughout the space were scantily dressed like the ones who entertain Dimitri's Arabian 'guests,' I'd suspect this establishment was a high-end brothel. Since they aren't, I'll settle on calling it a dance club for well-to-do patrons.

It's the fight of my life to keep a rational head when it dawns on me that Dimitri's buttons aren't the only things the blonde's hands are caressing. She's touching him everywhere—his pecs, his arms, the buckle of his belt. If it's a part of him, she's caressing it in some way.

The fact she can touch him so freely without fear of persecution has me switching tactics in an instant, and I throw more than just my morals under the bus in the process.

"Whoa, hold up, Princess P," Rocco pushes out, half amused, half panicked when I shove him into a bean-bag type seat across from Dimitri and the unnamed blonde before nuzzling into his side. "Aren't I supposed to get a final meal before I'm sent to slaughter?"

"I'm sure I can find you something interesting to nibble on if you'll follow my lead." While mimicking the tiptoe finger walk the blonde is doing to Dimitri's chest on Rocco's, I force my gaze away from Dimitri's slit eyes to the humorous pair peering down at me. "Unless you're scared about how Dimitri will react?"

With a smile that's as evil as it is sweet, Rocco sinks deeper into the flexible material cushioning his backside before he adjusts the span of his thighs. His stance is almost an exact replica of

Dimitri's. However, his eyes are nowhere near as narrowed. "I'm not scared of Dimi, Princess P. I'm just worried you don't understand what you're signing up for."

I hook my leg loosely around his waist before pressing my lips to the shell of his ear, shuddering when the scent of his cologne filters into my nostrils. "I'm well aware. I knew in the alleyway when he watched me come, in the woods when he spared my life, and I know right now even with him ripping my heart to shreds, Dimitri Petretti doesn't play games with anyone... *except me*."

Dimitri has an eye on every person in the room, but there's only one person he is paying attention to—me.

Good.

All is fair in love and war, and this is about as treacherous as it gets.

Pretending he doesn't want me is one thing, reminding me he's married is another, but this, allowing a woman to slobber over him directly in front of me is an entirely new kettle of fish, and I am done pretending I'm okay with it.

Even with my heart screaming at me to pull back on the reins, I match the blonde's seductive moves, tease for tease. When she presses her lips to Dimitri's ear, mine get super friendly with Rocco's. When she drags her nails across Dimitri's pecs, I scour Rocco's with mine. And when she finally succeeds in undoing the buckle on Dimitri's belt, I tug on Rocco's just as aggressively.

"Dammit, Roxie, you've got me all types of conflicted. I don't want Dimitri to slice my dick off if it gets hard at the thought of you stroking it, but if you're going to touch the hammer, I can't have you doing it while he's half-mast. That's an injustice I *cannot* allow."

I don't pay Rocco's witty-filled comment any attention. I can't. I'm too busy staring at Dimitri, shocked as hell I am seconds from sliding my hand into his number two's pants, and he's not going to do a damn thing about it.

The cropped hairs splayed across Rocco's pelvis are tickling my fingertips. I can hear the unease in the beats of Rocco's heart that we're stepping over the line, yet, Dimitri just stares.

He doesn't blink.

He doesn't move.

He. Just. Stares.

"Fuck you!" I shout at Dimitri while yanking my hand out of Rocco's pants like his 'hammer' scorched my fingers. "Someone in this room killed our baby! Maestro might have punched me in the stomach and kicked me over and over again, but he was acting on the orders of a *woman*. *She* told him what to do. *She* told him to do whatever it took to get rid of our child when the finger he forced inside of me came out free of carnage." I stand to my feet like I'm not sick to my stomach with disgust. "But I guess that doesn't matter to you, does it? Because the death of our baby means there's one less person for you to pretend you give a shit about."

I shrug out of Rocco's hold when he snatches my wrist. I'm not about to race over to Dimitri's side of the club to beg for his scraps like a fool. I'm going home to lick my wounds and refuel, then I'll start again on my quest to find the person responsible for the death of my child because despite what my heart believes, she isn't in this room.

The shocked sigh that collectively rolled around the no-longer thrumming space during the middle part of my confession was too loud to exclude a single patron. They were *all* horrified by my comment our baby was killed—even the blonde with her hand halfway into Dimitri's pants.

34

ROXANNE

"Can you please hurry the fuck up? It's a pimped-out Range Rover. How many could you possibly have in the lot?"

The valet excuses Rocco's foul language since it was said after a pleasantry. "Surprisingly, quite a few. Tonight's guests seem to be fans of that make and model."

"It's fine," I interject, stepping between Rocco and the valet before Rocco can sock him in the nose. "My flight was scheduled to depart hours ago. I doubt there'll be another one until dawn, so there's no need to hurry."

I twist to face Rocco when a *pfft* noise vibrates his lips. "What?"

For the first time since I've known him, he lies to my face. "I didn't say anything." Mercifully, my tapping foot and my crossed arms soon call him out as the liar he is. "Dimitri didn't organize for you to fly home commercially. He's paying five thousand an hour to have a jet fueled and on the runway. Has been since Wednesday."

"Wednesday." Although it sounds like I am asking a question, I'm not. "The day of my ultrasound?"

Unsure if I'm summarizing or seeking answers, Rocco half-heartedly shrugs. His lackluster response should ease my annoyance. It doesn't. Not in the slightest. I thought Dimitri believed my claims our baby was killed. The fact he's had a private jet on standby since the day India told him otherwise proves he doesn't.

"Then I guess you better hurry," I say to the valet. "I'd hate to waste another dime of Dimitri's hard-earned money." The way I spit out 'hard-earned' exposes exactly what I think about Dimitri's family business.

They're proof money can't buy happiness. They just rent it for a few hours and pretend their life is bliss, having no clue substance should always override quality.

"Finally," Rocco breathes out with a groan when our car rolls to a stop in front of us.

The darkness swamping me doesn't seem so dense when Rocco beats the valet to my door. He holds it open for me, his smile more welcoming now than when I used him as my pawn.

His grin would have you believing we won tonight. My nanna always said sometimes you must lose an occasional battle to win the war, but I don't feel anything close to victorious right now.

"Chin up, Princess P," Rocco mutters like he heard my private thoughts. "You've got more chance of jabbing the main players in the ass if you're tailing them from behind." He winks, shuts my door, then jogs around to the driver's side door by darting around the trunk.

Without speaking another word, he slips into the driver's seat, fires up the ignition, then commences our solemn trek to a private airstrip in the middle of nowhere.

It's a somber, unsatisfying twenty minutes filled with tension and unvoiced questions. I can feel the tension radiating out of

Rocco, smell the unease slicking his skin, but he remains quiet. That is as foreign as Dimitri not responding to my attempt to goad him and proves what should have dawned on me three days ago. My relationship with Dimitri was nothing but an arrangement to improve the odds of him getting his daughter back.

For some stupid reason, I'm okay with that. I never wanted to steal him from Fien, and I most certainly have no intention to do that now. I just wish I could be a part of their unit. I've always felt a little lost. I didn't experience that once while in Dimitri's realm. Even when he threatened to kill me or hurt those I love, I still felt wanted.

My watering eyes stray from the scenery whizzing by the window when Rocco shifts down the gears in the Range Rover. As stated, a gleaming state-of-the-art private jet sits halfway out of an airport hangar in a town bordering India's suburban mansion. It's fueled up and ready to go, meaning I only need to farewell Rocco with a kiss, and I'll be done with this life.

"Are you sure you don't want me to come with you?" Rocco asks before my lips have even left his cheek. "I'm not a fan of flying, but if it saves me facing Dimitri's wrath for a couple of hours, I'm all for it."

I'd laugh at his mumbled comment if I believed it held an ounce of truth to it. Dimitri would have to be jealous to respond to our horrible scam to make him jealous, and we both know that shipped sailed the instant our ruse was implemented with only the slightest hiccup.

No one was prepared for me to be actually pregnant—not even me.

With my shoulders hanging as low as my mood, I reply, "I'm only going to sleep the entire flight, so why bother?"

Stealing Rocco's chance to reply to my lie, I press a second peck to his cheek, snatch my clutch purse from the floor, then exit his stationary vehicle.

I don't look back while climbing the stairs of the private jet. I'm not a movie starlet, and this isn't a fairy tale.

When I break into the cabin that smells of wine and freshly baked cookies, a friendly voice greets me. "Good evening, Ms. Grace. We're pleased to have you aboard this evening."

"Thank you," I reply to the air stewardess, truly grateful for the sincerity in her tone. It is the nicest one I've had all week.

After removing my denim jacket, she folds it over her arm. "Can I get you something to drink? Perhaps a snack?"

"Umm..." I take a moment to consider the demands of my aching stomach before shaking my head. "I should probably take care of my sweaty body and face before eating. Is there a restroom I can freshen up in?"

Gratitude for perks I have no need to become accustomed to smack into me when the pretty brunette dips her chin. "I turned down the bedding in your suite earlier today. It's ready as requested." She steps closer to me, her eyes genuinely friendly. "While you freshen up, I'll instruct the pilot to finalize last checks. We should be in the air within the hour."

"Thank you," I reply through a yawn.

Once I have my purse dumped onto one of the dozen or more plush leather chairs lining the aisle, I head for the highly varnished door the stewardess pointed to when she mentioned my 'suite.' My steps are sluggish and slow, weighed down by exhaustion no amount of rest will cure. I honestly feel ill, like more than heartbreak is responsible for the shards of pain sluicing my veins.

The room at the back of the jet is small but fancy with silk sheets and hundreds of scatter cushions. I'm tempted to crawl into the middle of the mattress, roll into a ball, and pretend the world doesn't exist, but I need to use the facilities first. My face is covered with gunk I haven't worn since I thought black mascara and white powder would stop the uncomfortable gawks of my high school professor. It worked for almost a month, my ruse only ruined when he stumbled upon one of my erotic drawings in my school notepad.

I usually reserved my sketching for home, but Professor Lewis's constant after-school detentions saw me switching things up. I don't know what happened to him. He was constantly there, then he reported my artwork to my grandmother, and he disappeared not long after that. I didn't think much of it at the time, but now it seems a little odd.

Too curious to discount, I do a final wipe over my face before entering the main part of the cabin. "Smith..." I wait a few seconds, aware he's always listening, but also know I'm not the only person he keeps tabs on—*if* he's still keeping tabs on me. "Smith—"

"Is handling other matters right now."

With my heart beeping in my neck, I shift on my feet to face the voice that froze my heart. Since his Italian accent was heavier than I've heard it before, I assumed it belonged to Dimitri's father. If the dangerous pump of Dimitri's nostrils is anything to go by, I'm kind of wishing it was still him. Dimitri is bristling with anger, and once again, all his focus is on me.

I hate myself for running. I pledged on the way here that the rod in my back won't bend for anyone. But that doesn't count when the man you love is looking at you like he wants to kill you.

Besides, I'm not running from him. I am running away from what he represents. More than once he hurt me, yet all I want to do is smooth the groove between his brows with my lips.

That makes me as unhinged as Dimitri's growl when he slams the door shut before I get close to darting through it, then crowds me against it. I'm scared shitless, but for some stupid reason, I relish his big brooding frame looming over me. If he didn't care, he wouldn't be here. If he were done with me, he wouldn't have needed to check that Rocco drove away after dropping me off.

As I consider the possibilities of what his arrival means, my heart picks up speed. Will he beg me to stay? Will he tell me he's sorry? Will he introduce me to his daughter instead of pretending he hasn't noticed me watching their connection from afar?

The possibilities are endless, I just never considered this one.

With his big hand cupping the little pouch in the lower half of my stomach from eating too many carbs the past week, and his lips squashed against my ear, he whispers five words more important than any, "I cared. I still do."

35

DIMITRI

Every step I take away from the private jet feels like a knife is being stabbed into my chest. My words shattered Roxanne, she broke down in front of me, yet I still walked away.

I don't have a choice. I can't be who she needs me to be and protect her at the same time. She craves a monster, a bastard, a man who'd rather destroy her than have her ever believe she deserves better than him, but I need to be more than that.

I need to be the lowest of the low, the scum on the bottom of a seedy one-star motel shower stall, the man my father raised me to be. I need to rain terror down on those who have done me wrong and resurrect the innocent I burned along the way.

And I need to start with her.

Megan's eyes are as red-rimmed as Roxanne's. They're puffy like she's been crying, but not a touch of moisture is seen on her cheeks. She's scared she is about to meet with her maker but considering that couldn't occur until I broke her out of a mental hospital alters her perspective on things. She isn't close to being free, her wings are fully clipped, but it's better than being dead.

It's the same with Theresa. As much as I want her to be the villain of my story, that isn't a title I can give her just yet. She shared information with me tonight I couldn't have gotten elsewhere. Undeniable evidence that will have Roxanne returned to my bed even quicker than I'm hoping.

That alone will spare Theresa of my fury. It isn't a lifetime guarantee, but bearing in mind the many ways I had planned to kill her when her overzealous hands had Roxanne acting out, she should count her lucky stars. If she hadn't spilled a vault load of my father's secrets the past four hours, she would have been wearing concrete boots by now, and Rocco would be guzzling down saltwater right along with her. That's how much my blood boiled watching Roxanne and Rocco get cozy and how tenacious my itch to kill was.

It's just fortunate for them both, my wish to return Roxanne to her rightful spot at my side was greater than my urge to slit their throats.

It was a fucking hard feat—one I'm still struggling to maintain.

After sliding into the back of a prototype vehicle, I signal for the driver to go. We have a long trip ahead of us, and I want it done before Fien wakes. Since that's usually right at dawn, I better get a wiggle on.

"Do you recognize any of these people?" I remove a stack of licenses Smith printed when the drugs tracing through Theresa's veins couldn't stop the waggle of her tongue before twisting them to face Megan. "Whether in your family or outside of it."

I can't believe I'm playing into Theresa's suggestion Megan and I are related. The Petretti genes are strong, and Megan looks nothing like me. Her hair is mousy, her teeth are chipped and crooked, and her eyes are hazel. And don't get me started on the fact she's batshit crazy, or we'll be here all night.

I'm fucked in the head, but I'm not mentally challenged.

"I won't hurt these people, Megan. I just want answers." I'm such a fucking liar. If any of the thoughts running through my head are true, all these men are dead, then I'll move for their families like Clover is hunting Maestro's now. He broke the rules when he touched Roxanne, and now his entire existence will pay the price of his stupidity. I wasn't lying when I said I'd remove a man's legacy if he hurt Roxanne. I don't play games when it comes to people I love.

I work my jaw side to side to loosen its grip when Megan asks, "Are you from the hotel?" Her voice is as weak as the fragile mouse she's portraying, exposing I need to play on her insecurities. If she's a damsel in distress, I need to pretend I'm a hero. It's like good cop, bad cop, everyone has their role.

I unbutton my jacket before sinking into my seat, hopeful a blasé response will show Megan I mean her no harm. I don't even have a gun on my hip. It's stuffed down the back of my trousers, but that's not the point. "I don't own any hotels, but why would you ask that? Are you having trouble with some people at your hotel? I can help you with it if you'd like."

She licks her cracked lips before twisting them so they match her screwed-up nose. "They're okay. They are just *really* annoying." The woman seated across from me would have to be midtwenties at least, but she speaks as if she hasn't reached her teen years yet, furthering my proof she isn't a Petretti. Even when it could fuck her sideways, Ophelia was fierce.

After scooting to the edge of her seat, Megan drops her eyes to the stack of licenses. "Can I look through them?"

"Sure." I smile at her like she asked to suck my dick before handing over the pile of papers. It is stupid of me to do. She's more scared now than she was when Preacher snuck her out of a mental facility with a hessian bag pulled over her head and his hand clamped around her mouth. From what I heard from Smith, more than Preacher's hand is suffering bite wounds.

I join Megan in balancing on the end of my seat when she says, "The staff asks about him all the time. I don't like talking about him." When she swivels on the spot, it dawns on me that the heat on her cheeks has nothing to do with the heat pumping out of the vents. "Nick, though... I talk about him all the time. Have you seen him lately?" She stops, huffs, then folds her arms in front of her chest. "He wasn't with *her*, was he? I tried to fix his mistake. I gave her the drink like the man said. It didn't work. *She* still had her baby."

Her jump in and out of personalities gives me whiplash, but I attempt to maintain the momentum of our conversation. "What man, Megan?" I've shown her over a dozen images. She needs to narrow down the list of suspects for me.

She appears more innocent than insane when she brings her father's identification card to the front of the stack. Carlyle Shroud looks like a cruel, villainous man incapable of raising a rat, much less a daughter whose mother died before she reached womanhood.

"Your father gave you something to hurt a woman?" I sound like a fucking moron, but mercifully, it seems to be a language Megan understands.

"Not my daddy, silly." She laughs like I'm hilarious. "He is who the men in the white coats at the hotel asked about all the time."

"The hotel you just left?" I ask, finally clueing on to what she means. She has confused the mental hospital she was admitted in the past week with the Ritz Carlton. It makes sense when you see the conditions she grew up in. A pigsty would be glamorous compared to her family ranch.

While nodding, Megan pulls a second photo out of the stack

like she isn't about to unlock the treasure chest I've been hoarding the past almost two years. "He gave me the medication." She holds up an outdated photo of Rimi Castro in front of me—the once ringleader of the baby-farming syndicate who kidnapped my wife, held my daughter captive, and killed my unborn child. He's dead, so I can't get the answers I need from him. Megan, though, she's very much alive and very much on my radar.

"How long ago did you meet with Rimi?"

She takes a moment to contemplate. Her delay reveals she isn't as stupid as she wants me to believe. She's playing an act. I'm confident of that.

Don't get me wrong, she's fucking mental, but she could be a genius if her evil was harnessed the right way.

Once she's confident she has me on tenterhooks, she answers, "Last week."

"You saw Rimi last week?" I rush out before I can stop myself. I'm supposed to be portraying a cool and collected cartel leader, not a dweeb who comes after only two pumps.

Megan smiles, loving the shock in my tone. Since it places her on my team, I let the mocking gleam that arrived with her grin slide. "Yes. His home isn't too far from here." Just like earlier when she spoke about Nick, her expression perks up as she asks, "Do you think he'd like to see me again?" As quickly as her excitement bristled, it slips off her face with a groan. "*She* won't be there again, will she? I don't like her. She's mean."

"A woman was with Rimi when you visited him?"

She mistakes the shock in my tone as devious. "They're not like that. They don't do the things Nick does with *her*." She looks like she vomited a little in her mouth. "Rimi's *friend* sleeps in her own room." I feel as if our conversation is about to veer off course when she curls her hand over her basically flat stomach, but am proven wrong when she mutters, "Her baby is really cute. My baby will be cute, too. When she's born."

The full extent of her mental illness is showcased in the worst light when she coos to her 'baby' how she will see her daddy soon. She doesn't just have a brief conversation and move on.

She's so far down the rabbit hole, she doesn't blink when my 'imaginary friend' jumps into our conversation. "I told you." Smith's voice is a mix of remorseful and fretful. "Certifiably fucking insane."

I nod, agreeing with him. "But she could be onto something. Roxanne said the women at Rimi's ranch shared the same room. What if the woman Megan mentioned had her own room because she was a part of Rimi's team? She could be the woman we're seeking."

Although every member of Castro's team was taken down in the massive blood bath last week, over four dozen 'survivors' were registered in the CIA's recovery file. The women were an integral part of the baby-farming operation, but both Henry and I agreed they played no part in Fien's captivity nor his brother's family's downfall, so they shouldn't be held accountable.

"There's one person who can give you answers to the questions you're seeking, Dimitri. She's sitting right in front of you." Smith's tone is neither malice nor mocking. It is straight-up honest.

With my deadly insides hidden by a smile, I return my focus back to Megan. She's watching me, not the least bit confronted by the viciousness of my returned stare. "Did you have your own room at Rimi's farm, too, Megan? Or did you share a room with Rimi?" I scoff like I'm disappointed her innocent act is for show. "I wonder what Nick will think about you shacking up with another man."

"I didn't share a room with Rimi." She looks genuinely unwell. "My daddy told me what would happen if I shared a bed with a man who wasn't my husband. He'd sew my eyes shut like he did my mother when she let *him* sleep in their bed."

My eyes rocket in the direction she nudged her head, gasping like a man without a cock when I realize who she's referencing. The focus is no longer on Rimi's debunked crew. It has shifted to my father.

"Smi—"

"Cross-referencing any connection between Megan's mother and your father now." He sounds as shocked as me. I'm stunned, truly and wholly scandalized. My father fucked around long before my mother died, but that doesn't mean what I think it does, does it? Megan can't be my sister—surely.

"Furthermore..." Megan waits for my eyes to return to her flaming-with-anger face before she continues, "Rimi doesn't live on a farm." She talks about him as if he isn't dead. "He has a big house my mother would have loved. It has hundreds of rooms, a picture theater, and a special hospital in the basement. That's where the ladies have their babies. Rimi said I could have my baby there if I want." My thudding heart almost drowns out her next lot of words. "I can prove I had my own room. His house is close to here." She peers around like she's gathering her bearings. "Well, it was closer to the airport than here. Can we go back there?"

"Jesus fucking Christ," Smith murmurs out loud, matching my sentiments to a T. "Show her the photos I sent to your phone."

With my mind shut down, autopilot mode kicks in. I dig my phone out of my pocket, then fire it up. My thumb hovers over the message app when Megan grunts, "That's her, the woman who lives with Rimi. How did you get her photograph?" The absolute disdain hardening her features softens when she spots Fien on my screensaver. "Aww, now it makes sense. I told you her daughter is cute. I'd put her photo on my phone too... *if I had one.*"

My itch to kill turns catastrophic when the final piece of the puzzle slots into place. My screensaver is an image of Fien I snapped the first time I saw her in the flesh. Because Audrey clutched my hand most of the drive from Rimi's compound to India's house, Fien isn't cradled in Roxanne's arms. She's being held by India.

It doesn't take me even a second to do the math. India is in every scene even more than Roxanne. She has been in every single frame—even the ones before Fien was conceived. That fucking bitch orchestrated my daughter's captivity because I chose her roommate over her, and I'm going to kill her for it.

36

ROXANNE

I request the driver of my cab to pull over two houses back from India's country estate. Even with my gut warning me that this is a bad idea, I can't help but test the strength of the boundaries Dimitri lodged between us.

He could have let me leave thinking he didn't care about me. He could have walked away without telling me our baby meant something to him. He didn't.

That deserves recognition.

That deserves acknowledgment.

"Are you sure you're okay?" asks the driver when my hunt for bills in the bottom of my clutch has me grunting in pain. "You don't look real good."

Up until twenty minutes ago, I didn't know a broken heart could cause physical pain. I'm in as much pain now as I was when Maestro punched me in the stomach. It has me sweating up a storm and has my cab driver convinced I'm up to no good.

He was already suspicious when I said I would have to direct him to my location by taking a detour past a club that looks as shady as hell when it's minus its ritzy guests.

"Perhaps I could take you to the hospital?"

I lock my eyes with the kind pair glancing at me in the rearview mirror. "I'm fine. I think I ate something bad. It will pass soon." *I hope.*

He doesn't believe me, but I'm beyond caring.

After tossing a bundle of bills over the seat, I crank open my door and peel out of the cab. It's almost winter, so the chills racking my body should be from the cold. Regretfully, they aren't. I'm both burning up and shuddering like I am in an ice bath.

The unusual duo hitting me doesn't slow me down, though. Once I've ensured the cab driver has left, I cross the road, then head toward the back entrance I spotted Rocco sneaking out of many times the past week.

The secret passage could be lit up with surveillance, but I'm okay with that if it's being viewed by the man I'm endeavoring to spark a reaction out of. I still don't know Dimitri's cell phone number, and Smith is being as ignorant as my body begs for me to slow down.

Once the sweat beading my top lip has been wiped away, I push open the heavily weighted door in the far righthand corner of India's home. It takes everything I have to get the rusty hinges to budge, and even then, I have to squeeze through the gap since it barely opened a few inches.

"Smith..." I keep my voice low, hopeful my unexpected return doesn't startle the lady of the house. India isn't a fan of mine. I can't say I blame her. Audrey is more approving of my 'relationship' with her husband than her best friend. I can't help but wonder if that's because she's scarred from her ordeal. There's a pain in her eyes when she peers at Dimitri. It just seems more regretful than sad. "Smith..."

I get an answer this time around.

It isn't who I'm hoping, but mercifully, it also isn't India.

"Audrey, are you okay?" My last three words come out in a hurry when she stumbles forward at a rate too fast for me to catch her. She lands on her knees with a thump, her skidder exposing the cause of her fumbling state. Her wrists have been slashed. "Oh God, what did you do?"

I drag her into the open, positive if my screams don't reach Smith's ears, he will spot me on one of the many cameras Rocco pointed out late last night. "Help! Somebody, please help!" As I rip my shirt to make bandages for Audrey's gushing wounds, I choke out, "It's okay. You'll be okay. I promise."

My pledge should slacken the worry in her eyes not double it. The color drains from her face as quickly as it oozes out of her wounds. She looks truly panicked she's about to die, which is odd considering she attempted suicide.

"Finally," I push out with a relieved breath when the patter of footsteps racing my way sounds through my ears. "Call an ambulance while I lay her flat. If I raise her arms above her head, it should lower her blood loss." I've just got to pray she hasn't sliced an artery. If she has, help may not get here in time.

After removing my jacket, I place it under Audrey's head, then raise her arms as high as I can. It helps to lower the amount of blood gushing from her wounds, but she is still on death's door.

"Help me compress her wounds." When nothing but silence is heard for the next several seconds, my mood gets snappy. "Quick!" The shortness of my demand doesn't weaken the intensity of it. I'm beyond annoyed the person I hear creeping up on me isn't assisting me in making Audrey stable. "I get it's scary and that there's a lot of blood, but Audrey will die if you don't help me."

When a snicker overtakes the thud of the pulse in my ears, I crank my neck in the direction it came from. India is standing at the bottom of the stairwell that leads to the main part of her residence. Her hand is clamped over her mouth, and her eyes are fixed on the fading pulse in Audrey's neck.

"If you don't want your best friend to die, you need to help me... *now!*"

Unease melds through my veins when she remains standing at the foot of the stairs. She took charge last week when Audrey's injuries were much worse than this, so why is she acting like she's terrified of a little bit of blood?

When Audrey gargles out my name, my eyes jackknife back to her so quickly, my head gets a rush of dizziness. Her lips feebly move as she fights to warn me about the imminent danger I'm in, but not a sound seeps from her lips. She isn't just sinking into the blackness calling her name, someone hacked up her tongue as poorly as they did her wrists.

"Who did this to you, Audrey? Who hurt you?"

While searching her pockets for her phone, hopeful as fuck she has Dimitri's new number stored in her contacts, the shadow above my head doubles in size.

I duck with barely a second to spare, sending the vase India was attempting to knock me out with into the brick wall Audrey's forehead collided with when she stumbled to her knees.

As my sluggish head struggles to click on to what is happening, Audrey finally voices the name she was trying to get out earlier. "Fien."

Fien is not my child, but I love her father enough to wish she was, so I'll do everything in my power to protect her from the deranged woman attempting to kill her mother.

With a roar, I charge for India like Dimitri did Officer Daniel almost two weeks ago. My shove juts her so fiercely, a butcher's knife stained with blood falls from her back pocket. I snatch it up before racing up the stairwell as if my stomach isn't screaming with every pump of my legs. My plan could be a woeful waste of time, India could finish what she started with Audrey since I'm no longer in the room, but my intuition is telling me this is the right thing to do. India wants Audrey's death to look like a suicide. She can't do that without the weapon I'm clutching.

When I reach the top of the stairs on the third floor, I scan my eyes over the dozens of doors branching off the corridor. They're all identical, and there are far too many to search every one of them.

"Fien?" I call her name on repeat, unsure which room is hers. I only got to watch her connection with her father from afar. I was never invited into her inner circle. It wasn't just Dimitri shunting me from the festivities, it was India as well.

Now I understand why.

"Fien, honey, where are you?"

My heart races a million miles an hour when Fien sheepishly peers at me from behind a carved wooden door partway down the corridor. Her eyes are sleepy, and her beloved teddy is closer to the floor than her chest.

"Hey, baby," I say, optimistic she won't just recall how I ripped her out of Maestro's arms when he succumbed to a bullet. I helped her meet her father for the first time. Fingers crossed that gives me some additional brownie points. "Do you want to go see Dada? I'm sure he's dying to see you. I can take you to him."

The closer I pad to Fien, the more wetness fills her eyes. Even being raised in hell wouldn't see her eager to run into my arms. I have a bloody knife in my hand, and I'm sweating profusely. I very much look like an ax murderer.

After tossing the knife to the floor, I scrub a hand across my face, then hold out my arms. "That's it, Fien," I say on a sob when she moves out from behind her door enough I can see all of her adorable face. "I won't hurt you. I swear. We're just going to go see Dada."

I think I have her convinced.

I think she's on my side.

Then the mat is pulled out from beneath my feet.

While crying for her Mama, Fien sidesteps me with the agility of an up-and-coming state championship quarterback. She races to India at the other end of the corridor, smirking smugly about the devastation on my face.

How did she get past me? I haven't spent a lot of time here, but since I was lonely, and I pace the halls when I'm feeling that way, I know her floorplan intimately. There's no other entrance to the third floor except the stairwell I just climbed. Unless...

My mouth pops open when the truth smacks into me.

India's home has a secret stairwell like the ranch Fien was held captive at.

"You... you..." Come on mouth, put this bitch in her place. "You killed my baby!"

I snatch up the knife I threw down before holding it out in front of myself. Fien will most likely never forgive the murderous look on my face, but I'll do my best to erase it from her memories when I take down the conniving, two-faced bitch she has confused with her mother.

"Why did you do that to my baby? What harm could it have ever done to you? Dimitri was *never* yours. He didn't even sleep with you, so why do you think you have a claim to any children he has?"

Like the heartless snake she is, India says matter-of-factly, "My family's royal lineage hasn't been tainted in centuries, and I refuse to let it start with me."

"What?" Nothing she said makes any sense. Fien isn't her

child, so how could my child with Dimitri 'taint' her family's legacy.

It takes a little longer for the truth to smack into me this time around. The delay is understandable. This is as unkosher as it gets.

"You're Fien's mother." Since I'm not asking a question, it doesn't sound like one. "How? Dimitri went to Audrey's ultrasound. He watched Fien's brutal birth... more than once." The truth pummeling into me makes the pain in my stomach ten times worse. "You can't have children. That's how you knew about miscarriages and fibroids." I can barely breathe through the madness swamping me when disturbing thought after disturbing thought enters my mind. "Audrey was your surrogate. That's why Fien doesn't respond to her like she does you because she knows Audrey isn't her mother." When she doesn't attempt to deny my claims, my words get extra snappy. "You kept her from her father this entire time. Why would you do that, India? What did Dimitri ever do to you?"

Any chance of getting answers out of her is hit out of the park when the thud of someone climbing the stairwell two stairs at a time booms into my ears.

Dimitri races our way, his speed as brutal as the lies that fall from India's mouth when he reaches the landing. "Thank God you're here, Dimi. Roxanne killed Audrey before she turned the knife onto Fien." She sucks in breaths like she's on the verge of a panic attack before continuing with a sob, "I made it to Fien with barely a second to spare, but I'm scared, Dimi. She tried to kill your daughter. She tried to kill Fien."

"No..." The pain shredding through me becomes too much to bear. It sees me dropping the knife so I can cradle my aching stomach that's begging for me to bend in two. "I didn't hurt Fien. I'd never hurt her. *Argh...*"

I'm unsure if my gargled scream is from the intense sharpness hitting my lower stomach or from India using Dimitri's distraction to her advantage. She snatches up the knife wedged between us as quickly as Dimitri yanks his gun out of his trousers.

Instead of directing it at me, the supposed perpetrator, Dimitri aims his gun at the pleat between India's blonde brows, unimpressed she has the sharp side of the knife pressed against Fien's throat. "You will never make it out of here alive. I will gut you where you fucking stand if a droplet of blood beads on her neck!"

India is either an idiot, or she doesn't fear death. "One nick of her artery *will* kill her." Her voice is unlike anything I've ever heard. "You know this, Dimitri. We're miles from the closest hospital. Help will *never* get here in time."

When she pierces the blade in deep enough to make Fien sob for her daddy, I fall to my knees, both pained by the devastation on Fien's little face and the pain buckling my legs out from beneath me.

"Do you want your daughter to die!" India screams when my topple diverts Dimitri's eyes to me for the quickest second. "Is *she* more important than your flesh and blood?" Spit seethes from her mouth when she hisses out 'she.'

I shake my head at the same time Dimitri mumbles, "No."

I'm not only agreeing that I'll never be more important than Fien, I'm trying to relay to Dimitri that India won't do as she's threatening. She might be a callous, cold-hearted bitch, but that doesn't mean she will kill her daughter. I just can't get my mouth to work. I'm in too much pain to speak. I'm barely conscious, so I can't be expected to talk.

"Then, put down your gun, step away from the banister, and let me leave." Dimitri firms his grip instead of weakening it. It frustrates India to no end. "Do it or I'll kill your daughter like I did the bastard child you were going to have with *her*."

When she jerks her head to me during the last part of her

statement, something inside of me cracks. I'm on my knees, confident I'm on the verge of death, but I somehow manage to charge for India.

I stumble more than I sprint, but my fumbling movements are all that is needed for India to take her eyes off the prize for just a second. When she drops her knife to my stomach, preparing to maim me as she did Audrey, Dimitri snatches Fien from her arms, cradles her into his chest, then falls back while firing.

Bang. Bang. Bang, booms into my ears.

One bullet thrusts India into the wall with a pained yelp, the other pierces through the drywall next to my head, and the last one shreds through the pain that's been crippling me the past five days. It tears through my stomach, stunning me that it isn't as painful as anticipated.

That could have more to do with the fact the man I love shot me.

He. *Shot.* Me.

"No!" Dimitri falls to my side as quickly as he screams for Smith on repeat. "Stay with me, Roxanne... Smith!"

As I peer up at the ceiling, I gargle on the blood bubbling in my windpipe. Death is more peaceful than I predicted. It isn't filled with gore and horror. It's quiet and surreal, somewhat warm, or is that the blood seeping into my clothes?

"I swear to God, Roxanne, if you don't fight, I'll tan your fucking ass. By the time I'm done with you, your ass will be bleeding more than a little bullet wound."

I shouldn't laugh, the pain it causes is horrific, but it can't be helped. Just like Estelle searches for humor in every situation, Dimitri seeks darkness.

As my breaths shiver in the coolness enveloping me, I reach out to touch Dimitri's face, startling when my briefest touch smears his cheek with blood. I must be bleeding a lot because my hands were nowhere near my stomach before I moved them.

"What the fuck were you doing here, Roxanne? You were meant to stay away. That's the only way I could guarantee your safety," Dimitri mutters as he pushes on my stomach so painfully, I cry out. "I've got to hurt you, baby. If I don't hurt you, you'll die. You don't want to die, do you? You're too fucking strong to die now... Roxanne... Roxie... Rox..."

Dimitri slaps me two times—hard. He isn't meaning to hurt me. He's merely doing everything in his power to force my head out of the black cloud it's sinking into. "Fuck, Smith, hurry. We're losing her."

The absolute pain in his voice almost drags me out of the dark. I fight with everything I have, but the pull is too strong. I'm sinking into the abyss faster than my woozy head can keep up with. I barely get 'I love you' out before the blackness swamping me takes over the reins. Still, I swear somewhere between my float from reality to a much darker realm, Dimitri responds, "As do I, Roxanne. As do I."

37

DIMITRI

"How the fuck does a woman with a bullet wound get out of your city without you knowing about it?"

Henry doesn't get the chance to reply. My fist breaks through the drywall behind his head long before a syllable leaves his lips. I'm pissed, peeved as fuck, and since the person responsible for the anguish eating me alive isn't in my reign, I'm taking it out on the wrong person.

"She tried to kill my daughter and wife..." It feels like the final strand of the thread I'm clutching unravels when I force out, "I don't even know if she succeeded with Roxanne yet."

She's fighting—*my fucking God is she fighting*—but it's touch and go. The medics lost her twice during her transport to the hospital. If it weren't for Rocco and me holding our guns to their heads, they would have given up on her. They said she was clinically dead, that she was in cessation.

I didn't give a fuck what they called it, I wanted them to give her a chance to show she's stronger than her tiny frame and ageless face portrays. I wanted them to give her a chance to prove them wrong because if she can't do that, I'm dead too.

It was the jarring of *my* arm when I adjusted my fall to ensure Fien wouldn't get hurt that caused me to misfire. *My* bullet pierced through Roxanne's stomach, so if anyone is going to pay restitution for my error, it will be me.

Assuming my silence stems from believing he is incompetent, Henry says, "I have men combing every inch of my city looking for India. If she's still here, they'll find her."

The confidence in his comment should offer me some sort of comfort.

It doesn't.

Not in the slightest.

"What if she's already left?"

"Then we will find out where she's going and beat her there," Henry immediately fires back like he already considered the possibility our search for India will be longer than I'm hoping.

I rake my fingers through my hair, knowing it won't be as easy as it sounds, but hopeful I've been put through enough to ease Karma's nasty bite. India is smart, she has plenty of money at her disposal, and convincing-enough looks to make men disregard her hideous insides. She's a foreign version of Theresa.

"I have *all* my men on this, Dimi. The Albanians, the Italians, hell, even the Russians are looking for her. It might take longer than you're hoping, but we will find her... eventually." Henry squeezes my shoulder before stepping closer. His relaxed facial expression reveals why he was a good candidate for the boss of all bosses. He keeps politics out of the equation, and to him, it truly is family first of all.

He couldn't be more different than my father if he tried.

"But for now, your focus needs to be elsewhere."

When he motions his head to the flappy doors they wheeled

Roxanne through hours ago, I crank my neck back so fast, my muscles scream in protest. It's horrible for me to sigh in disappointment when my eyes lock with Audrey's across the room. The guilt is still horrendous, the angst won't quit, but I'd be a liar if I said I weren't praying for her to switch places with Roxanne.

What the fuck is wrong with me?

Audrey is the mother of my child, my wife, yet I still can't put her first.

Because you don't love her, screams a voice inside my head. *You never have, and you never will.*

Realizing what I need to do, I return my focus to Henry. I don't get one of the million words in my head out. He just squeezes my shoulder for the second time, wordlessly assures me he has everything under control, then leaves the Intensive Care Unit waiting room.

I'm not surprised when the number of people in the room remains the same after his departure. He has a reputation that doesn't require muscle. The fact he felt the need to bring backup to our impromptu meeting last week shouldn't make me smile, especially under the circumstances, but it does.

The boss of all bosses title isn't a handed-down legacy. It's earned through hard work and mutual respect—the very things my family's name was once founded on, and the very things I intend to return to it as soon as possible.

I just have to get a feisty redhead with gleaming green eyes out of the woods first because family comes first of all. Roxanne doesn't have the blood nor the Petretti title, but she has something more valuable than both those things.

She has my heart.

She stole it when she stood across from me with black, chunky smears rolling down her cheeks, earned it when she put her life on the line for a child she had never met, then secured it for life when she did it all again without the slightest bit of hesitation.

She went to the ends of the earth for me, and I'll do the same for her. She won't have to ask for a single thing. I will give her the world, and I might even occasionally smile while doing it.

I'm a cold, calculated killer, but Roxanne not only gives me purpose, she makes me want to be a better man. Since that will also make me a better father, I'm sure the weakening of my reputation will be worth the sacrifice.

I've faced worse things in my life, and look how well they've turned out for me.

38

ROXANNE

It takes me a few seconds to work out where I am. I can feel the thud of Dimitri's pulse even with no part of his body whatsoever touching me, hear Rocco's laugh, smell the slightest hint of Estelle's perfume, and the annoying thump of Smith tapping away on a laptop matches the mariachi beat in my head.

The thought of him always working forces a smile onto my dry, blistering lips. Smith wouldn't be Smith without a laptop balancing on his hand, just like I wouldn't be me without Dimitri's dark, mysterious aura igniting my senses.

While blinking to lubricate my eyes, I attempt to sit a little straighter. I'm already in a half-seated position, but since a pillow is wedged between my bed and the mattress, I'm not comfortable. I'm actually more uncomfortable than sore.

I barely move my hand an inch when a warm one slips over it. "Stay still. You'll pull your stitches if you move too much."

Stitches?

The figure that moves to stand in front of me is hazy, but I know who he is. A million droplets of rain couldn't hide his eyes from me, so I doubt a healthy dose of sedatives could.

Perhaps that's why I feel so spaced out?

Maybe I'm drugged up on the good stuff Dimitri reserves for his 'special guests.'

After swishing my tongue around my mouth to loosen up my words, I ask, "Where am I? And exactly how much did I drink to get here?"

Rocco breaks the news since the concern on Dimitri, Smith, and Estelle's faces steal their ability to talk. "You're in the hospital. Dimitri shot you." His last two words come out with a groan, compliments of Dimitri's fist landing in his stomach.

Always willing to push the boundaries when it comes to Dimitri, Rocco laughs before asking, "Was I supposed to keep that a secret? My bad."

I half groan, half laugh, the humor in Rocco's voice too strong for the bland white walls and antiseptic smell surrounding me to discount. I've awoken in a room like this before. Thankfully, this time around, I'm not alone.

"It was for the best," Smith says, not only jumping into the conversation but between Dimitri and Rocco before they come to blows. "Your appendix was a mess. When it ruptured, the infection spread to your abdomen. The sepsis was severe. In a way, it was lucky Dimitri shot you. It forced your stubborn ass to the hospital and allowed the doctors to treat the infection before it became life-threatening."

He's joking, right?

He honestly doesn't want me to believe being shot saved my life.

Actually, come to think of it, it sounds about right. I'm nothing close to ordinary, so why wouldn't a bullet be my savior?

As memories of what had me admitted slowly roll into my

head, my heart dives down low. So deep, I feel its thuds in my toes when I ask, "Is Audrey okay?"

"She's alive," Dimitri answers calmly. "Thanks to you."

"Did she..." I don't want to finish my sentence. I've given Dimitri enough reasons to hate me. I don't want more added to the stack. My parents hurt his wife. They treated his daughter like scum, so I really don't want to tell him everything isn't as it seems.

Dimitri scoops up my hand in his in an almost-nurturing manner. *Almost.* He still has a little bit to go in regard to being gentle. I don't mind. I like him rough and ready. His dominance is one of his most alluring features. "She told me everything."

"*Everything?*" I shouldn't be interrogating him. I'm neither his wife nor the mother of his child, but I can't help myself. The connection between us has always been explosive, and even with me being laid up in a hospital bed, it is the most blistering it's ever been. It has me thinking I can do no wrong and more than willing to risk punishment just to see how far my newfound abilities extend.

My heart sinks even lower than my toes when Dimitri signals for us to be left alone. Rocco and Smith are his closest confidants, so for him to want privacy from them means this must be big. It honestly makes me feel ill, like more than my life is on the line right now.

Dimitri waits for Estelle to press her lips to my temple and join the boys outside before he says way too casually, "Audrey told me everything. How India forced her to come to Hopeton to gather semen samples. The surrogacy. India's last-minute change of heart when she held on longer than expected after Fien's birth, and how you tried to save her even knowing she could one day be your competition." His gaze clings to my face as the slightest smirk curves his lips. "She even told me how India tried to kill her when she confessed to pouring a mixture of tomato soup, baby oil, and corn starch over your nightgown when you passed out so Maestro would believe you had miscarried."

What is he saying?

I don't understand what he means.

Dimitri doesn't laugh, joke, or glower at the shocked mask slipped over my face. He merely clears it away with the quickest brush of his fingers. It's a callous yet gentle touch that makes my heart rate soar as much as his murmured comment, "You didn't miscarry, Roxanne."

If he's about to say I didn't miscarry because I was never pregnant, he can stop right now. I saw our baby, clear as day, directly in front of me. I'm not skilled at pregnancy, and I've never trained to be a sonographer, but I know what I saw. Deep down in my heart, I know that the little black blob on the screen was our baby.

It looked almost identical to the jellybean on the strip of images Dimitri dangles in front of me. "Does this look familiar?"

I clamp my hand over my mouth to hold back my sob before nodding. "Is that..."

I can't talk through the frantic throbbing of my pulse. It's thumping out a crazy tune, stunned by the date and name on the ultrasound images in Dimitri's hand. If the date on Smith's watch is anything to go by, my scan was yesterday. Nine days after I was freed from the hell that killed our baby, and four days after learning Fien's true paternity.

It takes me a couple of seconds to talk, but when I do, my voice is so full of hope, I may very well die if I don't hear the answer I want. "Is that *our* baby?"

There's no chance in hell I can hold back my sob when Dimitri smirks, then nods. His response is almost too surreal, too calm, too fucking outrageous ever to believe it's true.

How is he not freaking out?

Why isn't he fuming mad?

I trapped him exactly how India tried and failed. Shouldn't that make him angry?

I take a mental note to have Smith scan me for mindreading devices when Dimitri mutters, "You can't snare a man in the trap he set, Roxanne." There's no trace of emotion in his voice when he says, "You can congratulate him on his victory, then hope like hell your stroke of his ego gives you a couple of months of freedom before he traps you again." He bites on my lower lip, slides his tongue across his teeth marks to soothe the sting, then presses his curved mouth to my ear. "The future belongs to those unscared to make it theirs. My future is with you, Roxanne, and whether you agree or not, yours is with me."

His comment should fill me with dread. It should make me panicked. I'm in love with a mass murderer who'd rather slay me than see me with any man who isn't him, but that isn't close to what I am feeling.

He killed my boyfriend, tortured my parents, and has threatened to kill me more than once, but I love him, and at the end of the day, that's all that matters.

DIMITRI

Four Months Later...

A tap sounds at my office door before Roxanne's head pops through the gap. "Hey, Smith said you wanted to see me."

I gesture for her to enter, loving that even walking past dozens of women paid to cater to our 'guests' every whim hasn't dampened the sparkle in her eyes I re-lit when I told her our baby had survived both the carnage of her captivity and his mother being shot in the stomach without the slightest scratch. She knows whores are a part of this industry, but she also accepts that I have no interest in them.

The latter is responsible for her blasé response.

No fear.

Even with my son growing in her stomach, and my daughter on her hip, Roxanne doesn't hesitate to put the women who step over the line she deems unacceptable into place.

If you touch what is hers, expect to pay for your stupidity with your life.

Same goes for me.

I won't just kill you, though. Your entire family will be extinct. Your father, your brothers, hell, I'll even kill your second cousin if you do my family wrong because family comes first of all.

If you don't believe me, ask Maestro's family. You'll have to find them first. Trust me when I say that won't be easy. The Italian Cartel doesn't leave bodies because corpses can talk. Take the toddler in the wall at the Shroud family ranch as an example.

Is Megan related to me? Unfortunately, yes. Is she my sister? Hell-to-the-fucking-no. Our connection is a consequence of the fucked-up world my father raised me in. Babies, made-to-order wives, underage whores, if you could make money from it, my family dabbled in it in some way.

That's all done and dusted now. My father is dead, killed in a way too deserving for him, but without a single ounce of remorse felt. Most people believed he died in a joint FBI/Ravenshoe PD operation, only I know that isn't the case.

I'm not a fan of dark, hidden crevices until it conjures up a way to take down the man responsible for my family's utmost turmoil.

Fathers are supposed to protect their children.

They're supposed to save them from harm.

My father did no such thing.

If he had the chance to profit from it, he ran for it, but shacking up the only surviving member of his family with a vindictive bitch who couldn't give her husband's actual royal lineage an heir was a new low for him. Mafia blood is royal, it has been around for centuries, but it isn't something you auction off to the highest bidder without expecting to pay for your stupidity with your life.

I hate what Smith unearthed about the agreement between India and my father after Agent Brandon James left his briefcase unattended within days of my crews' return to Hopeton. It made a mockery out of my family name even more than it was already facing, but it gave me plenty of motivation to kill my father without fear of punishment. Rules not even someone as high as my father could break were shattered, leaving me no other option but to re-invent the game.

The Petretti name still isn't what it once was, but it's getting stronger every day.

Smith makes it stronger.

Rocco makes it stronger.

And having it attached to Roxanne's name completely blows it out of the fucking water.

Yeah, you heard me right. Roxanne isn't just knocked up with my kid, all five-foot-four inches of her is also my wife. Audrey was more than happy to sign divorce papers without a claim to the child most people still believe is hers or my fortune. She was so grateful her life was spared for the part she played in India's ruse to forge an unbreakable unity of our family bloodlines, she would have signed anything I placed in front of her.

Do I still wish she were dead? Yes, for the most part. The only reason I didn't siphon the blood from her veins was because Roxanne asked me not to. She wanted her alive, and although Audrey technically hurt me before Roxanne, so the decision was out of Roxanne's hands, if it weren't for Audrey suddenly growing a conscience, Maestro would have killed my son. He may have even killed my now-wife.

That alone saw me offering leniency I don't usually give.

That alone also saw Audrey shipped back to her country of origin with the promise if she ever steps foot in my country again, all mercies will be null and void. She will be dead—as will India when I find her.

She's still hiding. I can't say I don't understand her objective. Her death won't be quick like my father's and Rimi's. I'll torture her for hours on end, perhaps even days. I would have said months if that wouldn't force me away from my family for longer than necessary.

Despite no one knowing of their existence, Roxanne and Fien haven't left my sight for a second over the past four months. Whether on a computer monitor, via my phone, or in the flesh, I have eyes on them no matter where they are. I'm not ashamed of my overprotectiveness. If anything, it makes me proud. My girls will want for nothing, and my son will be raised completely different than I was. He won't just be a contender for the boss of all bosses when he's my age, he will be *the* boss, point blank, and I'll guide his steps the entire way.

As will his mother.

Roxanne isn't scared of this lifestyle. She fucking loves it. Not as much as she does me, but I didn't lie when I said she doesn't want to be a lady any more than she wants me to be a gentleman. I killed her boyfriend, tortured her parents, yet she still takes my dick between her lips with a ghost-like smile on her mouth every single time without fail.

The same smile is curling her lips now. It makes the transfer of her ass from my extended crotch to my desk a real fucking hard feat. It's only done without anarchy because the high rise of her skirt awards me the slightest peek of her scant panties and the treasure they're hiding.

Alice spoiled Roxanne when she entered my realm with nothing but the clothes on her back and a hideous dressing gown tossed over her arm. Now she spoils her with remorse as well.

Alice is alive, breathing, and has sworn multiple times the past four months that Lucy will eventually forgive me. Fien is helping bring her around, so I'm sure it won't be too much longer until she reverts to calling me 'Uncle' again.

As the light in Roxanne's eyes shifts from sated to ravenous, she parts her thighs. Not wide enough for me to get my head between them, but wide enough to reveal she knows the reason she's been seconded to my office. Her fearlessness nearly killed her, but it's one of the things I love about her the most.

That doesn't mean I'll let her off easy, though.

"What was our agreement, Roxanne?"

I don't free my hardened cock from my trousers and stroke it to weaken the fire burning in her eyes. I do it for the exact opposite reason. I love her spark, her charisma, her spunk that is so fucking potent, a bullet couldn't dampen it. Just knowing I can unleash it with only a few strokes has me stroking my cock a little faster.

I run my thumb down the vein feeding the monster dick the alteration of light in my wife's eyes always causes before sliding it over the tip, collecting the bead of precum pooling there.

When Roxanne shudders, I realize I have her right where I need her. "What was our agreement, Roxanne?" I ask this question more sternly than I did the first time, strangled through both the brutal clutch I have on my cock and the grip Roxanne has had on my balls since the day I saw her with black smudges under her eyes and chunky, wedged boots on her feet.

With her teeth gnawing on her bottom lip, Roxanne slowly raises her eyes from my cock, rocking in and out of my fist to my face. Her eyes are fucking fascinating. They have cum racing from my sack to the crest of my cock like my pleasure can come before hers.

That will never happen, but I fucking love that she can convince my cock otherwise.

I lessen the severity of my pumps when Roxanne purrs out,

"That I'm to do as you ask, when you ask, for *exactly* how long you ask."

Her last five words come out with a quiver when I grip the back of her neck with my spare hand so I can drag her delectable lips to within an inch of mine. As predicted, they taste like candy. They're the sweetest thing I've ever sampled. I crave them *almost* as often as I crave her cunt. "And what did you do tonight?"

"I did as you asked." Her minty fresh breath mingles with the whiskey bounding from mine when she murmurs, "I read our daughter a bedtime story..." I'm not surprised she calls Fien 'ours.' She is ours. Has been since Roxanne put her life on the line to free her from captivity, will be until the day we say our final farewell. "Then raked my fingers through her hair until she fell asleep in her big girl bed, then I came downstairs for an alcohol-free nightcap with some friends."

"Friends, eh? Who *exactly* were these friends?"

I know her answer.

I don't like her fucking answer.

And once I've shown her exactly how displeased I am that she took a detour on the way to my office tonight with my cock, I'll teach Rocco the same lesson with my fists.

I'm still pissed about how cozy he and Roxanne got four months ago. He shouldn't test my patience. I've killed men just for looking at Roxanne in the wrong manner, and I'll do it again because family comes first of all, and to me, Roxanne is the very definition of the word.

No fear.

The end...

The next explosive part of the Italian Cartel Series is Maddox's Story. **Maddox** will release January 13, you can preorder it NOW!

If you want to hear updates on the next books in this crazy world I've created, be sure to join my **readers group**: Shandi's Book Babes

Or my **Facebook Page**: www.facebook.com/authorshandi

Join my **newsletter** here: https://www.subscribepage.com/AuthorShandi

Rico, Asher, Isaac, Brandon, Ryan, Cormack, Enrique & Brax stories have already been released, but Grayson, Rocco, Clover, and all the other great characters of Ravenshoe/Hopeton will be getting their own stories at some point during 2021.

If you enjoyed this book please leave a review.

ACKNOWLEDGMENTS

I always say the acknowledgement page is one of the hardest pages of a book to write. *I'm not lying.* A lot of things go into the production of a book. From my kids understanding I can't hose them off after school everyday because I have a deadline, to my editing team who make a high school dropout's stories shine more brightly than she could have imagined.

It takes sacrifice, time, money, and a shit load of patience to write a single book, and even with *all of that*, we're still human, so mistakes are bound to happen.

They occur all the time. In books, in real-life, and even in our dreams, but it is how you rise above them that shows your true strength.

I will never be the best writer, just like I will never be the best mother, but as long as I am giving it my all, I am okay with that.

I have a story to tell. Whether that's words on a piece of paper or my husband catching my sneaky, admiring watch, I'm telling my story.

Are you telling yours?

Until next time.
    Shandi xx

Facebook: facebook.com/authorshandi

Instagram: instagram.com/authorshandi

Email: authorshandi@gmail.com

Reader's Group: bit.ly/ShandiBookBabes

Website: authorshandi.com

Newsletter: https://www.subscribepage.com/AuthorShandi

ALSO BY SHANDI BOYES

Perception Series

Saving Noah (Noah & Emily)

Fighting Jacob (Jacob & Lola)

Taming Nick (Nick & Jenni)

Redeeming Slater (Slater and Kylie)

Saving Emily (Noah & Emily - Novella)

Wrapped Up with Rise Up (Perception Novella - should be read after the Bound Series)

Enigma

Enigma (Isaac & Isabelle #1)

Unraveling an Enigma (Isaac & Isabelle #2)

Enigma The Mystery Unmasked (Isaac & Isabelle #3)

Enigma: The Final Chapter (Isaac & Isabelle #4)

Beneath The Secrets (Hugo & Ava #1)

Beneath The Sheets (Hugo & Ava #2)

Spy Thy Neighbor (Hunter & Paige)

The Opposite Effect (Brax & Clara)

I Married a Mob Boss (Rico & Blaire)

Second Shot (Hawke & Gemma)

The Way We Are (Ryan & Savannah #1)

The Way We Were (Ryan & Savannah #2)

Sugar and Spice (Cormack & Harlow)

Lady In Waiting (Regan & Alex #1)

Man in Queue (Regan & Alex #2)

Couple on Hold (Regan & Alex #3)

Enigma: The Wedding (Isaac and Isabelle)

Silent Vigilante (Brandon and Melody #1)

Hushed Guardian (Brandon & Melody #2)

Quiet Protector (Brandon & Melody #3)

Bound Series

Chains (Marcus & Cleo #1)

Links (Marcus & Cleo #2)

Bound (Marcus & Cleo #3)

Restrain (Marcus & Cleo #4)

Psycho (Dexter & ??)

Russian Mob Chronicles

Nikolai: A Mafia Prince Romance (Nikolai & Justine #1)

Nikolai: Taking Back What's Mine (Nikolai & Justine #2)

Nikolai: What's Left of Me (Nikolai & Justine #3)

Nikolai: Mine to Protect (Nikolai & Justine #4)

Asher: My Russian Revenge (Asher & Zariah)

Nikolai: Through the Devil's Eyes (Nikolai & Justine #5)

Trey (Trey & K)

The Italian Cartel

Dimitri

Roxanne

Reign

Maddox

Rocco

RomCom Standalones

Just Playin' (Elvis & Willow)

The Drop Zone (Colby & Jamie)

Ain't Happenin' (Lorenzo & Skylar)

Short Stories

Christmas Trio (Wesley, Andrew & Mallory -- short story)

Falling For A Stranger (Short Story)

K (A Trey Sequel)

Coming Soon

Skitzo